CHRISTOPHER BUSH
THE CASE OF THE FOURTH DETECTIVE

CHRISTOPHER BUSH was born Charlie Christmas Bush in Norfolk in 1885. His father was a farm labourer and his mother a milliner. In the early years of his childhood he lived with his aunt and uncle in London before returning to Norfolk aged seven, later winning a scholarship to Thetford Grammar School.

As an adult, Bush worked as a schoolmaster for 27 years, pausing only to fight in World War One, until retiring aged 46 in 1931 to be a full-time novelist. His first novel featuring the eccentric Ludovic Travers was published in 1926, and was followed by 62 additional Travers mysteries. These are all to be republished by Dean Street Press.

Christopher Bush fought again in World War Two, and was elected a member of the prestigious Detection Club. He died in 1973.

CHRISTOPHER BUSH

THE CASE OF THE FOURTH DETECTIVE

With an introduction
by Curtis Evans

DEAN STREET PRESS

Published by Dean Street Press 2019

Copyright © 1951 Christopher Bush

Introduction copyright © 2019 Curtis Evans

All Rights Reserved

First published in 1951 by MacDonald & Co.

Cover by DSP

ISBN 978 1 913054 13 7

www.deanstreetpress.co.uk

INTRODUCTION

Labouring under Suspicion
Christopher Bush's Crime Fiction in the Postwar Years, 1946-1952

Seven years after the end of the Second World War, Christopher Bush published, under his "Michael Home" pseudonym, *The Brackenford Story* (1952), a mainstream novel in which a onetime country house boots boy, having risen for some time now to the lofty position of butler, laments the passing of traditional English rural life in the new postwar order, as signified by the years in which the left-wing Labour party held sway in the United Kingdom (1945-51). The jacket description of the American edition of *The Brackenford Story* reads, in part:

> *The Brackenford Story* is the story of a changing England. William saw the political enemies of the Hall gradually successful, whittling away the privilege it stood for. He saw squire begin to sell his land, the taxes increase, the great Hall sold, the beautiful trees along the drive cut down. And then with a Second World War, nationalization, rationing, pre-fabricated houses and queuing. William recalled with gratitude the kindness of his masters and their sense of responsibility for others. He saw that the bad old days of Toryism were not so bad after all. And he never lost his sense of outrage at the loss of something he felt was worthy of preservation.

A few years earlier, in July 1949, Anthony Boucher, the postwar dean of American crime fiction reviewers and a highly socially conscious liberal (small "l"), wrote with genial bemusement of the conservatism of British crime writers like Christopher Bush, in his review of Bush's latest crime opus, *The Case of the Housekeeper's Hair* (1948), making topical mention of a certain anti-Utopian novel penned by a distinguished dying tubercular English writer, which had just been published in June. "However much George Orwell, in *Nineteen Eighty-Four*, may foresee the forcible suppression of 'crimethink' under 'Ingsoc,' English socialism in 1949 takes pleasure in exporting mystery novels which disapprove of the Government and everything about it," Boucher observed with wry irony. "Like most of his colleagues, Christopher Bush is tartly critical of the regime; and an understanding of his unreconstructed Tory attitude is necessary if you're to hope to understand the motivations of this novel."

In both the detective novels and mainstream fiction which Christopher Bush published between 1946 and 1952, Bush, like many other distinguished mystery writers of the Golden Age generation (including Agatha Christie, Dorothy L. Sayers, Georgette Heyer, John Dickson Carr, Edmund Crispin, E.R. Punshon, Henry Wade and John Street), indeed was critical of the Labor government and increasingly nostalgic about a past that grew ever more golden in blissful, if perhaps partially chimerical, remembrance. Yet keeping Bush's distinct anti-left bias in mind, fans of classic crime fiction will find between the covers of the author's crime novels from these years--*The Case of the Second Chance* (1946), *The Case of the Curious Client* (1947), *The Case of the Haven Hotel* (1948), *The Case of the Housekeeper's Hair* (1948), *The Case of the Seven Bells* (1949), *The Case of the Purloined Picture* (1949), *The Case of the Happy Warrior* (1950), *The Case of the Corner Cottage* (1951), *The Case of the Fourth Detective* (1951) and *The Case of the Happy Medium* (1952)--fascinating observation of postwar social malaise in the age of British imperial decay and domestic austerity, as well as details about the rise of rationing, restriction and regulation, the burgeoning black market and, withal, that ubiquitous flashily-dressed criminal figure from Forties and Fifties Britain: the spiv (dealer in illicit goods).

Puzzle-minded mystery readers also will find some corking good no-nonsense "fair play" mysteries. "Few writers can equal Christopher Bush in handling a complicated plot while giving the reader a fair chance to solve the riddle himself," avowed the American blurb to *The Case of the Corner Cottage*, while Anthony Boucher applauded Bush's belated return to the American fiction lists after the Second World War, declaring: "It's good to have Mr. Bush back after too long an absence . . . he presents the simon-pure jigsaw-puzzle detective story with unobtrusive competence." Concurrently in the United Kingdom, author Rupert Croft-Cooke, who himself wrote fine detective fiction as "Leo Bruce," pointedly praised Bush's "urbane and intelligent way of dealing with mystery which makes his work much more attractive than the stampeding sensationalism of some of his rivals."

In the pages which follow this introduction by all means attempt, dear readers, to match your keen wits against those of that ever-percipient gentleman sleuth, Ludovic Travers. Frequently in tandem with his old friend Superintendent George Wharton and with occasional input from his smart and sophisticated wife Bernice Haire, the former classical dancer, Ludo continues to hunt, in his capacity as a sort of special consultant to Scotland Yard (or "unofficial expert," as he puts it), more not-quite-canny-enough crooks. Additionally Ludo, a confirmed fan of American crime films like *The Blue Dahlia* (1946) and *Call Northside 777* (1948), comes to find himself in ownership of the Broad Street Detective Agency, perhaps the finest firm of private inquiry agents in London. In these old and new capacities in the postwar world Ludo confronts his greatest cornucopia of daring and dastardly crimes yet.

THE CASE OF THE FOURTH DETECTIVE

"Yes," Ramplock said. "Life's pretty grim for quite a lot of us. We don't want to start talking about the government, but you'll guess what I mean. Still, there we are. Beer and skittles were pretty good while they lasted."

"Now the beer's coloured water, George [Wharton] said, "and if you want to play skittles you'll probably have to get a licence."

People will do all sorts of things for money. It's still the best motive for murder.

During the nineteenth century canny newspaperman William Henry Smith and his equally canny son, likewise named William Henry Smith, established a remarkable newsstand and bookstall empire--named, appropriately enough, WH Smith & Son--at railway stations across the United Kingdom. Train commuters, avidly devouring detective fiction and thrillers in the form of Hodder & Stoughton yellow jackets and green and white Penguin paperbacks during the twentieth century heyday of classic crime fiction in the Thirties, Forties and Fifties, often had purchased their prose treasures at WH Smith & Son bookstalls. The company remained privately held until 1948, when, upon the death of the third Viscount Hambleden (the original William Henry Smith's great-great grandson), shares had to be sold publicly in order to cover the costs of the ravaging inheritance tax (aka "death duties") that had laid waste to the company's once burgeoning coffers. This event--much noted at the time, when the tax policies of Britain's lately-installed Labour government were the subject of contentious debate --inspired Christopher Bush's 39th Ludovic Travers detective novel, *The Case of the Fourth Detective* (1951).

In previous detective novels that Christopher Bush had published since the Labour Party took power in 1945, the author through his genteel sleuth Ludovic Travers had taken potshots at Labour's confiscatory tax policies, making withering asides about the depredations of "Comrade" Hugh Dalton and Stafford Cripps, successive Chancellors of the Exchequer in the Labour government during the years 1945-50. However, in *The Case of the Fourth Detective*, Bush, like contemporary crime writer and Detection Club member Henry Wade in his detective novel *Diplomat's Folly*, likewise published in 1951, put Labour tax policy front and center in his book. Some writers of classic British crime fiction felt so strongly about the estate tax issue that they continued to elaborate upon the dread theme even after Winston Churchill and the Tories were restored to power in 1951, the modern British welfare state having proved a hungry creature indeed—see, for example, Henry Wade (yet again) in *Too Soon to Die*, 1953, and Margery Allingham in *The Estate of the Beckoning Lady*, 1955, whose titles suggest their authors' agendas (as does "Taxman," the title of a 1966 Beatles song about the 95% supertax introduced by the government of Prime Minister Harold Wilson, Labour having finally ousted the Conservatives from power again two years earlier). However, in *The Case of the Fourth Detective* tax policy feels like more of a key plot point than an occasion for a jeremiad.

In the novel Ludovic Travers--now the owner, since the sudden demise from a heart attack of Bill Ellice, of the Broad Street Detective Agency--finds his firm called in by Owen Ramplock, who has succeeded to the chairmanship of Ramplocks, the chain of thirty-four provision shops he has inherited from his late magnate father, old Sam Ramplock. By the time Ludo arrives at Warbeck Grove, the block of palatial flats where Owen Ramplock resides when in the City, however, Ramplock lease on life has expired. Ludo finds him on the floor of Flat 5 "as dead as they make them: deader than last year's hit-song. At the side of the skull was a bloody gap where the bullet had done its work. Messy work, but only too efficient."

Ramplock's call was taken by the Agency's manager--Jack Norris, formerly a Chief Inspector at Scotland Yard—and he reports that Ramplock's last words on the phone were "Prince! . . . What the devil are you doing here!" So now Travers, rather than taking on a juicy job with posh Owen Ramplock, is tasked with trying to find Ramplock's killer, by helping his old friend Superintendent George Wharton and young Sergeant Matthews of Scotland Yard to discover the identity and whereabouts of the mysterious man named Mr. Prince, who left behind him at the scene of the crime a cryptic calling card. In bold letters on the back of the card is a terse message warning "You'll be Sorry".

Certainly there were plenty of people whom Owen Ramplock --a former playboy turned POW in Italy who until recently had never faced up to real work in his civilian life--had antagonized. There are, for example, his wife Jane, from whom he was estranged (it appears Ramplock may have had a mistress) but with whom he had recently tried to effect a reconciliation, and Jane Ramplock's uncle, lately returned from Canada, a character with a large stock of (tall?) stories by the name of Solversen. Then there are various officers and staff at Ramplocks: Henry Dale, managing director; Richard Winter, head of sales; Charles Downe, chief accountant; and Miss Haregood, Ramplock's highly efficient secretary. "A schoolmarm to the life was what I thought her," dismissively comments Ludo of Miss Haregood. He is rather more taken with company typist Daisy Purkes, whom he deems "cute as a kitten with a black nose," and he finds opportunity over the course of the case to interview Miss Purkes more than once on the premises of Ramplocks. It seems that the company's directors were trying to determine just how to deal with the crushing death duties imposed on the business after the demise of old Sam Ramplock. Before his untimely demise was Owen Ramplock trying to cut a deal for survival with Herringswoods, a mammoth concern with over one hundred shops in London and the Home Counties?

Kevin Burton Smith of the Thrilling Detective website, a devotee of the American school of tough crime fiction, has asserted that while Travers' murder cases "may lean towards 'hard-boiled' they don't lean far enough." For murder fiction fans happily steeped in the more genteel traditions of Anglo-American detective fiction of the between-the-wars period, however, Bush may have timed things just right. Certainly in *The Case of the Fourth Detective* Ludo seems to have developed something of the more casual attitude about sex which is associated with American hard-boiled detective fiction. "Ramplock's morals didn't interest me beyond their possible connection with his death," Ludo confides at one point. "I've skidded about a bit myself in my time and in my furtive moments I've thought monogamy a harshly Christian virtue." Recalling Ludo's romantic revelations in *The Case of the Magic Mirror* (1943) and Christopher Bush's own amorous flings (at least before he settled down with his longtime partner Marjorie Barclay), this seems an honest enough assessment. Perhaps now we know why Ludo's wife Bernice appears to spend so much of her married life away visiting friends.

By this time, indeed, Ludo seems in many ways to have merged with his creator. In *The Case of the Purloined Picture* (1949), for example, we are reminded that Ludo's native ground is found in East Anglia, just like the author's, and it is claimed that Ludo is "middle class," putting him closer in social origin to Bush, who was descended from generations of humble Norfolk farming stock (though the claim that Ludo is of middle class origins is belied by earlier novels). On American book jackets in the 1950s, underneath photos of the author, readers were informed that Bush was, like Ludo, a Cambridge man, though in fact this claim was untrue. Bush himself admitted in his memoirs that he had missed his chance to go to Cambridge; evidently that lost opportunity long rankled.

In having to forego his chance at obtaining an elite English education, Christopher Bush resembled another prolific mystery writer and Detection Club member who created a popular genteel surrogate detective and has been reprinted by Dean Street Press: E.R. Punshon. With his Newcastle sugar broker father having gone bankrupt and apparently left his family, Punshon at the age of sixteen was forced, he recalled in mid-life, "to work in the accounts office of a railroad. . . . After a year or two my office superiors told me gently that they thought I was not without intelligence but that my intelligence and my work did not seem somehow to coincide. So I thanked them for the hint, gracefully accepted it, and departed to Canada . . ." During the waning years of the reign of Queen Victoria, Punshon had a great many larger-than-life adventures in Canada and the American West--including, he claimed, an escape from a ravening pack of wolves--before he returned to England and settled down to a writing career of over a half-century's duration. As any good novelist would, Punshon drew on these New World experiences in one of his early novels, *Constance West* (1905).

In his later years, ill with a wasting terminal disease, the now elderly Punshon spent some time, in the fall of 1949, recuperating from an operation at Little Horspen, the charming

East Sussex Tudor home of Christopher Bush and Marjorie Barclay. (Later that year Bush succeeded E.R. Punshon as the Detection Club's treasurer.) The next year, when Bush was writing *The Case of the Fourth Detective*, he amusingly included, in the person of Jane Ramplock's uncle Matthew Solversen, a character that may well have been partly modeled on Ernest Robertson Punshon:

> "He's a delightful person but you may find him . . . well, just a bit original. . . . He was a natural born wanderer. He tells the most marvelous stories of all the things he did in Canada and the States."
>
> "I know," I said. "Bar-keep, prospector, hobo, farm-hand—everything."
>
> "But how did you know?"
>
> "I didn't," I said. "But they always do, at least in books."

As for the matter of the identity of the titular fourth detective, there are Ludo, Wharton, Matthews and . . . Why don't you read on right now and see for yourself?

Curtis Evans

Chapter I

MAN IN A FLAT

As soon as the taxi moved off I was leaning back in the corner and trying to concentrate on what I knew of Owen Ramplock. When you are—nominally at least—head of a detective agency and a man wants to buy your services, and when that man is prepared to pay but prefers to keep you in temporary ignorance about what it is he wants to buy, then it's up to you to dig down deep. You may not find many answers but at least you should have something ready when the real talking starts. The customer may be always right but it's just as well to have a trick or two up what he considers an empty sleeve.

In the office there had been only a few seconds to wait for the taxi and I hadn't even had time to consult *Who's Who*. But words didn't matter so much as the personal contact, and I began thinking back to the time I'd seen Ramplock. It was at Morecombe Hill golf course on a dry dull day of March, and since it was October, there was a gap of seven months for memory to bridge.

I'd been playing with—of all people—George Wharton: known to you, maybe, as Superintendent Wharton of Scotland Yard. George, six feet of burliness, had up till then been content to regard golf as a matter of three clubs, and he had an immense scorn—especially when he had beaten me—for the dozen or so that filled the average bag. His tools were a massive niblick for general emergencies, and an old-time cleek with which he could outdrive me by anything up to fifty yards, and, with my six-foot-three of reasonable lithe leanness I'm far from a mean hitter. A stroke every other hole was what I'd give him and it used to make a goodish match. Put us within seventy yards of the green with me still a stroke down, and the hole had a good chance of being mine. And the reason was George's third club—a rusty old steel putter. To pitch he scorned. His trust was in a sort of jab with that putter, and he was as likely to be short or over as that New Year's Day comes after Christmas.

Sometimes, of course, if the ground was smooth and flat between his ball and the hole, he would do that run-up shot with considerable skill, and then he'd be cock-a-hoop. But the agonised look on his face and the sway this way and that of his body as his ball careered over hummocks or through short rough or round the edges of bunkers was as good as most music-hall turns. And I'm telling you all this because that method of approach was George himself to the very life: never taking a risk where seeming cautiousness would pay: being simple and obvious and direct on the face of things but actually crafty as a zoo full of monkeys and as full of tricks and dodges as a yellow dog's full of fleas.

Take that game at Morecombe Hill. I rarely play nowadays, nor does George, and I was surprised when he rang me up and suggested a morning off. What I didn't know was that his daughter had bought a bag of quite good clubs at some auction or other and had given them to George as a Christmas present, and that as things that spring had been none too hectic at the Yard and he lived within a mile of a public course, he had been practising under the pro on the lighter evenings and putting in some time by himself. You should have seen the look of studied indifference on his face when he drove off that morning with wood, and when we neared the first green and he took out a mashie-niblick, he reminded me of a spinster going down to the sea for the first reckless moment in a bra-and-panties suit. He squinted round to see how I was taking it when he put the ball within putting distance.

"A regular pro shot, George," I said ironically.

"I don't know," he told me, and with that false modesty which always infuriates me. "Didn't know the ground was so hard or I'd have been right on the pin."

But to get to Owen Ramplock. I'd heard and read about him, of course: who hadn't, if it came to that. The British public loves the sporting type and he was pretty good copy for the papers. Good-looking too, by the photographs, which made him a hit with the women. At Cambridge he got his cricket blue and then for two years played uncommonly well with one of the counties. Then he had dropped cricket for golf. Twice he'd started favourite for the amateur championship, but had been knocked out in the semi-finals in each case. Then he had switched to tennis, which he had also played at Cambridge, and he had actually got through a round or two at Wimbledon. His latest idea, just before war broke out, was to put England on the map again in Continental road-racing, and there was a lot of talk about a special car. The war stopped all that and he joined up. But he didn't have too good a war. He did get an M.C. in Libya and then he was captured by the Italians.

That was most of what I knew of Owen Ramplock: his taking up this sport and that and always contriving to make the headlines. As for the gossip, it was said that his father—old Sam Ramplock of the chain of provision shops—thought the publicity good enough value for the young fortunes he must have handed out. I didn't know. What I did know was that Sam Ramplock had died in the December prior to that golf game. I never saw the amount of his personal estate but there should have been a pretty good sum for his heir, even after Cripps had dipped both arms in it up to the elbows.

But to come back to that morning at Morecombe Hill. Ramplock was playing with a tallish, beefy-looking chap of forty—his own age, by the way—who was showily dressed in plus-fours and a pullover in the nature of a strong emetic. I didn't know that Ramplock was on what had looked like a deserted course till the pro told me so in the shop where I'd gone to buy a couple of balls.

"The course playing well?" I'd asked him.

"Not too badly, sir," he'd said, and then his voice had taken on a kind of awe. "Owen Ramplock's playing this morning. He's just gone off. Nearly drove the first green."

So somewhere, in spite of the intervention of the war, the magic still lingered. I asked if he played much golf.

"He's too busy, he was telling me." He shook a regretful head. "A pity he didn't stick to golf, you know, sir. He'd have had the championship in his pocket."

George and I made our fortuitous way through, along and round the wide open spaces. We came eventually to the rough and the gorse bushes of the blind eleventh and were looking for a ball of mine which some malignancy of fate had kicked uncannily a good twenty yards off the fairway, when there was a sort of sizzling whistle and a ball came high over us and plopped somewhere just beyond.

"You're not the only one who can't keep 'em straight," George told me unctuously, and then Owen Ramplock came in sight over the hill. His partner's chauffeur was caddying for them both, and the three of them were hurrying forward and looking the wrong way. The caddie laid down the bags at a fairway ball.

"Someone's ball's just gone over here," I called to Ramplock.

"That'd be mine," he said, and he and the others came over. George called that he'd found my ball—I hate to say it but I'm almost sure he trod it hard in—so I gave Ramplock a rough line on his ball, and I was just poking about with a mashie when there the ball was. It was the devil of a lie but open enough for the swing of a club.

"Thanks a lot," he said. "I'm sure I'd never have found the damn thing."

He had a charming smile and the good looks hadn't altogether gone, even if the hair was just greying at the temples and his middle had the beginnings of a spread. The eyes were just a bit puffy too, though it didn't look as if it came from a lifting of the elbow.

The chauffeur had fetched the bag. Ramplock took a heavy niblick and we stood still while he made his shot. There was no lingering about it. Up went the club and the whole of his six foot and twelve stone was behind it. Up went grass and a miniature gorse bush and the ball dropped a hundred yards down the fairway.

"Dam' good effort!" his partner said.

"Thanks again," Ramplock told me, and the smile seemed wholly for me rather than a satisfaction at the shot.

George and I went on. At the thirteenth he was dormy five and he won the next hole. I didn't mind the new ball but I could have belted him with an iron when he said I'd been playing better than usual. He took three sixpences from me on the byes, and even then he wasn't quick to stand me a drink when we got to the bar.

"Won't you have a drink with me?" a voice said.

Ramplock had been sitting at a table to our left. His partner had evidently gone, for through the window I saw that the Buick was no longer there.

"You have one with me," I said, and hoped it might put George to shame. "I'm just ordering."

"Not a bit of it. If I'd lost that ball on the fifteenth it'd have cost me a fiver."

"You won?"

"Just did it on the last green."

We all had beer. I introduced George and myself. We took the drinks to a table near the fire.

"Don't think me too personal," I said, "but aren't you connected with Ramplocks, the provision people?"

"That's right," he said. "As a matter of fact I'm chairman of the company now. Have been since my father died."

"The reason I mentioned it," I said, "was that the particular business with which I happen to be connected did a job for you people about a year ago. The Broad Street Detective Agency."

"Don't remember it," he said. Then he frowned. "Wait a minute, though. Wasn't it some black market business or other?"

"That was it," I said. "The manager of one of your depots was doing rather well for himself. We did the investigation."

"That was in my father's time," he said. "I just remember him mentioning it."

Then he was suddenly giving me a curious look. It was as if my eyebrows were all at once shooting sparks, and he couldn't believe his eyes.

"You don't look much like a detective if you don't mind my saying so?"

"Probably because I'm not," I told him. "There's a first rate managing director. I'm only the chairman—and the owner. A dam' sight less important than it sounds."

"Rather like myself," he said, and gave a rueful grin. "Or so I used to think."

His tankard was empty and I asked if he'd have another. George hastily took a last swig. The steward brought three more beers and Ramplock resumed where he'd left off.

"I've got a first-class managing director too. Chap who's spent his life in the business. I thought that being a chairman was a figure-head sort of business, but, by God, I was wrong."

"No fun at all?"

"Don't get me wrong," he said. "There's the hell of a lot of fun. A hell of a lot of hard work too."

I hope you haven't got *me* wrong—about George Wharton, I mean. George is a good enough mixer when he's incognito as he was that morning, and suddenly it was he and Ramplock who were monopolising the talk. The war was mentioned and Ramplock was saying what he'd planned for himself if he ever got out of that Italian prisoner-of-war camp, and how wide of the mark he'd actually been. George said that the war had changed the outlook of a whole lot of people. The between-war years now seemed fantastic.

"Yes," Ramplock said. "Life's pretty grim for quite a lot of us. We don t want to start talking about this government, but you'll guess what I mean. Still, there we are. Beer and skittles were pretty good while they lasted."

"Now the beer's coloured water," George said, "and if you want to play skittles you'll probably have to get a licence. You get much golf nowadays?"

"Far too little," he said. "Wish to God I could get much more. Lack of exercise plays the very devil with the figure."

Then he was getting to his feet. He'd have to hurry, he said, as he was lunching with a business acquaintance in town.

A smile and a nod and out he went. I heard his car start and—unashamedly curious as ever—looked out of the far window. He was driving what looked like a just pre-war Rolls with a special sports body, and it was fine to watch how it seemed to glide through the gates and accelerate effortlessly up the steep hill.

We'd ordered lunch and when we took our table George tried to pull my leg.

"Rather summed you up, didn't he?"

I didn't get it for a moment, and then I knew he was referring to Ramplock's remark about my not looking like a detective. And he'd certainly been right. That length of mine, the hatchet face, the Roman nose and the horn-rimmed glasses give me the look—as a newspaper reporter once wrote—of an amiable secretary-bird.

"What about yourself?" I asked him, for if George looks like anything it's a harassed father of a swarming brood who has the devil's own time trying to make ends meet. When he sags his shoulders and puts on his antiquated spectacles and purses his lips reflectively with the huge moustache as an awning, the unsuspecting take heart and even feel a surge of pity. That's only one of the acts he can put on for the undoing of the unwary, but it's his best.

"That's different," he told me, and I might have known he'd beg the question. I didn't press the point. The lunch had come for one thing, and in twenty years of association with George on murder cases I'd learned at least the folly of expecting a straight answer to a straight question. But we did go on talking for a short time about Owen Ramplock: for a short time because there was little more about which to talk than you've already heard.

In the months that followed, Ramplock never came back to my mind, if only because I was exceptionally busy and had never a game of golf. There was the Agency, for one thing, and having to act as stop-gap during staff holidays, and during the whole of August there was a case where the Yard—for some eccentric and philanthropic reasons of its own—called me in to work with George. It wasn't one of our successful shows, which was why it kept us so tied down. Then at the end of September I'd managed ten days' holiday and I'd been back only a couple of days.

My taxi had turned left towards the Park but I wasn't aware of it. What I was trying to do was to make something of those seven months since I'd seen Owen Ramplock, but there was almost nothing on which to work. All I could tell myself was that since Ramplock had made neither the headlines nor, as far as I knew, the back pages, he must be sticking close to business. He'd said there was a whole lot of fun in it, and so maybe there momentarily was for the sporting, hither-and-yon kind of playboy that his father's money had once made him. Would he tire of the new toy, I wondered? Was his March outlook a sort of death-bed conversion, or had those months in that prison camp changed his outlook and sobered him down for good? I didn't know, and then suddenly I didn't have to worry about it, for the taxi was slithering round into an open court and the driver was telling me we were there.

Warbeck Grove was a block of palatial flats. There was a kind of superior solemnity about the place that spoke of snobbery and money. It was coldish that morning of early October but the sun was just coming through and it mellowed the deep red bricks and lighted to a decorous colour the window boxes with their dwarf dahlias. A solitary Rolls stood just beyond the spacious entrance porch and a uniformed chauffeur came out as I was entering and there was a superciliousness about his level glance. I halted for a moment and looked back across the Park. An autumnal haze was just lifting from the distant elms, and there were splashes of colour from the distant beds of flowers. Something nostalgic stirred inside me—God knows for what, unless it was a lost youth and vanished fields—and I gave a peevish grunt as I went through the swing doors.

Maybe I was suddenly in an awkward mood, and there was something about those flats that was to keep me that way. Unreasonable of me, perhaps, or even frivolous, but there it was. I haven't that inverted form of snobbery that envies other people's money, if only because I've enough of my own. It was just a something that I didn't even try to place. Maybe everything was just too self-satisfied and sleek.

Take the large entrance hall with its tessellated paving and the wide stairways at each side. An aura of repression seemed to hang over it, as though, if I'd dared to cough, the sound would have echoed hollowly and with a grim reproof. To my right were the open doors of an obviously recherché restaurant and, though it was nearer ten o'clock than nine, I could see a sprinkling of people, women mostly, still at their meal. Somehow that restaurant oozed money: it looked the sort of place where to look at the menu would set you back quite a bit.

Flanking the lift were a couple of palms in huge brass pots that reminded me of Ali Baba and the forty thieves. To the left was the office with a kind of magazine and newspaper kiosk at its far end. There was no need for me to consult the sleek-haired gentleman who was running his eye over his nails, for an elegant indicator told me that Flat 5 was up that stairway. The pile of its carpet reminded me of Sinai and ploughing a way through soft sand.

On the first landing I had to go left again. Flat 5 was at the very end, which meant that on one side, at least, it had no neighbours. A palm in another Ali Baba pot stood at the far end and through the tall window which it partly masked, the sun sent flickers of light. Then I saw that the bottom of the window was just open and a tiny breeze was flickering the leaves of the palm. I took a quick look through the window. It opened on a kind of side courtyard. A fire escape ran past and beneath it from above and it was painted red to match the weathered colour of the bricks.

On the door was a number but no name. I pushed the bell and in a couple of minutes was wondering if Norris by any chance had made a mistake, for there wasn't a sound beyond that door. I rapped with my knuckles, glanced along the wide corridor and listened with my ear hard against the door. I rang again and listened again. Then I went down to the office. The sleek-haired gentleman who had finished with his nails gave me a look of polite perplexity. Maybe he was wondering if I was real.

"Number 5 is Mr. Ramplock's flat, isn't it?"

"Yes, sir."

He had the look and tone of a butler who'd never need references. The face and the manner would have brought him a ducal job.

"Has he gone out, do you know?"

"Not to my knowledge, sir."

There had been a gentle reproof, and a slight emphasis on the *my*.

"Then where is he?" I said. "He made a most urgent appointment with me and I've rung and rung and no one seems to be there."

He gave a little bow and said he'd try the telephone. I stepped back a yard or two from the presence and waited. Things were getting hectic in that hall. A couple of plump dowagers were coming out of the restaurant and it seemed blasphemous that high-heeled shoes should be clattering on the mosaic. Then a waiter with a tray appeared from nowhere and glided like a ghost up the other stairway.

"Sorry, sir, but no one seems to be there."

"Dammit, there must be. I came all this way at Mr. Ramplock's urgent request and he said he'd be waiting in his flat."

His brow wrinkled decorously in thought. He said he'd speak to the manager. I drew back again but nothing seemed to be happening in the hall. Then a messenger boy came in with what looked like a flower-box. Probably orchids, I thought, just flown in specially from Brazil. A gent in a natty morning suit popped out and collared him before he could do much harm, and the two disappeared.

"The manager's just coming, sir."

I thought his name would be Something-*vitch*, but it wasn't. It was just plain Goodge, and that seemed a kind of *lèse majesté*. Nor was he wearing a cutaway suit, though the grey worsteds were handsomely pressed. His face was shiny and clean-shaven, even to the last of the chins. It spoke of good-living and maybe an odd drink or two, for it had the veined colour of a red peony when the sun's at last through with it. His hands, unusually white, were so pudgy that the signet ring on a finger was buried almost out of sight.

I told him my name. I expected it to convey nothing, and I was right. But I did feel almost at home with him. On the way up the stairs he was quite talkative about the weather. Maybe he'd had a hand in it. As for his rap on the door, I doubt if he felt it on his knuckles, so tactful was it and so suave. His greyish eyebrows lifted perplexedly and he ventured to ring. His lips pursed. A key was produced and noiselessly inserted. Even then he cleared his throat gently before he opened the door.

He looked cautiously in and I was at his heels. I caught sight of quite a large, well-lighted lounge and then things happened. He made a curious little noise like a lot of water going down a narrow pipe, and instead of going forward, he moved, or almost fell, back. I went smack into him but he didn't seem to notice.

That was when I saw the body on the carpet. I didn't need to move more than a couple of yards to know whose body it was, and then I went forward towards the electric fire. I took a quick glance at Goodge. There was a horror on his face and the face seemed a shade or two lighter. Then I switched off the electric fire, and for the life of me I don't know why. Maybe it was the sickly oppressiveness of that room, and its vague connection with the horror of Ramplock's head. He was as dead as they make them: deader than last year's hit-song. At the side of the skull was a bloody gap where the bullet had done its work. Messy work, but only too efficient. Goodge was at my elbow and having a quick look. I heard that gurgling noise again and then he fairly shot past me and through to the bathroom.

CHAPTER II

MAN NAMED PRINCE (?)

There was a telephone on a Sheraton card table at one of the two large windows. I dialled 999, gave my name and asked to be put through to Superintendent Wharton. In half a minute George was on the line.

"This is Travers, George," I said. "Remember Owen Ramplock playing golf that day last March at Morecombe Hill?"

"Why?"

"He's dead, here in his flat," I said. "Someone blew the top of his head off. Flat 5, Warbeck Grove, Regent's Park. All sorts of curious things about it. Think you'd better come along yourself?"

I waited for him to answer and at last he gave a grunt which seemed to indicate agreement. As I replaced the receiver I saw Goodge watching me from the bathroom door. He didn't look too good and he was wiping his mouth with his handkerchief.

"A nasty business, this," I said. "Murder's always a nasty business."

"Murder?" His fat hands were trembling like a jelly in an earthquake. "But it couldn't be!"

"Take it easy," I said. "Sit down here and let's have a quiet talk."

He didn't move for a moment, then he sidled in. His eyes were on me as if I was a dog and he the postman.

"I didn't murder him," I said. "I've just rung up the police. A few minutes and they'll be here."

He sidled on and into a chair. You could see him realise what a poor chance he had of bolting past me to the door.

"I'm connected with Scotland Yard," I said, "though that wasn't what I came up to see Mr. Ramplock about this morning. That was purely personal business. Have a cigarette."

I passed him the case and held the lighter. His hands were still trembling and from under his thick greying eyebrows he'd shot me a none too happy look. He took a draw at the cigarette and then he actually spoke.

"It wasn't . . . suicide?"

"Where's the gun?"

That hadn't struck him.

"Tell me this," I said. "When did he have his breakfast— if at all."

There was a second telephone: a natty little wall affair with two plugs—one for the office and the other for the restaurant. You just plugged in, pushed a knob, and hooked off a miniature receiver. That was what Goodge did and he was facing me all the time. It was curious how he changed as soon as he'd made contact with the world outside that room.

Ramplock hadn't had any breakfast, it seemed. I got him to ask when he usually had it, and the answer was at any time after nine, though there had been rare occasions when he had it as early as eight.

"Maybe he was waiting for me," I said. "Thought I might have breakfast with him while we talked. But tell me about these flats. What's the rent of them?"

He said it varied from three-fifty to seven-fifty. Every kind of service was included, and, of course, there was the attraction of a first-class restaurant.

"What did this one cost?"

"But it was Mr. Ramplock's," he said, and spread his pudgy palms.

"I gathered that," I told him dryly. "But what rent did he pay?"

"It was his own flat." he said, and he couldn't help a quick impatience. "The property's his. He kept this flat for himself."

"Sorry," I said. "I just didn't get it. I take it now that his father bought the property and Mr. Owen Ramplock inherited."

That was almost it. Sam Ramplock had actually built that block of flats in the early 'twenties and on the site of a large house and gardens where his mother had lived. Just before the war the flats had been refurnished and modernised. During the war the whole building had been taken over by a branch of American Air Administration, but Sam must have had a few anxious moments when the bombs really began to drop.

"That's clear enough, Mr. Goodge," I said. "Now there's something you might have ready for the police. A man called on Mr. Ramplock this morning, at precisely nine-twenty. I don't know his name but it might have been something like Prince. Mr. Ramplock wasn't expecting him, not that that matters. What you'd better do is see if he went to the office and if he's been here before and if any of your staff know him. Try to get a description."

"Prince?"

"It sounded like it," I said. "And one other thing. Get ready a list of the occupants of the nearest flats. Anyone who might have heard a shot. Doesn't matter if they're on the premises now or not. And one last thing."

I motioned him to the door and out we went. He didn't sidle at all as he went past me.

"This window," I said. "Find out if any of your staff opened it."

I said that was all and he turned to go. He turned back.

"You must have thought it pretty weak of me—I mean, seeing him . . ."

It was almost pathetic the way he hated to lose face. I told him it'd been a nasty sight. There'd been times when I'd been almost voluptuously sick myself.

"The publicity," he said. "There won't be . . ."

"Why should you worry?" I told him. "You've probably got a queue lined up for these flats. And you're the boss—till the will's read."

A mournful cringe of the shoulders and off he went. I had a good look at Ramplock's flat, and the first thing that struck me about it was its comparative smallness. It was handsomely furnished but that wasn't the point. Ramplock was married, that was something that at least I knew, but this flat had only the one bedroom. It was true it had a double bed, but there were pillows only for one, and Ramplock alone had occupied it that previous night. The lounge was a fine, airy room and the bathroom was modern and well equipped, but there that flat ended. A bachelor establishment, on the face of it, and about that there seemed something wrong. Even if his wife was living out of town and the flat was his business dormitory, then that was no reason why the wife shouldn't make use of the flat after a dinner in town and a show.

But except for what they call a faint elusive scent, there was never a trace of a woman's having ever been in that flat. And the scent was probably Ramplock's face powder or shaving soap. He had shaved that morning—all the traces were there even to soap on a towel—and I went back to the lounge and felt his smooth cheek with a finger. Then I noticed the other door.

Ramplock's body lay with head towards the electric stove, slant-wise across an oriental rug which in turn was on a heavy-piled carpet. The stove was between the twin windows, so the body was central to that outer wall. Across the room, just the bathroom side of the facing wall, was the door. I tried the handle and it was locked. Maybe that was a second bedroom, no longer used. Maybe it was Mrs. Ramplock's bedroom, and locked when she had no use for it. Then something made me go back to the bathroom, but there was no second door there that led to the locked room. And that seemed odd. Why should Mrs. Ramplock have to come through the lounge to get to her bath? And then I wondered something else, and went out into the corridor. That bedroom—if it was a bedroom—had a door that opened on the corridor. There was something else that it had—a Yale lock. I walked back along the corridor and looked at the other doors and never one had a lock like that. And as I glanced down into the entrance hall I saw Wharton coming through the swing doors.

George looked up and I beckoned. He gave me a grunt as he reached the landing. Sergeant Matthews gave me a bit of a grin.

"The circus here?" I said.

George grunted a something I took for yes. I led the way to the flat. George spotted the open window, pursed his lips but said nothing.

"The door handle's smudged past hope," I told him as he went through. "There he is, as you can see. Still easy to identify."

George had a good look. He stooped and turned the body and looked underneath. He let it fall again. He shook his head, then cocked an ear as the circus was heard outside. Matthews went out and I stopped him as he was closing the door.

"Get them to try that window for prints. And the fire-escape rail outside."

George took out his pipe, felt for a match, then rammed the cold pipe in his mouth. He was wearing the same old navy blue overcoat with the velvet collar, and a bowler hat that I'd known for years.

"How'd *you* come to find him?" he was asking me.

I told him. What I told him, a shade more elaborately, was this. It's my custom to drop in at the Agency of a morning, usually at about nine-thirty, to have a word with Norris and, if necessary, to lend a hand. That morning I was early. It was just a quarter-past nine when I arrived, and scarcely before I'd opened my mouth to Norris, Miss Munney—the receptionist-secretary—put a client on the line. Norris naturally took the call.

What the client was saying, I didn't know. All Norris said was, "Yes, sir," and, "Certainly, sir," and he had a pad on which he wrote things down. Then he said this:

"Can you give us any idea, sir, just what it is you're likely to want, so that we can send a suitable man?"

The client said any responsible man would do, and Norris was to regard it as a matter of urgency. Norris said it would be done straightaway, and just as he went to ring off I saw his eyes pop a bit. Then his mouth gaped and he seemed to be listening intently. Then he shook his head, and that was that.

As I told George, Norris is the boss. I hadn't intruded because it was Norris's job. In fact, I'd got up from my chair and had been looking at something across the room. That was why I was so surprised when Norris mentioned Ramplock as the client's name. In a moment or two I was to be more surprised still.

"That the Broad Street Detective Agency?" Ramplock had said. "This is Owen Ramplock. You did a job for my firm some time ago and I want you to send a man here at once. I'm speaking from Flat Number 5, Warbeck Grove, Regent's Park. It's extremely urgent."

That was all, except what you've heard, and the explicit mention that he'd be in and waiting. Then, just as everything was settled and Norris expected Ramplock to say goodbye and ring off, Ramplock said something extraordinarily strange.

"Prince! . . . What the devil are *you* doing here!"

That was all, and then the receiver had been replaced, and without the usual goodbye. Norris, as I told Goodge, wasn't certain that the name was Prince, but that was what it sounded like. Then, to cut the story short, I was a bit intrigued, and I thought Ramplock might like *me* to see him, and there wasn't in any case a suitable operative around, so I told Bertha Munney to ring the stand round the corner and have a taxi sent at once.

George gave a grunt and his lips pursed with a faint contempt.

"Seems open and shut. This chap Prince must have killed him. Probably bolted through that window outside."

"Maybe," I said. "But we've still got to find Prince."

The lips pursed again. As if to show me just how easy it was, he gave a leering sort of smile as he riffled the pages of the Telephone Directory. Then he dialled a number I soon knew as that of Warbeck House, the headquarters of Ramplocks.

"That Ramplocks? . . . Give me the managing director. . . . Superintendent Wharton of New Scotland Yard."

He was humming a little tune to himself, though his eyes were all round the room—a bit furtively perhaps, like a shoplifter's in the mink department.

"Yes? . . . Not in? Who are you, then? . . . I see. I'm Superintendent Wharton of New Scotland Yard. I want to know if you have anyone named Prince on your staff?"

He spelt it out and gave another snort. The eyes were round the room again.

"Yes? . . . Not that you know of. Well, what about a customer? . . . Not that you can recall. Well, then, have you ever heard Mr. Ramplock or anybody mention the name? . . . I see. Well, let me know if anything occurs to you. Goodbye."

"Must have been some other name," he told me. "They've never heard of a Prince."

Not that he was at all deflated. When I told him what I'd done about Goodge he asked me to get him in. I used the natty house phone. The police-surgeon came in while I was talking.

"Nine-twenty to the dot when he rang me from here," I told Anders, who was an old friend of mine. "That electric stove was on. I turned it off. You couldn't breathe in the place."

Anders got down and had a look. George drew a chalk line round the body. Goodge looked in and was asked to wait outside.

"Probably an Army Colt," Anders said. "Rammed clean up against the skull. He never knew a thing. Like the end of the world that hit him."

George nodded for me to fetch Matthews. Matthews said there were old prints on the window but none on the rail. George told him to get the body stripped and the pockets emptied.

"What's through there?" he asked me.

I said there was a bedroom and a bathroom. He moved on through then called back that I might as well bring my pal, the manager. You can guess the mood he was in.

We sat in the bedroom and Goodge wasn't the same man who'd desecrated the bathroom basin. George was suave too: handing out compliments and saying a man could only do his best. That was after Goodge said the maid hadn't opened the window and nobody knew anyone named Prince.

"Mr. Travers tells me that Mr. Ramplock owned this property," he told Goodge. "That flat was his own, so to speak. A bit small, though, isn't it?"

Goodge said Ramplock had had one of the larger ones with three bedrooms, but some months ago he'd changed to Number 5.

"Any special reason?"

Goodge looked away. He moistened his lips and said he didn't know a reason. Wharton leered and his mouth was like a dirty story.

"Sure? . . . We're men of the world, you know. Everything you tell us is strictly confidential."

"Well," he said, "strictly between ourselves I think it was something to do with Mrs. Ramplock. I mean it was no business of mine but that's what I've thought."

Maybe Wharton leered again. I didn't look till Goodge got some more revelations out of his system. Not a lot, but enough. There was probably some kind of separation. No mention of a divorce, at least as far as he'd heard.

"Any children?"

"A baby boy," Goodge said, and then corrected himself It was interesting that whereas he'd professed to be so poorly informed about the marital relationships of the Ramplocks, he should take care to tell us that the baby was hardly a baby but over two years old.

"Mrs. Ramplock used to spend some time here when she was in town?" I asked him.

"Yes," he said, "when there was the larger flat."

"Then what's in that room which is locked?"

You'd have thought he was Bluebeard. His shoulders gave a cringe. It was no business of his, he said. He didn't know what was in it.

"You've got a key," Wharton said. "Let's have a look inside."

But Goodge hadn't a key. Ramplock had given orders when he moved into the smaller flat for that room to be incorporated. It used to be a linen cupboard.

"The devil of a big linen cupboard?" I suggested.

"If you'll pardon me, sir"—that was the first time he'd addressed me like that—"this is the devil of a big place. I should have said that cleaning apparatus and so on was kept there as well. Then Mr. Ramplock had the Yale locks put in."

"Then who cleans the place?"

He could only shrug his shoulders at that one.

Wharton went to the door. Were there any keys in Ramplock's pockets? Matthews said there were. Wharton nodded back for us to come.

The faintest light came through with us from the lounge but beyond it that room was dark as death's night. Wharton found the light switch. Goodge began doing some more elaborating. Mr. Ramplock had had that door made, and the lighting arrangements altered, and the furniture brought in. Not that there was a lot of furniture: just a wardrobe, a dressing table and a chair, and a carpet on the floor.

"You see?" Goodge said, and smiled relievedly. "It was just a dressing-room."

What he meant was that there wasn't a bed. Wharton was sniffing, and I caught another whiff of that scent I'd noticed when I'd gone through the other rooms. We looked inside the empty wardrobe and the scent was stronger there. Wharton's eyes screwed up ironically.

"A dressing-room, you call it, and he kept all his clothes in the bedroom."

He waved a hand at the door and back we went to the lounge. There was a flash as a photograph was taken. We waited for a second one before Wharton got out his notebook.

"What's Mrs. Ramplock's address?"

It was near Watford, Goodge said. The house was called Timbers and the village was Fareholt, just north-west of Watford. The telephone number was Fareholt 556.

"Any letters for him this morning?"

Goodge didn't know. Usually the letters were on the breakfast table.

"You might find out," Wharton said. "And go on asking about Prince." A finger wagged playfully. "And keep all this to yourself. All you know is that he was found shot in his room."

The door closed on Goodge. Wharton gave a grunt.

"Wish I had the money it took to get his face that colour."

"Probably all on the house," I said.

Wharton waved an impatient hand at Matthews.

"Get your people in there. Go through it with a small-tooth comb."

Two of the circus went through to that dressing-room. Ramplock's body went out to the ambulance. Anders said he'd let us know whether the time of death tallied. A pity he hadn't had his breakfast. Corpses are sixpence a bunch, like radishes, to Anders and Wharton. I've never quite got used to them. In the presence of death—that great overwhelming finality—I can't even assume my usual protective colouring of a flippancy.

I began looking at the contents of Ramplock's pockets. A visiting card caught my eye and Wharton spotted it just as I did.

Mr. A.W. Prince
CENTRAL PALACE HOTEL

The name was printed in italics. The name of the hotel was printed in ink by hand. There were two good prints on it and one or two smudges. Wharton slipped on his gloves and turned it over. On the back something was printed, and again by hand:

YOU'LL BE SORRY

That was all, and it was underlined. Just like that. Wharton gave a prodigious grunt and hollered for Matthews.

"Where'd you find this card?"

"In his waistcoat pocket, sir. Right-hand bottom one."

"The prints his?"

"Yes, sir. And only his."

Wharton gave me a look. A hand waved Matthews back to the dressing-room.

"Queer business," he said. "What do you make of it?"

It's funny how he will invite me to theorise. Mine is one of those brains that act like lightning or not at all, and when George asks a question and I come back with a theory, it's long odds that he'll pooh-pooh it, or worse. If the holes he finds in it are yawning enough to be obvious, even to myself, then it's labelled contemptuously as one of *my* theories. If it is good enough to be tried out, then it's *our* theory while the trying out is going on. If it's a winner, then in some curious way it's *his* theory. And as far as the duds are concerned, he never ceases to be heavily sarcastic about the speed with which they were produced. George is not without an elephantine wit. Once he told me that at a second's notice I could account for the gullet of Jonah's whale or the vocal organs of Balaam's ass.

"What do I make of it?" I said to gain a second's time. "I'd say he's some sort of agent who travels about a lot. That's why he has blank cards and fills in the hotel address where he happens to be staying at a particular time. It seems odd that he should have been wearing gloves when he gave Ramplock that card or sent it to him. That might mean he had a criminal record. The threat on the back of the card isn't exactly confirmation, but it gives the same sort of feeling."

I looked to see how he was taking it and I might have known he wouldn't commit himself; all he did was grunt and go on looking at what was on the table. And those were just the things you'd have expected to find in the pockets of a man like Ramplock. Even the wallet had nothing but notes and some visiting cards. I looked at the label of the suit he'd been wearing, and it was made by a first-class man.

"Well, what next?" I said.

"Check up at that hotel," he said, and I waited while he began ringing the Yard. I had a look at the rest of Ramplock's clothes. Good quality, every one of them, and the shoes handmade. Nothing flamboyant about anything. Even his cigarette case was of stainless steel, though beautifully turned at that, and the wallet was good pigskin with no fancy work like a monogram.

"Well, we'll see what that brings forth," George said as he hung up. "Far too cluttered up, this case, already."

"What d'you mean?"

He shrugged his massive shoulders. George's mother was French, by the way, which accounts for the gestures and maybe the showmanship. Cluttered up with all sorts of irrelevances, he said. We'd heard about the love life of Ramplock and God knows what, but his idea was that there was nothing to do but cast the net for A.W. Prince. Just as simple as that.

"Then I might as well be pushing along," I said. "It's been nice seeing you, George. Mind if I tell Norris what's happened to our client? We might want to recover expenses from the estate."

George glared. He didn't say a thing, and because Matthews came in. Matthews is the quicksilver type, like myself, and he didn't come in—he bounced in.

"Two lots of prints in there, sir. His and another lot. Look like a woman's. And what about these, sir?"

There were three long black hairs and two small hairpins.

"Yes," George said, and almost beamed. "But go on looking. You may turn something else up."

"The love life of Owen Ramplock," he told me slowly and sarcastically. "And Goodge knew nothing about it. Oh no."

"Ramplock was the boss," I reminded him.

"I know, I know," he told me impatiently. Then he reckoned he might do worse than break the news to the wife. George rather fancies himself with women. He thinks he can handle them—purely in the way of business, of course.

"You get hold of Goodge downstairs," he told me. "Stir him up about those enquiries." The hand waved impatiently when I didn't move. "You know what to do. Don't want me to tell you everything, do you?"

"Only one thing, George," I said. "To whom shall I mark up my time? To the Broad Street Detective Agency, or whom?"

"What d'you want? An autographed letter from Buckingham Palace?"

"That might be rather nice," I said. "Meanwhile who am I working for? Myself, or Scotland Yard?"

"You will have your little joke," he told me, and it must have taken a force-pump to ooze out that smile. "What do you think I'm giving you orders for?"

"Good enough, George," I said, and waved a cheerful hand as I went out. I didn't walk along that corridor. It was more of a dainty trip. The peevish mood of the morning had gone. Ludovic Travers was himself again. He was working on a case again with George Wharton. The two old Musketeers were in action once more; each for both and both for each. Or me for George and George for himself. Not that it seemed to matter.

Chapter III
BOARD OF DIRECTORS

I ASKED about Goodge at the office where the sleek-haired gentleman was suddenly most courteous. Maybe someone had quietly passed along the information that I was public school and Cambridge, for he actually left his sanctum and scurried off in search of the missing manager. I had a change of feelings too, and I mean about Goodge. I'd thought him too dapper and smug and overfed, but now I could view him from a different angle.

Life for Goodge must have been nothing but putting up a front—of obsequiousness towards the clientele and of dignified aloofness towards his staff. Probably too there had to be nice graduations—from civility to servility—according to the monetary importance to the management of this tenant and that. As for him and Ramplock, when Ramplock whistled he would have to gallop. And now Ramplock was dead, he was facing a new orientation. Who was to be his new employer? If Mrs. Ramplock, then what would be her reactions to a manager who'd been well aware of, and even pandered to, the association of her husband and the woman who'd used that dressing-room. Naturally it would depend on the kind of woman Mrs. Ramplock was. If a prude, and that scandal reached her, then I imagined that Goodge would be looking for another job. No wonder then that, he was pretending an utter ignorance of most things that concerned the Ramplock flat.

A couple of minutes and Goodge had been run to earth. A uniformed nurse was with him. She was looking after an old lady in Flat 3, and it was she who had thought the corridor stuffy and had opened the window. But she made no objections about giving me her finger-prints. I put the paper in an envelope, with a covering note, and had it sent up to Wharton. With it went, or so it seemed to me, the idea that Prince had made himself scarce by the fire-escape, for she claimed that it was at least half-past nine when she opened the window, and it looked a certainty that Ramplock had been shot almost as soon as Prince entered the room, and that was definitely at nine-twenty.

Goodge also produced two letters which had been waiting on Ramplock's usual table. I opened them. One was from his tailors confirming an appointment and the other from a M. Solversen. It was addressed simply from Fareholt, and bore the previous day's date. I scanned it casually for Goodge's benefit, but it seemed to me a remarkably curious letter.

DEAR OWEN,

I figure from what I've learned from Jane that your trip down here was pretty much a waste of time. Looks to me as if you've gotten yourself in a hole that's going to be mighty hard to wriggle out of.

I'm not so sure about you myself, but we always got along pretty well, you and me, and I'd like to see things back where they were. If you think of seeing her again, you might do worse than have a word with me. That is *if* I don't happen to see you first, and *if* you're prepared to put all the cards on the table.

Yours,

M. SOLVERSEN

I gave a shrug of the shoulders as if neither letter was of any importance at all.

"Might as well keep them," I told Goodge, and put them in my pocket. "Anywhere we can talk quietly? And any hope of a cup of coffee?"

We went to his own office, a snug little room that looked out over the Park.

"You don't happen to have seen here with Mr. Ramplock, or heard him mention a man by the name of Solversen?" I said.

He'd never heard the name.

"He's probably an American, if that helps."

He still didn't know.

"He might be a close friend of the family. I rather think he lives in the same village."

That didn't help so I switched to Mrs. Ramplock. What sort of a woman was she.

"Very nice indeed," he told me. "Very charming."

"Any money?"

He nipped back into his shell. He just didn't know.

"Good-looking?"

"Very good-looking," he said. "Quite tall and what I'd call— well, gracious, if you know what I mean."

A waiter brought coffee and half-a-dozen delicious little macaroons: the sort for which you need only one bite.

"All this is very palatial," I said. "But to get back to Mrs. Ramplock. Was she what you'd call a prude?"

His pudgy palms spread at that. He said again she was a very charming lady. His face brightened when he remembered that all women ought to be prudes where their husbands were concerned, if I knew what he meant. I said I had some idea.

"Suppose you and I get down to things," I said. "It's snug in here. The perfect place for a confidential chat. Suppose, for instance, that Mrs. Ramplock inherits this property, and she does happen to have strait-laced ideas. Doesn't like her husband sleeping with other women, for instance. Some women don't, you know. And suppose she happens to find out about the goings on in Flat 5. Aren't you going to be on a spot?"

"But how could she!"

"Then there *were* goings on," I said. "But she won't hear it from the Yard. We don't ask dirty questions because we love dirty answers. We're not a collection of pornographiles"—I rather liked that word—"if you know what I mean. We're after facts. Things that have a bearing on this murder."

"But why bring her in?" he wanted to know. "I thought it was just something between Mr. Ramplock and this man Prince." The hands shook in a quick, flustered gesture. "I mean I don't know a thing, but that's how it looked to me. I mean when I thought about it."

"I know," I said. "Everything open and shut. Prince walks in and shoots. But how did he get in?"

That was something else that he'd missed.

I finished the cup of coffee, poured out another, and gave him a friendly little nod.

"All nice and confidential," I told him in the best Whartonian manner. "Mrs. Ramplock's never going to know a thing—if she doesn't know it already."

His eyes popped. I held up a soothing hand.

"Which is hardly likely. But you take my word for it that she's highly important as far as getting hold of Prince is concerned, so suppose you tell me everything you know or suspect about Flat 5. From that moment, shall we say, when Ramplock had the special adjustments made."

He still didn't like it. I ought to have been hurt at the ingratitude.

"The black-haired lady who used such attractive scent," I said. "Surely you'd rather talk about her confidentially here than have to be questioned at Scotland Yard."

That shook him. His tongue was moistening his lips. I poured him out some more coffee and offered him a cigarette.

"Well," he said. "I never knew any such lady but there *was* something. But you do understand, Mr. Travers, it was more than my place was worth to—well, to know anything."

I said I knew only too well. I was actually getting a liking for that fat little man. He was human. I could even think of him when things were slack on a warm afternoon, sunk in a chair with his feet up.

"There was something Mr. Ramplock said," he was going on. "It was when I was with him in that room seeing everything was satisfactory."

I could picture the scene. Ramplock knowing that Goodge must have ideas.

Ramplock: "By the way, you like the work here, don't you, Goodge?"

Goodge: "Yes, sir. I must say I like it very much."

Ramplock: "Good. I hope we shan't have to part company."

That was all. Goodge read the implied threat. That, he said, was why he sacked the waiter.

"What waiter?"

"Well, sir, it was just after that room was ready and Mr. Ramplock rang down to me that he wasn't feeling too well—I think he mentioned a hangover—and I was to send breakfast up. Nothing but plenty of toast and marmalade."

"And where did the waiter come in?"

"Well, sir, he noticed a thing or two, and there was that scent, as you said. I believe there was a lady's handbag. Then he got to talking and the head waiter heard of it and reported it to me."

"I see. And that waiter's name wasn't by any chance Prince?"

"Oh, no. Max Johnson was his name."

"His real name?"

"Yes, sir. We're most particular here."

"And Mr. Ramplock never had breakfast sent up again?"

He looked surprised that I should guess that. But it seemed logical enough. Ramplock had had a lady friend and the new set-up had been with her in mind. The first time she'd spent the night in his flat he'd sent down for a breakfast which was intended for two, but maybe he'd noticed the waiter's suspicions or had realised the *gaffe* about the handbag, or else he'd thought breakfasts were too dangerous.

"And no one ever saw the lady?"

He explained with a great deal of volubility. The block of flats must be thought of as a series of private houses. Not only were there the tenants and their families: there were also friends and acquaintances and chance callers. When some tenants were away they let friends from the country use their flats. There could be no such thing as a challenge to strangers. The only communal thing about the flats were the restaurant and the sharing of a maid. Robbery or burglary was not the concern of the management.

I'd guessed as much, if only because I own a block of flats myself. Something quite small and for the *hoi polloi*. I should know. I've lived in one of those flats—St. Martin's Chambers—for over twenty years. But I didn't tell that to Goodge, especially as he'd begun addressing me as sir.

"How could Prince have got into the flat?" I asked him. "We know that he just walked in, when Ramplock was in the act of telephoning. Ramplock was flabbergasted."

Goodge hadn't an idea. He couldn't have entered by what I'll call the dressing-room, for Ramplock had the key.

"Presumably Ramplock also had the key of the main entrance," I pointed out. "I can't imagine him having that door ajar. Mind you, I daresay I could pick that lock myself in a couple of ticks if I'd come prepared."

That horrified him. I don't quite know why but I gave him a pat on the shoulder as I got to my feet. He was a busy man, I said, and it'd been an unsettling morning. But he'd been most helpful, and we'd remember it.

I left him there and went slowly up the stairs to Wharton. I was thinking of Ramplock and how I didn't like him in the least. I'd seen a certain amount of superficial charm that morning on the golf course, but charm is an easy thing to have on tap. But don't get me wrong. Ramplock's morals didn't interest me beyond their possible connection with his death. I've skidded about a bit myself in my time and in my furtive moments I've thought monogamy a harshly Christian virtue. What left a nasty taste in my mouth was that subtle threat that Goodge hadn't failed to catch. There'd been in it egotism, a petty sense of power and a sneering disregard, and those, thank God, are none of my vices.

Matthews and his circus were still pottering around. George was in good spirits. Prince had stayed the previous night at the Central Palace Hotel. It was a huge caravanserai of a place and he wasn't hopeful of a description. But it was being worked on, and they were getting a photostat of the form he'd had to fill in. He'd rung Mrs. Ramplock and she hadn't seemed too distressed. She was not to come to town, he'd advised her, but he'd be seeing her some time in the afternoon. He'd also arranged at Warbeck House—headquarters of Ramplocks near St. Paul's—to see all the heads of departments at twelve o'clock sharp. That left us half an hour.

I began telling him what had been said by Goodge and myself. He was very non-committal but at least he didn't disapprove.

"That point about the key's a good one," he actually told me. "You got any ideas?"

"Far too many," I said.

"Oh?" He gave me his usual glare. "Such as what?"

There I was, being asked to theorise. I gave a little grunt of my own before taking the header.

"Begin with the lady," I said.

"Why?"

God knows, I said, "except that one's got to begin somewhere." Then I looked him clean in the eye. "Personally I don't think this Case is as open and shut as it looks on the face of it. Besides," I went hastily on, "if we get the reasons for the existence of Prince we might have a much better chance of finding him."

"Well?" he said, as if that wasn't unreasonable.

"Take the lady then," I said. "She couldn't have been what one might call a regular, or else Ramplock would have installed her in an establishment of her own. She was someone who was ready to spend a night here when they both felt like it. That must mean that he couldn't very well go to her place for fear of attracting attention or compromising her. The logical trend of all that is to make her a married woman. That room there was for her to dress in. Maybe she kept an evening frock and so on there in case they wanted to do a dinner or a show. It was also a handy room for her to nip in by with her own key. It also was a handy room to nip into if Ramplock happened to have an unexpected caller."

"Isn't that all obvious?"

"Maybe," I said. "But let's get to the Yale key she had. Neither she nor Ramplock might have been as careful as they ought. Her husband might have seen that key and managed a duplicate. He might have had her watched. In other words the lady's name might be Prince because her husband's name was Prince."

"Yes," he said, and his lips pursed out.

"Or Ramplock might have been framed. Prince might be the lady's boyfriend. Prince might have been doing a spot of blackmail. That's why he told Ramplock on that visiting card that he'd be sorry at not being prepared to pay."

"Yes," George said again. "It's far from unlikely."

"But there's a sort of confirmation," I told him. "The lady's belongings aren't in that room any longer. Therefore, presumably, she's gone. The liaison's over. And why? Because she was in the business of putting the screw on Ramplock? Because there was a husband and he found out? I don't know. But something tells me there's the devil of a lot of sense in the idea."

George grunted. He shook his head.

"It's worth bearing in mind if we don't collar Prince direct. It might be useful if we have to arrive at him the back way." Then he was shrugging his shoulders. Maybe he'd shown too much interest; committed himself to something that didn't look like being a certainty. "But we'll get him all right. He can't have got far. Wouldn't be surprised if he gives himself up."

It was time to be on the way to Ramplocks and we were in Camden Town before I remembered that Solversen letter. I gave it to George. I wish he wouldn't try his tricks with me but he put on his antiquated spectacles though they're nothing but plain glass. I guess they've become a kind of second nature. He's like one of those temperamental racehorses that won't gallop unless there's a favourite Billy-goat or something about.

"Who's Jane?" he wanted to know.

I said it might be Solversen's wife, or daughter, who was friendly with Mrs. Ramplock. It might even be Mrs. Ramplock herself. George didn't seem interested any longer. He was wondering what the hole was that Ramplock had got himself into.

"Might be something to do with why he rang the Agency this morning," I said. "It was some urgent reason. He wanted a man as soon as we could make it."

"It's all too muddled," he told me impatiently. "No use chewing the rag till we get things clearer in our minds. We'll pick up something where we're going, or my name's Robinson."

In another minute we were there. Warfare Street is on the City side of St. Paul's. I got out of the car, stretched my long legs and had a look at Warbeck House. It was like a stout, squat, homely old lady who hasn't done too badly for herself in her time. It was five stories high but its breadth made it seem less, and it had what I might call a comfortable sort of grime: something that wasn't an excrescence but had become a part of its yellow brickwork. The tall entrance doors, one of which was open, were of stout mahogany, and the floor of the spacious hall was of yellow and white tiling.

There was an air of bustle. Two people were at the enquiry office and I wondered if George would rush the queue. Then I saw something just beyond by the lifts—a bronze bust of a man on a rather ornate pedestal.

JAMES WARBECK
(Opened his first shop in 1872)

He was a bewhiskered man who looked something like Ibsen. Somehow it didn't seem incongruous in that building to be still extolling the Victorian virtues, and then it struck me that old Sam Ramplock's mother must have been a Warbeck. His son was Owen Warbeck and he'd called that block of flats Warbeck Grove.

"They're waiting for us," George was telling me. "Better take the lift."

We went up but only to the first floor. A man was apparently on the watch.

"Here you are, gentlemen. Dead on time."

"You're busy men and so are we," Wharton told him. "You're Mr. Drale?"

"That's right, sir. Henry Drale."

"I'm Superintendent Wharton and this is Mr. Ludovic Travers. Where do we talk?"

We went a few yards to the left, past the rising stairway, and to a room with MANAGING DIRECTOR in black on the frosted glass of its door. Drale held the door for us and in we went. It was a largish room as workmanlike and solid as the building itself. There were the usual desk, filing cabinets and plenty of chairs. On three of the walls were what looked like photographs of shops and staffs, and on the other an immense map of the London area, stuck with red, amber and green flags. Three people were in the room: two men and a woman. Drale did the introductions.

I couldn't conceive of three men being so dissimilar. Whereas one might have expected that similarity of work and maybe the slow assimilating influence of the building itself would have fashioned three directives to something of the same mould, those three might never have met till that morning in Drale's room. Maybe it might save time if I told you most of what we subsequently had to learn about them.

Drale himself was a man of just over fifty and he looked what he was—the managing director of a firm of provision dealers with whom he had spent his working life. He was of medium height, clean-shaven and with hair greying only at the temples. A self-made man obviously and one who had not only made a good job but had finished it off well. He was a good mixer. You could see he liked a drink, and whisky for preference. His dress was careless and almost shabby; his manner friendly but not boisterous. But his voice was just a bit hearty, as if he was used to men who liked the bluff, John-Bull attitude to things. His voice was pleasant and I placed him, rightly, as a Londoner. He was a widower, his wife and daughter having been killed in an air-raid. He lived at West Hampstead.

Richard Winter was something I never really understood, but I'd call it head of the department of sales, which meant that he overlooked all buying and timed the regular stocking of the Ramplock shops. He was thirty-nine and a second cousin of Owen Ramplock, and had been brought into the business after Cambridge, learning it the hard way from the ground floor up. In the war he had served in the tanks—he still wore a desert-rat moustache—and he looked as much out of place at his job as I should in the pulpit of St. Paul's. A tall, fine-looking fellow—I'd even call him distinguished-looking—and I was almost surprised to learn that he was uncommonly good at his job. His clothes were unobtrusive but quality and he was wearing an Old-Reptonian tie. His voice was disappointing. It was all right, so to speak, but just a bit foggy, as if he suffered from catarrh, and that wasn't likely by the look of his tanned face which seemed as if it had been left in the sun and forgotten. He was a bachelor with a flat at St. John's Wood and his hobby was book-collecting.

The third man, Charles Downe, was very near fifty, and life in an office was written all over him. He was the firm's Chief Accountant and, unlike the others, had only joined it during the war. His hair was reddish and he had a peaked, foxy-looking face, with little deep-set eyes as restless as his nervy self. His clothes were the neat greenish-grey of a thousand other professional men and if you had met him in the entrance hall you'd have taken him for a clerk, what with the quick shuffle of his walk, and the stuffed outside pocket of his coat with its pencils and pens. He too was a first-class man at his job. He was married, with a grown-up family of four, and lived at Willesden Green.

"This is Miss Haregood," Drale said. "She's Mr. Ramplock's secretary. I thought you might like to have her along."

She had given Wharton and myself a prim sort of bow. A school-marm to the life was what I thought her, though her age rather puzzled me. I put her, tentatively, at forty. She was tallish and slim, though far from making the best of her figure. The face was a neat oval, and spoiled by the hair that was drawn too tightly back. Her eyes I couldn't see, for they were masked by the horn-rimmed glasses. Had she been what she wasn't—

though what that might have been I couldn't quite imagine at the time—she'd have been a far from unpresentable brunette. Had one of the swagger beauty places got really down to work on her, and that had been followed up by a consultation with Hartnell, say, or Worth, the result might have been something more than passable. How she was at her job I never knew; only Owen Ramplock could really have told us that, but my own guess was that she was coldly efficient. Her voice was quiet and pleasant enough, with now and then a touch of aggression. She was unmarried, as you must have guessed, and shared a fiat with an aunt near Golders Green.

"Sit down, please," Wharton said briskly, and the five of us grouped ourselves a bit self-consciously. Wharton kept on his feet. He took his time in hooking on those antiquated spectacles and peered round at us over their tops.

"A tremendous shock, this," he told us tragically. "It must have come as a great surprise to you all. I suppose none of you could tell us why it could have happened?"

Eyes went almost furtively round. When Wharton talks it's my function to watch, and for the life of me I couldn't see a trace of real regret on a single face. Susan Haregood's face hadn't a trace of tears, but she wasn't wearing make-up and if she'd been womanly in spite of herself when she'd heard the news, then she'd done an admirable job of repairs.

Drale cleared his throat.

"I don't think any of us have any idea why he could have done it, Superintendent."

"No business worries?"

"None whatever as far as we know here."

"Any private worries?"

Eyes went round again. I just caught Drale nodding at Winter.

"Well," Winter said, in his rather husky voice, "there might have been. If there was, I still don't understand it." Wharton peered at him. His voice had just a touch of authority. No one can be more dignified when he chooses. "Hadn't you better elaborate?"

"Well," Winter said, and still with the same shuffling on his chair, "I could do so, if it's all confidential."

Foxy-faced Downe was peering round at him. A look of expectancy was there. Almost an avidity.

"Everything's confidential," Wharton told him. "Nothing said in this room will ever get out of it."

That shows the unblushing liar George can be in the cause of justice.

"Well," Winter said again, "he was trying to get a divorce from Jane—his wife"—that was a hasty correction—"and she wouldn't give him one. I rather think he then changed his mind and was trying for a reconciliation. He saw her last week-end but what happened I don't really know."

"But you think she turned him down."

Winter shot him a look. He smiled rather feebly and shuffled again in his seat.

"Well, yes . . . I imagine she did."

Wharton grunted. He looked patiently round but there was nothing else. He peered over the spectacle tops.

"Well, gentlemen—and Miss Haregood—you've all been frank with me"—there wasn't a trace of irony in the bland statement—"so I've come to a decision. I ought to be equally frank with you. Mr. Ramplock didn't kill himself. He was murdered."

Mouths gaped: eyes popped. Drale opened his mouth to speak, then closed it again.

"Who shot him we don't know," Wharton went on. "There's more than the chance that a man named Prince may be able to give us some information if we can get hold of him. That's why I rang here to see if anyone knew a man of that name. Prince, I should add, was definitely in Mr. Ramplock's flat at nine-twenty this morning."

Drale's mouth opened again, and shut. He got to his feet, decided it wasn't necessary, and sat down again.

"Yes, Mr. Drale?"

"I think I might help," Drale said heavily. "But not much. I think I may have seen this man Prince."

Chapter IV
"TIMBERS"

Drale had to do some explaining. He'd been out most of the morning at the Holborn warehouse—trying to settle some threatened labour trouble—and hadn't returned till just before Wharton last telephoned. It was after that that he'd heard of the Prince enquiries. It was about a month previously he'd seen the man.

"What morning was it when you went to Curtis Street, Miss Haregood?"

She frowned. It was a Friday—she was sure of that. Then she remembered. It was Friday, the 30th of September.

You'll follow Drale's story if I give you the set-up of Ramplock's room at Warbeck House. It had a private lift at what I might conveniently call the back, and one stepped out of it into a cloak-room and through that to the room itself. But to get to that room in the ordinary way one went through a sort of annexe, occupied by Miss Haregood and a typist—a Miss Purkes—who acted as watch dogs and admitted callers to the presence. Miss Haregood, by the way, had an inner sanctum of her own and there was also another cloakroom. Once the watchdogs had rung through and Ramplock was prepared to see the member of the staff or caller, then that particular person went through a baize-lined door and through a second door to the room. In some cases, if the caller was highly important, Ramplock would come through to the annexe room to give a special and individual welcome. All that hedging in had been old Sam's idea, for he hated noise.

The special lift was because he was fat and scant of breath—he died of a sudden heart attack—and because he liked to turn craftily up at that head office at hours unexpected by the staff.

But Drale wasn't too partial to all the mumbo-jumbo. He'd got so that he'd come into the annexe, give a hasty, "Is he alone?" and at a nod go straight through. That was what he did that morning. He barged, as it were, straight into the room, and there was Ramplock talking to a stranger, and a stranger who could only have entered that room by using the private lift. Drale hastily apologised. Ramplock frowned, and made no attempt at introductions, so Drale apologised again and backed out. But he'd heard Ramplock say something, and just as he'd entered the room.

"No you don't, Prince. You can't play that game on me."

"Interesting," Wharton said. "And you saw him plainly?"

"Not plainly," Drale said. "I sort of caught sight of him and that's all."

"Tell us what you know," Wharton told him coaxingly.

"Well," he said, and his forehead furrowed in thought, "he looked about forty, far as I remember. He looked more like a friend than a business acquaintance."

"Yes, but his looks. What sort of a face had he?"

"He had his hat on—I know that—and he was wearing glasses. Like Miss Haregood's, only smaller. And he had a rather thick, dark moustache."

That was all. Wharton began prompting again. Drale said he wouldn't call Prince a gentleman. As far as he remembered there was something commonplace if not seedy about him. Something that made him rather an oddity in that room. Ramplock, one rather gathered, took himself very seriously.

That was all Wharton got except that Drale hadn't mentioned the caller to a soul. Nor had Ramplock referred to it when Drale saw him that afternoon. The caller apparently was something purely private, and it was fairly important to note that the call had been made on the one day in weeks when Miss Haregood was out. She, by the way, had the right of entry.

"I hardly expect an answer," Wharton told us almost jocularly, "but I suppose no one else ever saw this Prince or heard him mentioned? You now, Miss Haregood. You opened Mr. Ramplock's correspondence?"

"Not letters marked Personal," she told him severely. I noticed how pale her face had suddenly become, but I wasn't prepared for the faint. Her eyes suddenly closed before Wharton could speak, and then she keeled over, just like that. Even

Winter, sitting next to her, only just caught her as she reached the floor.

A fluster was on. Wharton was saying that he needn't keep any of them any longer. But Drale might stay for a minute or two. Downe was coming back with water and Winter was holding the secretary's head in air.

"Take her to her room," Wharton said. "Or better still, Mr. Drale, let's you and me go to Mr. Ramplock's room. She should be all right in a moment or two."

I took it that the invitation included myself. As we walked the few yards to the annexe I was thinking about that faint. Had the Haregood's corsets been too tight, or had those revelations about Prince been too sudden and frightening? Had she been designedly away that morning when Prince had called? I didn't know. What I did know was that she hadn't looked like fainting when Wharton had mentioned murder, and the murder of a man with whom she'd closely worked.

I followed the other two into that annexe room. It was quite large and had the usual furnishings of an office, and its only occupant was a girl who'd been typing.

"Nothing happening, Daisy?"

"No, Mr. Drale," she said, and her voice seemed cheerful and eager. She was still smiling as I passed her. Our eyes met and I smiled. She kept on smiling and gave me a little nod. I liked her. She was cute as a kitten with a black nose. But hers was a pert little nose, and she was dainty and delightful as a young May morning.

I went on to Ramplock's room. It looked as if Sam's furnishings had been removed, for the new desk and chairs were definitely modern. So were the cabinets and the rather showy Indian carpet. Three or four water-colour drawings broke the flatness of the distempered walls: three walls, that is, for the fourth was almost covered by a map like the one in Drale's own room.

"What're the Stop, Caution and Go signs," Wharton wanted to know.

Drale smiled. They marked the thirty-four shops in London and the suburbs that constituted Ramplocks. A red flag meant that to date a shop was behind with its sales compared with the previous year: an amber flag that it was holding its own, and a green that it was ahead.

"Very neat," Wharton said, and waved Drale to a seat. His eyes were round the room as he stoked his pipe and lighted it. I offered Drale a cigarette.

"No use asking you gentlemen to have a drink?" Drale said.

"Not at the moment," Wharton told him. "As a matter of fact we're rather in a hurry. I wouldn't be surprised if we don't have our hands on this chap Prince at any moment. But about this firm of yours. How'd it start? Just give me a quick idea. All I want is to get a kind of background."

Drale told us what I'd guessed. James Warbeck had begun with the one shop. Then his wife had come into money and he had opened a second shop and enlarged the first. Sam Ramplock married the only daughter and by the time Sam inherited, there were seven shops. Sam, who never kept an idle penny and lived in the pre-Crippsian days when what a man made was practically his own, expanded the firm to the present thirty-four shops.

"And Mr. Owen Ramplock?" Wharton said. "Why did he take over when his father died? Speak well of the dead and all that, but surely he never was a business man?"

Drale said that Owen had got back from Germany—his camp had been transferred from Italy by the Germans—early in 1946. He'd had none too good a time and it was not till 1947 that he was fit again. Sam, feeling the twist of the taxation rack, didn't feel like pouring out money on this sporting hobby and that, and Owen himself seemed to have settled down. At any rate, he entered the business. He didn't have to go through the mill like Drale himself who'd begun as an errand boy in one of Warbeck's shops, but his was rather a series of conducted tours through the departments and some of the most important shops. Then he spent some time with Sam in the room where we then were, and then Sam died. Owen, who held almost a controlling interest by his father's will, took over.

"What's your own job?" Wharton asked.

Drale pointed to the map.

"That's my job, sir. Every one of those shops has to be as much under my eye as that pipe of yours is now. If it isn't burning right, I have to know just why."

"And your late chairman: what did he do?"

There was a hesitation. His lips moved and I wondered if there'd be a smile or a sneer. There was a smile: the sort of smile one might give as one watched a small boy kidding himself that he was an airman.

"Well, sir, he sort of kept a grip on everything."

"He chivvied you all round."

"I wouldn't say that exactly," Drale told him. "He was what I'd call a working chairman. Chairman-proprietor, so to speak."

"This is a private concern," I said. "Any objection to telling us who holds what shares?"

He made no bones about it. Owen Ramplock, by the terms of his father's will, held forty-five percent. Drale, by the same will held five per cent. Mrs. Ramplock had forty-five, Winter three and Downe two, and all by the terms of the same will.

"Let's suppose something," I said. "If someone—your chairman, for instance—had thought it best for all concerned to make this a public company, he couldn't have done it without getting a controlling interest. If his wife had been of his opinion, their two holdings could have easily outvoted the rest."

"That is so," he said. "It has to be so. But believe me, sir, we'd never have done what you suggest. We've customers who dealt with old Mr. Warbeck. We pride ourselves on giving personal attention. A public company's a different thing. It's just an impersonal machine, dividends first and dividends last."

"Exactly," I said. "But it was purely a supposition. I just wanted to be clear about how things stood. Just part of that background that Superintendent Wharton's trying to build up. If, for example, your late chairman was on bad terms with his wife, he'd have been on a spot if he wanted to control her shares as well as his own. If he couldn't have got the votes of yourself, Mr. Winter and Mr. Downe, for instance."

He made no comment at that.

"How's the firm doing?" Wharton cut in.

Drale said it was doing well, considering the times. Profit margins were heavily cut by costs and taxation but there were reserves and the financial position was strong.

I'd glanced at a sheet of business paper on the table by where I sat.

Directors

O.W. RAMPLOCK, M.C.
(Chairman)

H. DRALE
(Managing Director)

R. WINTER
C. DOWNE
J. RAMPLOCK

It prompted a question. Did Mrs. Ramplock take any active part in the business?

"None whatever, sir," Drale said.

"I see," I said. "It just makes the list a bit more impressive."

Drale smiled at what he considered a joke. Wharton said he was grateful for his help and might we go down the private way. Drale showed us through the lavatory cloak-room and the three of us just managed to get into the smallish lift. A touch of the button and we were at the ground floor. A turn to the left and there was a private door that opened on the entrance hall.

We shook hands and Drale went back up the stairs. I don t know what made me look round just as I was going through the main door, but I did. Downe was there, and I wondered what he was doing in that entrance hall, for his offices had been on the first floor, and he was peering out from a kind of passage that led to the staff cloak-rooms.

"Just a moment, George," I said to Wharton's back, and I turned and went through the hall, and just why I didn't know. Downe's sharp, foxy face crinkled in a smile as I came up.

"Goodbye, Mr. Downe," I said. "Afraid we've bothered you people considerably this morning, but you were all very kind. How's Miss Haregood, by the way?"

"Quite recovered," he told me. "Most distressing for a woman, you know, to be mixed up with all this."

"She thought a lot of Mr. Ramplock?"

"I wouldn't say that," he said. "The man had charm, of course, but she's a very level-headed person."

There had been a slight curl of the lip at that mention of Ramplock's charm. And then his fingers went to that pocket where I had time to count the three pencils and two pens. They went down again. It was rather like that nervous trick of my own when I'm at a mental loss or on the edge of discovery, but my fingers always go to my glasses.

"Some time we must have a chat about things," I told him suggestively.

"My dear sir, there's nothing I'd like better." The words were coming in a spate. "Don't let them draw the wool over your eyes about Ramplock."

I glanced back and there was Wharton impatiently looking for me at the door.

"We'll fix up a chat," I told Downe. "A confidential one, of course. I'll give you a ring—tomorrow, perhaps."

The thin lips had a self-satisfied grimace. His hand was bony and unresponsive as I shook it, and when I gave another quick glance back at the door, he was still standing where I'd left him, and I'd have wagered that on his face was still that smile of gratification and expectancy. It reminded me of what I call Wharton's Colosseum smile—the drooling smirk on the face of the lion who's espied a particularly plump Christian.

"Where the devil have you been?" George was asking as I got into the car.

"Having a word with Downe," I said. "Everything in the garden isn't so lovely as Drale made out. Or so I guess. Downe would like a strictly confidential talk with me some time."

"What's he getting at?"

"Don't know," I said, and then I was suddenly leaning forward and telling the driver to wait a moment. Daisy Purkes had come out of the main entrance and who should be following almost on her heels but Winter. I craned round and saw her cross the road and Winter nip across as the traffic surged forward. He caught her up and the two passed out of sight together round the bend.

"Remember that pretty little typist—Daisy?" I said to Wharton. "Looks as if Winter's taking her out to lunch."

He gave a grunt as the car moved on, then lugged out his note-book. I was glad he wasn't asking me to contribute, for all sorts of ideas were floating through my mind. I thought about Goodge and I thought about that hour we'd spent in Warbeck House. I thought about Mrs. Ramplock and the share set-up, and I did some useless guessing about the unknown Solversen and wished I'd asked someone at Warbeck House about him. I thought of Daisy and the fresh young charm of her and I wondered if Winter were really taking her to lunch, and why, and what was it that Downe was so anxious to tell me. And I was looking forward to the afternoon's visit to Fareholt as a boy looks forward to a birthday.

"If you feel like a spot of lunch you might as well get out here," George suddenly said, and I realised we were at the traffic lights in the Strand. "See you at the Yard at half-past two."

My wife was staying on with the friends with whom I'd spent that ten days' holiday, so I grabbed a taxi and had a quick meal at my club. Then I rang Norris at the Agency and gave him a shrewd idea of what had happened. Then I had to wait for another taxi and I was a bit late when I got to the Yard. George didn't notice. Sergeant Matthews was with him and all the exhibits were spread out on the table. As I came in they were having a look at that photostat copy of the form that Prince filled in at the Central Palace. I didn't see much connection between the writing and what had been on the visiting card, but, of course, one was writing and the other neat printing.

"Get a description?" I asked Matthews.

The chambermaid had given one, for Prince had rung her at about seven o'clock and asked if he might have an additional pillow. The description she gave was much like that we'd had from Drale, but she thought him a tallish man whereas Drale—who'd only seen him seated—thought him under the medium height. But he was dark-haired, full faced, had a thick moustache and had been wearing horn-rimmed glasses. And, according to her, he spoke with a northern accent.

I didn't argue that point. Matthews knew his job well enough to have been satisfied about her reasons. I asked if Prince had dined at the hotel.

"No means of checking," he said. "Dinner doesn't go on the bill. You pay for what you have."

"Did he have breakfast?"

The same again, he said. "Breakfast's included in the charge whether you have it or not. But we're trying to check up."

There was some other news. Anders said the time of death checked roughly with nine-twenty. The gun had probably been a Webley, Mark VI, and that throws a slug that would stop an elephant.

"Funny no one heard the shot," I said.

Matthews said there might have been a silencer. In any case there were only flats one to five along that corridor. Flat 4 was vacant after a quarter to nine, and neither the nurse nor the invalid lady in Flat 3 had heard a thing. George thought there must have been a silencer. Prince couldn't have been aware that Flat 4 was vacant—if it had been he who had done the shooting.

A whole lot of things that I'd never seen were on the table: a partly used cheque book and a book of stubs, for instance, and various letters which Matthews had thought might have something in them. I asked about the prints of the black-haired lady, but they weren't on record.

"Go over all this stuff again and see what you make of it," Wharton told him. "And get that broadcast description in hand. We ought to have been half-way to Watford before now."

Into his pocket went the spectacles, on went the blue overcoat and the bowler, and he was bustling downstairs to the car. We moved along more quickly after the irritating traffic lights of the Edgware Road, and we fairly shot forward when we left it for Fareholt, and ten minutes later we were entering the village, and we might have been fifty miles from town instead of just off the fringe of the outer suburbs.

"Look out for a post-office," Wharton told the driver.

We were on one at once—a post-office shop. I hopped out and made enquiries. Timbers, I was told, was through the village on the left, about a quarter of a mile on, and I'd spot it by a lodge at the entrance to its drive.

"Is there a Mr. Solversen living here?" I said.

The girl smiled.

"Oh yes. He lives at the lodge. He's Mrs. Ramplock's uncle—or something."

"I thought he was an American."

"Oh no," she said, and smiled again. "He's English, really. They say he was in Canada ever so long and he talks sort of funny."

"Good," I told her. "I like people who talk funny. You don't mean that he talks like an American or a Canadian? Like the people on the movies?"

"Well, yes," she said. "Like some of them."

"Good," I told her again, and gave her a smile as I went out.

There was no missing that lodge, if only because it was the only building after we'd left the last cluster of houses. It was a hideous little place: squat and yet fatuously ornate: one-storied and with Victorian-Gothic windows and surrounded about as much garden as gave room for a second-class spit. The door was shut as we went through the open white gate, and there wasn't a sign of life.

The drive went straight on through what must once have been lawns but now were just an untidy meadow. Then it turned under some elms that had hidden the house, and almost at once we were at the house itself. It was a monstrosity even more emetical than the Lodge. Old James Warbeck had built it, we were to learn, and there it stood as an epitome of what an architect could really achieve in the 1880's when up to his neck in the pseudo-romantic. It didn't sprawl—I will say that for it—but it reared up like the anti-macassared kind of castle it had been meant to be. Maybe James Warbeck had added a few ideas as well. Once, too, it had swarmed inside with maids in pink print dresses and outside with gardeners in baize aprons. Even now it was keeping up a certain dignity for the lawn that fronted it was nicely kept, the gravelled drive had no weeds, and the Michaelmas daises and dahlias were colourful in the autumn beds.

"Fine-looking place," George mumbled to me as the car halted at the turreted porch. "Wonder how the devil they get the help to keep it up."

Down a side drive leading to the back premises, I caught sight of a smart little coupé outside what had once been the stables. Ichabod, Ichabod, I almost said to George. Once there'd been handsome carriages there, and a coachman with a cockaded hat and underlings that hissed through their teeth as they curry-combed sleek horses or polished harness.

George was out of the car and giving a quick look round. He grunted at me as if to warn me to mind my manners, and his finger went to the bell-push. It seemed a long while before the door was opened, and by an elderly maid. She had a neck like an aged turkey's, and when Wharton spoke she peered as if she were deaf.

"Yes, sir," she told him. "Madam is expecting you. Will you come this way, sir. And you, sir?"

That afterthought had come when she had given me a quick look as if trying to place me. We followed her across the entrance hall where she ushered us into a room that faced the lawn. It was a lovely room, and it was hard to imagine it as it must have been in its heyday—crowded with furniture and knick-knacks, frilled covers and macrame-work, and its walls so thick with pictures, plates and photographs that the flowered wallpaper must have been a sheer waste. Now, but for a few fine period pieces, everything was modern and suitably sparse. The fireplace was new and above it hung a portrait of Owen Ramplock. It was vaguely familiar, and maybe I had seen it in some earlier Academy. I warmed my hands at the cheerful fire and then had a look at it. It looked just pre-war, and he was standing hatless and wearing a vivid green tweed coat, with one foot on the running-board of a maroon-coloured car.

From the fire-place I looked back at the room. A scent like summer lavender lingered about it. It had charm and colour.

The huge bowl of dahlias on the window table harmonised curiously with the softer tints of the carpet. A mirror reflected it like a Dutch interior.

"A lovely room," I said quietly to George.

I could have said that it was a woman's room: a room on which someone with exquisite taste had spent a loving care. And that was when the door had suddenly opened.

"So sorry you've been kept waiting."

The door framed her for a moment and then she came forward.

Wharton had got hastily to his feet and I noticed he hardly knew what to do with his hat.

"Mrs. Ramplock, is it? I'm Superintendent Wharton. This is Mr. Ludovic Travers."

The smile was quiet.

"Won't you sit down," she said. "And do take off your coats. Or are you cold?"

We took the overcoats off. The chesterfield was drawn up to the fire and the chair she took made the late afternoon light fall on her. It was almost as if Wharton himself had placed her— we almost in the shadow and she in clear light. Or was it that she had placed herself out in the vivid open where not even a thought could be concealed. And yet Wharton seemed finding it hard to begin.

CHAPTER V

TWO PEOPLE

IT WAS curious that a man like Goodge—a man one could never credit with a feeling for words or a happiness of phrase—should so aptly have epitomised Jane Ramplock in that word gracious. I was thinking how exquisitely or fortuitously right he had been. There was a sense of quality about her, a poise and an unforced charm and ease, and yet when she spoke or gestured it seemed as if it were with some special consideration for yourself: as if the words were said or the gesture made because you would know and understand.

She was thirty-four, and she had married Ramplock soon after Dunkirk. I've seen many women far more beautiful but few with so exquisite a charm. For a woman she was tall, and still slim. Her face was rather pale, but maybe that was accentuated by the sheer blackness of the hair and the dark brown eyes. The mouth seemed always to hold the suspicion of a smile.

"You haven't lived here very long," Wharton began. "Or did you live here when your father-in-law was still alive?"

"We moved in almost immediately afterwards," she said. "We were actually living in Sunningdale."

"This is a lovely room," I told her. "But how on earth do you manage to get the indoor help?"

"Most of the house is shut up," she said. "There's just Mary—the maid you saw—and a young nursemaid—you can hardly call her a Nanny—for my small son."

She had smiled at the mention of the boy. That smile still lingered quietly when Wharton spoke again.

"This must have been a distressing day for you, Mrs. Ramplock. I apologise humbly if I was too abrupt over the telephone. We try to break things gently but we can't always succeed."

"I thought you were perfectly charming," she told him. "It must be very difficult."

"But we're not going to trouble you now," he said. "Just a question or two and only because you might help. First of all, did you ever hear mentioned a man named Prince?"

"No," she said. "I can't say that I ever did."

"Mr. Ramplock never mentioned him?"

"Not in my hearing."

Wharton said there was nothing he hated so much as to cause distress, but he thought she ought to have the bare details of what happened where the unknown Prince was concerned.

"I really don't know him," she still said. "But he must have had some dreadful grievance against . . . my husband." That quick hesitation had been the only sign of the things we knew, and guessed.

"Undoubtedly," Wharton said. "But you, Mrs. Ramplock. When did you last see your husband?"

"On Sunday," she said. "Perhaps I'd better tell you about it."

"Please don't," Wharton said. "Not unless it has a bearing on what—on what happened."

"I think I prefer to tell you," she said. "For over six months now my husband and I have been virtually separated. Please don't ask me about it but I believe he was attracted by some other woman. He asked me to divorce him but I refused. I wasn't sure, you see, that he was sure of himself. Perhaps you see what I mean. There was also Peter—our boy. What I would have done ultimately I don't know. It would have depended on so many things. And then early last week he rang me up and asked if he might see me here. He hinted that he wanted to come back to me."

I wouldn't have put the question if it hadn't been for that slow shake of the head.

"But he was too late?"

"How did you know?" she said.

"I had the feeling that it might be so."

"Yes," she said, and slowly moistened her lips. "It *was* too late. You can hurt a person even quite a lot and still it doesn't seem to matter, and then they do just something else and at once everything's changed."

"And he did that one thing?"

"Yes," she said. "Something purely personal. I was wrong to let him come here on Sunday. I knew, even before he came."

There was a quietness as thoughts weaved and hovered in that lovely room. Wharton cleared his throat.

"Well, Mrs. Ramplock, we won't give you any more trouble. If anything should occur to you, you might be so good as to let me know. But, before I forget it. Who were your husband's solicitors?"

They were Quimper, Hove and Quimper of Old Broad Street, which was right on the Agency's doorstep. Wharton got to his feet.

"But won't you have tea?" she said. "I assure you it will be no trouble."

"Wouldn't dream of it," Wharton told her. "Not that it wasn't good of you, madam. The fact is we're in rather a hurry. We'd like to get back before dark and we have to see a man named Solversen."

"Solversen?" she said, and looked almost startled. "You don't mean my uncle?"

"This is an M. Solversen," Wharton told her guilefully. "We found a letter he'd written to Mr. Ramplock. Found it unopened at the flat. We hoped this Mr. Solversen might be able to help."

"He lives at the Lodge as you come in," she said, and behind the poise there seemed for the first time a suspicion of disquiet.

"Extraordinary!" Wharton said, and gave me a look.

"We're calling on a man we don't know and he turns up on the doorstep."

"If one can mention anything so vulgar as doorsteps in a house like this," I said.

There'd been no irony but she must have guessed what was in my mind.

"It *is* a monstrosity," she said. "I'm always having to apologise for it. We'd never have come here if it hadn't been for the will. Our own house was so much nicer."

"And this Mr. Solversen's your uncle?"

"Uncle Matthew," she said. "He's a delightful person but you may find him"—she frowned amusedly—"well, just a bit original. I love him, and Peter adores him."

I said that certain expressions in his letter gave the hint that he must have lived some time in America or Canada.

"Practically all his life in Canada," she said. "Between ourselves, he was what was known as a black sheep. Something foolish or other he did when he was a young man and the family shipped him over there. I believe that's the expression. He was just a natural born wanderer. He tells the most marvellous stories of all the things he did in Canada and the States."

"I know," I said. "Bar-keep, prospector, hobo, farm-hand—everything."

"But how did you know?"

"I didn't," I said. "But they always do, at least in books."

"You'll like him," she said. "He should be in now. If it's fine he always goes for a walk in the afternoon with Betty and Peter, but they were back some time ago."

We thanked her again and she went with us to the door. It seemed a curiously different world when the door closed: a world in which I, at least, was suddenly at a loss. Dusk was in the sky. A last sun was gilding the autumnal elms. Long shadows ran across the lawn.

"Matthew Solversen ought to be good," I said to George as I got into the car. "Did you see how her eyes lighted up when she talked about him?"

"Hope to God he'll be able to tell us something," George told me, and brought me down to earth. "Wonder if that broadcast will be out about Prince."

The car drew up just short of the Lodge. A light was showing through a curtained window. The door was open and we stepped into a brick-floored kitchen. Everywhere was spotlessly clean.

George opened his mouth as if to give a call, then closed it. Through the door facing us was coming the sound of a voice. It was a drawling voice, and it was clear.

"Sure, sure," it said, and, "Now, Jane, don't you be sorry, I've handled bigger things than this in my time. . . . Sure, sure . . . Yes, I'll remember. . . . Yes, I'll be along."

There was even the faint click of the receiver.

"Anyone at home?" George called.

The door opened and a man stood as a scarcely distinguishable blackness against the sudden light. He was of medium height and loose limbed.

"Come in, gentlemen," he told us. "I understand you want to see me. About some dam-fool letter or other I wrote to Owen Ramplock."

We went through to the living-room, and it too was almost uncannily tidy. A telephone stood on an oak desk and by it was a tray on which was a tea-pot. There was a horsehair sofa and a couple of horsehair chairs. The floor had coconut matting and an Axminster rug. Framed spotted prints were on the walls and a fire burned up brightly in the old-fashioned grate. A cat was curled up asleep on another rug along the steel fender. The stove shone, the kettle shone, and the cat looked sleek.

"Reckon it's more homely than smart," Solversen said in his drawling voice. "Haven't gotten around yet to smartenin' up, same as Jane have done at the house."

He was a man of about seventy, with a homely, humorous, clean-shaven face. I've never seen more wrinkles at the corners of a man's eyes and all the time it was as if he were peering at the sun. Then I placed his voice—why it had seemed so friendly and familiar. It was the echo of Lionel Barrymore's: Barrymore, the grandfather, say, in *You Can't Take It With You.*

Wharton lowered his bulk into one of the chairs. I chose the sofa. And if I try to reproduce that Barrymore hoarseness of Solversen's, I'm taking a risk. To you it may sound phoney, but it's the best I can do. And it's the general impression that will have to count.

"Jane tells me you folks have had no tea. Won't take long to make you a cup."

"No, sir, thank you all the same," Wharton told him. "We ought to be getting back to town. A cosy little place you've got here."

Solversen said we knew how it was. He hadn't made a lot of money in his time but he had enough to get along on. He liked Jane and the boy and the house was just big enough. We knew what getting houses was like. He'd jumped at the chance of the Lodge. And he liked it there. A real pretty part. People friendly too. He reckoned, in fact, that he might end his days there. And so the voice drawled on till Wharton slipped into an opening.

"This murder business must have been a bit of a shock."

"Sure," he said. "Murder's always a shock."

"This isn't your first murder?" George's tone had just a trace of irony.

Solversen admitted that it wasn't. He didn't claim to be in the same class as us two gentlemen—or did he say folks?—but he'd been a lot of things in his time. When he was a younger man he'd even put in a year or two with a Montreal Detective Agency.

He gave a slow shake of the head as if there were things he knew and could tell.

"Then you ought to be a God-send," Wharton told him. "Someone who can help keep his eyes and ears open. Did you ever hear, for instance, of a man of the name of Prince?"

"Prince?" The eyes wrinkled. "There was a feller named Prince I once knew in Montana but I guess he wouldn't be the one."

"Owen Ramplock ever mention the name?"

"No, sir. Not no one of the name of Prince."

Wharton told him all he knew about Prince. He said there'd be a broadcast description just before the six o'clock news. Solversen nodded but his eyes were wary.

"Now this letter?" He took it out of his wallet. "I wonder if you'd tell us just what was behind it. What was the hole that he'd got himself into?"

"You've seen Jane," he said. "She's a good woman, is Jane. A fine woman. Any man ought to be proud of Jane. Once you've left a woman like Jane you can't get her back just by whistlin'."

"And what did you think about this sudden wish for a reconciliation?"

Solversen said dryly that it was bad medicine to involve one's self in a dispute between husband and wife. I was as keen as George on getting information, and yet somehow I was enjoying things. Solversen had a shrewd brain. I guessed he was going to be even a match for George.

"Whose side were you on?"

Solversen said he was impartial. It was an affair between husband and wife. After what had happened he hadn't a tremendous lot of respect for Ramplock, but men were men and women were women. Wharton let out a patient breath, and it was pianissimo.

"You knew he'd got himself mixed up with some other woman?"

Solversen said mildly that he didn't know, but wasn't that usually the case?

"But no real evidence to go on?"

He guessed not.

"I see," Wharton said. "You never saw the lady. But about this final paragraph. Why did you want to see him first if he came down here again to see Mrs. Ramplock?"

Solversen said that you never knew. There was such a thing as oil on the waters.

"But isn't that the opposite of what you just told us? Wouldn't that be stepping in between husband and wife?"

Solversen crinkled up his eyes and reckoned it was and it wasn't.

"Isn't it a fact, as you just said, that you hadn't much use for Ramplock after the way he treated his wife and when he came down here you wanted to tell him just what you thought? Just the kind of skunk, shall we say, that he'd been?"

Solversen gave that a quick consideration. He might have. A man's temper often made him say things he didn't intend. On the whole he was reckoning it would have been better if he'd never written that dam-fool letter. No fool like an old fool, and somehow he'd never learned when to keep his mouth shut.

Wharton put the letter back in the wallet. The lips clamped tight, then slit to a smile.

"You didn't shoot Ramplock?"

"No, sir. I guess I didn't."

"And you've no idea who did?"

"No," said Solversen slowly, and rubbed his chin. "But what about this feller Prince?"

"We don't know," Wharton told him frankly. "But if you've been a detective in your time, you'll not be offended if I ask you where you were at, say, nine o'clock this morning."

"Nine o'clock." He fingered his chin reflectively. "At nine o'clock I was sort of talkin' things over with Jane. I thought there might be a letter."

"But there wasn't."

"No, sir; there wasn't. So we just talked."

"Well, that seems to be all," Wharton said, and got to his feet. On his face was that other Colosseum smile—that of the lion when the first spring has missed the Christian. "Glad to have met you, Mr. Solversen. We may be seeing you again. You never know. Meanwhile, goodbye."

If Solversen gripped his hand as he gripped mine, then even George must have winced. The light was switched on in the kitchen, and as I looked back from the car Solversen was only a black shape framed in the light of the open door. Then his voice came. George was in the car so it was I who went the few yards back.

"Something I just thought of," he said. "You might make a few enquiries at that office of Owen's. Wouldn't be surprised if you dug up something there."

"Such as what?" I said, but the door had closed.

"What the devil was he getting at?" Wharton wanted to know as the car moved off.

"Maybe Downe will tell us," I said.

"Downe," he said, and, as if that reminded him, "Solversen's a downy bird. I'll lay a fiver he knows a dam-sight more than he let on. And why'd Jane Ramplock ring him up? What'd she want him to keep his mouth shut about?"

The phrase was still almost a vulgarism. If George had felt in that drawing-room at "Timbers" a vision and a gleam, it had been less than momentarily. I could still feel the charm and the graciousness that had been Jane Ramplock's. That's why I said people had every reason to guard against intrusion into purely private and personal affairs.

"Wasn't her husband personal?" he cracked back at me.

"Once, maybe," I said. "She was uncommonly frank about all that."

"Frank!" he said, and snorted, and after that we didn't talk for quite a time. We were back in the Edgware Road before he suddenly announced that he'd been thinking.

"What was it that happened between her and her husband?" he was wanting to know. "Didn't she say in so many words that she'd have taken him back even up to the last minute if he hadn't done something. Something like . . ."

"A sin against the Holy Ghost?" I said as I waited for words.

"That's it," he told me. "What'd he do? I've an idea it might be important."

"Maybe the answer's at Warbeck House," I told him. "Even our clam-like friend Solversen hinted as much. Or was he trying to throw us off the trail? Get us away from 'Timbers'?"

George hunched himself well into his corner and begun thinking again.

I was thinking too, and about the two people we had seen back there at Fareholt, and there was something that suddenly struck me about Jane Ramplock. Her face had shown no signs of grief. Admittedly it had been hours since Wharton had broken the news to her, and yet, even after those hours, to talk about Ramplock should at least have brought back some faint emotion. Stoicism, poise, reserve—call it what you liked: somewhere there should have been a slight breaking point, if only a flush of the face or a hesitation, or a catch in the voice. Ramplock was her husband, her boy's father, and the man she'd have been prepared to take back and forgive only a few brief days ago, but she had spoken of him with a concern that seemed largely for herself: to justify the very absence of grief that she was demonstrating. The only time she had shown concern was when she had as good as asked us not to force her to say what that unpardonable thing had been which had set her irrevocably against him.

You see where all that was leading me? Absence, even of minutes, was lending disenchantment to the view and I was having furtive doubts about Jane Ramplock. Was it not only an infatuation for another woman that had made Ramplock leave her? Could a man tire of too much grace and poise? Was it only one facet of her that I, like Goodge, had seen? Why, for instance, had she rung Solversen so urgently? And why, during our interview at the house, had her only sign of disquiet been when Wharton had talked about seeing Solversen?

And what about Solversen himself? I had to admit that I'd liked the man. Jane Ramplock had warned us that we might find him odd, but all I had found him was only too natural, and because he seemed to me the logical product, so to speak, of the life he had led. Fareholt might find him odd, as that girl in the post-office had thought his way of talking was queer, because he didn't conform to a recognised pattern. I'd seen him as a kindly, honest soul who'd achieved a philosophical outlook and acceptance—something more valuable than life had given myself. Yet now I couldn't but wonder if he'd been just a little too obvious and transparent. If he had planned a deception, then everything had been in his favour; the very ungainliness of him, the wrinkled eyes and the dryly humorous twist of the mouth. Weren't they curiously at variance with the brain that had parried and warded off those questions of Wharton's with a deft agility and a smoother reticence?

It wasn't strange that Wharton should have been thinking along the same lines. We were not a long way from the Yard when he suddenly spoke. I had been so busy with my thoughts that his voice almost startled me.

"A queer cove, that Solversen. I don't know that I've ever run up against anyone quite like him."

"Yes," I said. "What was he? Just being his natural self or overdoing it for our benefit?"

"I've been wondering," he said. "Did you notice something fishy about his alibi?"

"Can't say that I did."

"Well, didn't he go out of his way to give Mrs. Ramplock an alibi tied up with his own?"

"You're right," I said. "But you're not looking for collusion?"

He grunted and settled back in his corner again. I did an internal chuckle. So George was beginning to cast the net wider. The Case wasn't open and shut. Prince wasn't the only fly who might finally have fouled the ointment.

"It's that business what he called you back for that's puzzling me," George said. "If he wanted to draw us away from Fareholt he couldn't have done it more clumsily." He gave a click of the tongue. "There we are, you see. All goes back to whether he was putting on an act. Was he genuine about digging up something at Warbeck House?"

It was too late to argue for we were back at the Yard. Matthews was waiting for us in George's room and he had nothing to report. Ramplock had drawn no large sums of money on his private account and there wasn't a thing of consequence among his papers. The broadcast appeal for Prince had duly gone out.

"In connection with the death of Mr. Owen Ramplock, the police are anxious to interview a Mr. A.W. Prince, last heard of at the Central Palace Hotel. . . ."

That might bring something at any time, or it might not. Wharton said that the first thing in the morning he'd be seeing Ramplock's solicitors. The will might give us some new ideas.

"You'd better see that chap Downe," he told me. "While you're there you might get a few alibis as well. Get in touch with me or Matthews when you've finished."

I said that mightn't be till the afternoon. And I had an idea. "Surely Ramplock and that lady of his must have had some other forms of relaxation," I said. "They must have gone to a theatre, say, or some sort of show. If she'd got so sure of him that he wanted to divorce his wife and marry her, then she wouldn't have been content merely to go on sneaking into that flat and sneaking out again?"

"What're you getting at?" George said.

"Well, why not do the rounds of the booking agencies. Find out if Ramplock rang up for seats. Find a show that the two went to and so get a line on the lady."

"A waste of time," George told me. "Who's to give us the line? Theatre attendants don't know names. All they see is numbered tickets."

"Tickets bought beforehand have names on them," I said, but he still wasn't enthusiastic. I didn't press the point. You don't when you're hungry and it's time to call it a day. But he stopped me at the door.

"Something I wanted to ask you about. What was that business about Ramplock being left forty-five per cent and his wife forty-five per cent? Why wasn't the son left the lot?"

"Perhaps Sam Ramplock wasn't sure of him," I said. "Perhaps he was surer of the wife. But I can't say. He might even have foreseen a marriage break-up."

"Ramplocks," he said, and pursed his lips. "It's what you call a private company. You know all about these things. Just explain it. Simply. Layman's language."

He seemed serious, but you never know with George—what he knows and what he's pretending not to know.

"A private company," I said. "The shares weren't obtainable by the general public. You can't buy them on the Stock Exchange. Sam owned Ramplocks. He may have had figurehead directors, but he owned it. Now it's owned in the proportions you heard this morning."

"And what'll happen now Owen Ramplock's dead?"

"That's a long story," I said. "When Sam died he had probably enough salted by to pay death duties. There're ways and means—legitimate and not so legitimate. Now it's different. The Commissioners of Inland Revenue assess the value of Ramplocks and death duties have to be paid. I'd say at a rough guess that those duties will be over a million." George gave a whistle.

"Remember when W.H. Smith and Sons became a public company last month?" I said. "That was because of death duties. The holding was valued at nine millions. Six millions had to be found for death duties, so they became a public company."

"That means what?"

"Shares were sold to the general public through underwriters to the tune of six millions. Preference shares and ordinary shares. The firm's now owned by the shareholders. The family, of course, would also retain shares. And that sort of thing will have to be done by Ramplocks. There *is* another way. They could sell out to another and bigger firm. That's just a bare outline. There's plenty more to it than that."

"I get it," George said. "I just wanted to know, that was all. And to get an idea of what might be attached to Owen Ramplock's will."

"If his wife gets everything, then she'll have control. Almost as much as old Sam Ramplock did. She'll have to decide how Ramplocks raise the death duties."

"Or someone will for her."

There'd been something enigmatical about that remark. I didn't query it. As I've said, I was only too anxious to call it a day.

CHAPTER VI
THE BUSY BEE

I THOUGHT that Downe, as an important cog in the Ramplock machine, mightn't get moving till well after nine o'clock, and it was half-past nine when I rang him. He still seemed anxious to see me and we fixed things for half-past ten, at a certain tea-shop near St. Paul's. I was on the dot but he was there first.

It was an L-shaped room and it seemed suggestive that he should be at a table round the bend out of sight of the entrance door. I didn't know if other executives from Warbeck House had morning coffee there, but even if they didn't, Charles Downe was taking no chances on being seen. He held out his hand as I came up and gave me his foxy smile.

"Any idea yet who did it?" he was asking me as soon as I sat down.

"Not yet," I said, and the answer seemed to be giving a certain gratification. A waitress came up and he asked if I'd have tea or coffee. In a subtle way that summed him up, Downe was suburban-minded, whatever his salary from Warbeck House. His wife, I cynically imagined, would be the sort who peeps from behind lace curtains. She would allude to him as *hubby* and their children would still be *the kiddies*. And that's not snobbishness even if you're thinking so. I'm middle-class myself. I flatter myself that I can talk as a brother man with a dustman. But a dustman hasn't the artificialities and the false pretensions of quite a lot of suburbia.

"I'm afraid I'm going to be a highly unpopular person this morning," I told him when my coffee came. "You probably know all about red-tape, and jackdaw bureaucrats. Well, I've got to get a whole lot of facts this morning about all you people at Warbeck House. They'll probably go into some pigeon-hole or other, but there it is. I've got to earn my keep."

"What sort of facts?" he wanted to know.

"Oh, alibis and things. Whether you all loved your late chairman or not."

Up went a finger and he was leaning forward. There was almost a gleam in his grey-blue fishy eyes and his tone was meant to be impressive.

"Don't let them fool you. You know what they'll be like: trying to make out he was this and that. Take my advice and form your own judgments."

"Thanks for the tip," I said. "As a matter of fact I'm rather the susceptible kind." I gave a wry shake of the head. "I've been fooled too often in my time. But about Ramplock. You suggest I'll be told what he wasn't. You tell me what he was."

"What he was," he said, and gave a little snort. "He was a spanner in the works, that's what he was. Thought he was a second Sam Ramplock. Nothing he didn't interfere with. Thought he knew more than those who'd spent their lives at a job."

"To be frank and vulgar, he was a first-class bitcher-up."

"My dear sir, you've got it." He was quite triumphant. Then he frowned. "What was that remark someone made about Dr. Johnson? Or was it Goldsmith? *Nullum qui tetavit non ornavit*—or something like that. My Latin's rusty but you see what I mean. Only he was the opposite."

"I know," I said. "Everything *he* touched he far from adorned. A bitcher-up, as I said. He must have been popular."

The lip drooped with the smile.

"He was hated. Everyone got to hate the sight of him. You'll be told about his charm. Charm—my God! Far as Ramplocks was concerned, the man was a menace."

"You're the sort of evidence I pray for," I told him in one of Wharton's guileful enthusiasms. "But let's begin at home, like charity. Just why did *you* hate him?"

He didn't even question it.

"I told you," he said. "Old Sam was a bit of a tartar. Secretive, you know, and a bit dictatorial, but by God he knew his job. He didn't pick your brains and then give you back your own ideas as if they were his own. He gave you a job and let you get on with it. Besides, I've got to like Ramplocks. It used to be what I'd call a happy ship, Mr. Travers. It's hard for a man to stand by and see it the other way."

"Coming from you, that's real evidence," I said. "You're an important man. A pretty big staff working under you and so on. You'd hear a lot of opinions. By the way, I wonder if you'd mind telling me in strict confidence what Ramplocks paid you?"

"Fifteen hundred," he said, "for what it's worth with things as they are."

"And Drale?"

"Two thousand."

"And Winter?"

"Twelve hundred. And, of course, we all get something from our holdings."

"Thanks," I said. "I just wanted to get a kind of background. Drale, of course, must have hated him because there can't be two managing directors. If two men ride a horse, one has to be behind."

"You've hit the nail right on the head."

"And Winter? He hated him because of Mrs. Ramplock, his cousin?"

"Yes," he said, but rather dubiously. "And again because Ramplock couldn't keep from interfering with his department. No use giving authority, Mr. Travers, and then perpetually in-terfering. It's irritating. It gets a man down. What's worse, it gets his job down. It got all our jobs down."

"Yes," I said. "Either a team, or nothing. You can't have a half-way house."

"You saw our Miss Haregood yesterday morning," he was going on. "There's a woman who knows her job. She hasn't been with us long but she was most competent. She felt it too. There were things she used to let drop from time to time when we were together—the rest of us, I mean." He shook an almost bewildered head. "Funny how things can settle on your nerves. We got so we couldn't even meet on a friendly occasion without sooner or later talking about Ramplock. Airing grievances and so on."

"More coffee?" I said.

He wouldn't have any more. I thought I'd better get down to cases.

"What you've told me has been invaluable. And yet, you know, we've got to arrive at this. We're conducting an enquiry into a murder. Did any of those people you've mentioned hate him enough to murder him? Had any of them got to that vital breaking point?"

"Don't know," he told me heavily. "You can't tell, Mr. Travers. People react differently. Even the most unexpected people."

"But what I confidentially suggested isn't impossible?"

"No," he said. "All the same I wouldn't like to commit myself."

I let out a deliberate breath.

"Ah, well. I've got to enquire into everyone's alibi. I may know more after that. And by the way, wouldn't it save bothering you at the office if you gave me yours now?"

He made no bones about it at all. He'd been a bit late that previous morning. Both he and his wife had over-slept. They'd spent the evening at the annual general meeting of a literary society of which he was secretary, and had got home late. So he'd not left home till half-past nine and had reached the office at a quarter-past ten.

"Good enough," I said, and got to my feet. I let him pay the bill and we walked together down the stairs. He said it might be as well if he went back first.

I gave him five minutes, then made my way to Warbeck House. I didn't take the lift but went up the stairs and into that sort of annexe office. Daisy Purkes was typing away but there was no sign of Susan Haregood. Her pert little nose seemed to lift as she gave me a smile.

"I dropped in to ask if Miss Haregood was quite fit again," I told her.

"She's absolutely all right," she told me. "Did you want to see her? She's in there, with Mr. Drale."

In there was Ramplock's room. I said I might see her later. Then I produced a roguish smile.

"Have a good lunch yesterday?"

Her eyes popped. But she didn't blush.

"You saw us?"

"More or less."

She smiled: her natural smile.

"The first time I've ever been to lunch with Mr. Winter. We just happened to meet, and he asked me."

"He's rather nice, isn't he?"

"Oh, awfully nice."

"I'm rather nice too."

She might be cute but she knew things. There was a quick appraising look before the smile came.

"Are you?"

"Nice enough to like to ask you to lunch."

"Uh-huh?"

"And what about doing ourselves well? Stefanoff's, in Causeway Street. Say at half-past twelve."

"Uh-huh?"

But there was a look that said she'd be there. I gave her a smile and went out. I turned at the door and she was watching me. Her own roguish smile was still there.

Winter was the next port of call. He was in conference and I had to wait a few minutes. The same old map was on the wall of his office and his desk seemed cluttered up with work. We had a friendly handshake.

"Shan't keep you long," I said, and spun him the tale about red-tape and getting a background. It was funny, I thought, that he didn't ask me for news about the murder. "You've a happy ship here?" I began.

"Well,"—he frowned—"if business can ever be really happy."

"Whistle while you work," I told him flippantly. "Did you all used to whistle?"

"Dam' little time for whistling," he told me, and a knuckle smoothed back that desert rat moustache. "Still, I suppose it wasn't worse than any other place. Things are sticky everywhere, you know. Never know where you are from one minute to the next."

"Ramplock popular?"

He shot me a look at that.

"Why shouldn't he be?"

"Oh, just things."

"Someone's been blowing the gaff?"

"That's not giving me much credit," I told him. "But why not be frank? Everything's confidential."

"Well," he said, and the knuckle was at work again, "I must say we were happier in old Ramplock's time. The trouble with Owen was that he thought he'd learned too much too soon."

"I know," I said. "He was atomic business sitting in his room with telephones all round him. Right at the heart of things. Finger on the pulse. Quick diagnoses."

"Yes," he said. "And quack remedies."

That might have been clever if he hadn't spoken so pontifically. It was as if he wanted me to treasure it up and tell it to my grandchildren.

"I know," I told him sympathetically. "And, by the way, I saw Mrs. Ramplock yesterday. A charming woman. So charming that I couldn't help thinking what a miracle her rival must be."

"Must we talk about that?" he told me coldly.

"Why not?" I said. "You don't want me to be brutal and say better here than at the Yard. You ever see the other lady?"

"Never," he said tersely. "We weren't even sure there *was* one. We merely deduced it from his wanting a divorce."

That seemed to tell me something else. A second ago I'd guessed he was in love with Jane Ramplock and now I thought I knew why that business at Ramplock's flat had been so ultra-cautious.

"I saw the uncle—Mr. Solversen—too."

He actually smiled.

"Quite a character, isn't he. I like him. He's frightfully gone on Jane and the boy."

"He was telling us he'd been a private detective in his time."

He smiled quite broadly.

"Between ourselves he's a bit of a windbag. I wouldn't be surprised if he hadn't been half the things he says."

I got to my feet. I said I wouldn't take up any more of his valuable time.

"Just the one thing," I added. "Same old red-tape. Just that little matter of an alibi."

"Yes," he said. "Where were you on the night of the fourteenth of January at seven o'clock."

There wasn't anything resembling a sneer: it was more as if he were prattling to gain time.

"That's it," I said. "Only it's yesterday morning at nine-twenty."

"In that case it's just the usual," he said. "Except that I got here a bit earlier. I think it was half-past nine. May even have been a quarter to ten."

"Time enough to have bumped Ramplock off and got here," I said, and I didn't make it too jocular.

He seemed rather amused.

"Now I come to think of it, you're right. I know I left my flat just before nine."

"And where's that?"

"St. John's Wood. Handy for cricket, if you've got the time."

"Handy for Regent's Park too, if you make the time."

"Yes," he said, and still seemed faintly amused. "All the same I didn't shoot Owen Ramplock. Mind you, I'll tell you strictly off the record that I wouldn't have minded something of the kind on occasions. Sorry I can't be more helpful."

"Don't let it spoil your lunch," I told him, and nodded genially as I went out. But I was in a bit of a sweat when I did get out. Like old Solversen I hadn't quite learned when to keep my mouth shut, and it had been on the tip of my tongue to add, about that matter of lunch, that I hoped he'd enjoyed his lunch of the previous day. And if I had, then he'd have been hot-foot along to Daisy to warn her to do no talking.

I thought I'd better call next on Drale. He wasn't in his room so I went back to Daisy. This time we were both rather solemn. He was still in the chairman's room, she said, and Miss Haregood was there too. I didn't see why two birds shouldn't be killed with the same stone, so she rang through. I was told to go right in.

The two were at a table which had been drawn out to the middle of the room and there wasn't much of it that wasn't occupied with papers. Drale, I gathered, was trying to get acquainted with the way Ramplock had mismanaged the office. Susan Haregood gave me a prim smile and said she was quite better. Drale actually fetched me a chair and cleared a space on the table. I said my piece about red-tape and alibis. Neither seemed alarmed.

Susan Haregood said she had followed the routine of a normal morning. She shared a flat at Tellier Park, Golders Green with an aunt who would vouch for the fact that she had left at half-past eight. Miss Purkes could say that both had arrived together at just before nine-fifteen.

"All dam nonsense, this," I said as I jotted the facts down. "So is asking you for the exact address."

It was No. 11, Tellier Park. I apologised again and turned to Drale. He lived at 7, Estover Road, West Hampstead. He'd lived there for twenty years, he said, and had hated to give it up when his wife and daughter were killed in that air-raid—a daylight raid when they were visiting friends at Camberwell. As for his alibi, he said I'd have to take his word, for the woman who looked after the house never arrived till he'd left. And he'd left a bit earlier because he wanted to be at the Holborn depot at nine.

"You ask Harmer, the manager," he said. "I'll get him for you."

I said it wasn't necessary. He insisted. He didn't want us going over all that business again.

Harmer came on the line.

"Morning, Charlie," Drale said. "Some necessary enquiries going on about Mr. Ramplock. A gentleman from Scotland Yard would like to speak to you."

He gave me a business-like nod and handed me the receiver.

"Mr. Harmer?" I said. "We're sorry to trouble you but these are routine enquiries and no reflection whatever on the people concerned, especially Mr. Drale here. We just have to be clear where people were at round about nine o'clock onwards yesterday morning. Mr. Drale was with you, I believe."

"That's right, sir," he said. "He was here just before nine and he and me were together till best part of eleven." He gave a little chuckle. "And didn't I know it!"

"That's all," I said, "and I'm very grateful."

"What'd you do at that depot?" I grinned at Drale. "Twist this chap Harmer's tail?"

"Shook him up a bit," Drale said wryly. "He's an old employee but he let things get slack. Miss Haregood knows all about Harmer."

"Well, that seems to be most of what I know," I said: and very casually: "I suppose there's some truth in what I've gathered about this not being altogether a happy ship?"

"Who said so?" Drale asked me sharply.

"A little bird. But suppose you tell me. Was it a happy ship?"

"Mr. Ramplock was a very charming man," Susan Haregood told me angrily, but there wasn't an angry spot on her cheek.

"So was Landru, or so one gathers," I told her sweetly. "But let's stick to the point. Why can't you two people give me a direct answer? What have you to fear? Some hoodoo about speaking ill of the dead?"

Drale let out a breath.

"Well, I'll say this, Mr. Travers. It was better when old Sam Ramplock was alive. Owen might have been charming to his own personal staff. He could be charming—if you'd call it that—with me, in his own peculiar way, but the fact is he thought he knew more than he did."

"What was your opinion of his business ability, Miss Haregood?"

"He used to work very hard. I think he enjoyed it, or most of the time."

She had a nice voice, I thought, when she forgot to be prim.

"Look," I said. "Let's finish all this with one ridiculous question. Did anybody here, in your highly confidential opinion, get so driven frantic by Ramplock that he thought the only way to stop it was murder?"

"Preposterous!"

"Too far-fetched," said Drale heavily.

"Ah, well," I said. "I never expected any other answer. But you two people tell me something else. You must have known all the ramifications of Ramplocks. You'd call this an exceedingly valuable property? What would it be capitalised at, for instance, if it were a public company? A million? More?"

The two exchanged a quick look. I thought she gave an even quicker shake of the head.

"Might be much more," Drale said. "But why did you ask?"

"We have to look at all angles," I told him enigmatically, and left it at that. "But just one other thing, and it's largely tittle-tattle. You know Mrs. Ramplock, Mr. Drale?"

"Very well indeed," he said. "I've known her ever since she was married. A very charming lady."

"Who was she?"

"Percy Solversen's daughter—his only daughter. He was a stockbroker. Killed like my wife, in an air-raid. A highly respected man in the City."

"You ever met her, Miss Haregood?"

"Just once," she said. "I thought she was very nice."

"Have you ever met the uncle?" I asked Drale.

He smiled.

"Matt Solversen? Yes. I think I've met him twice when I was at The Towers seeing—"

"You mean Timbers," Miss Haregood quietly corrected him.

"Always think of it as The Towers," he told me amusedly. "It always was The Towers till Owen changed it. Don't know why. The place is nothing else but towers."

"And what did you think of Solversen?"

"A most interesting old chap. Been in Canada all his life, you know, then thought he'd like to end his days back in the old country."

"He's really a genuine character?"

"Genuine?" he said, and laughed. "You pinch him and see."

I said that was all—at the moment—though I hoped we'd not have to pester people again.

"I heard that broadcast about Prince last night," he said. "I suppose you've had no answers?"

"Plenty of time," I said. "It's just as hard for a man to bolt as ever it was."

There was little time left so I went to Downe's office. He too seemed to be up to his eyes but as soon as I came in he dismissed the elderly woman who I found out was his secretary. My own voice was suitably impressive.

"Thanks again for that tip of yours. There was a certain amount of hushing-up."

His thin lips smiled in gratification.

"You'll see," he told me. "I'm in rather an awkward position or there're things I might say. But you'll see."

"You and I have got to get together confidentially on all this," I said. "I'm not suggesting you should be a spy or anything like that, but you would be doing me a personal favour if you kept your nose to the ground. If you find anything, just give me the private tip. I'll see that your name's never mentioned."

"I'll do that," he said.

I gave him the hush-hush sign and got to my feet. The Yard would find me, I said, or if he wanted to make it ultra-confidential, he could try my private number in the late evening.

It was twenty-past twelve. I walked round to Ludgate Hill and hopped a bus. It dropped me at Stefanoff's with two minutes in hand. I had to wait ten minutes more, and I was thinking she'd turned me down, till I saw the saucy little hat with the pheasant feather that I'd noticed in the office. But for that I'd hardly have recognised her five-foot nothing in the New Look coat. She was just a mite nervous in spite of the smile.

I ought to have rung for a table, but they know me there and we had a good one in the far corner with a window overlooking the Embankment. I gave her the menu and she said she'd rather leave it to me. I ordered boiled Surrey fowl with peas and new—from God knows where—potatoes for the main dish. She led off with *hors d'oeuvres* and I with thick soup, and when the time came we finished with an ice. She wouldn't have coffee. She said she liked lager, and because her father liked lager, so that's what we drank.

"Well, here we are then," I said, when we'd ordered. "How am I doing? As well as Mr. Winter?"

"He was just a bit stuffy," she said, and made a little moue. "Did nothing but ask me questions."

"Ridiculous," I said. I wasn't going to rush her. "Who wants to ask questions. Let's talk instead. You know my name's Travers and—"

"You live at St. Martin's Chambers." She giggled. "I looked it up in the directory."

"And quite right too," I told her. "Always check up on the forest where the big bad wolf hangs out."

I said I was old enough to be at least her uncle and I ought to call her Daisy. That seemed all right in Stefanoff's, though she told me, with more amusement than alarm, that I hadn't better forget if I came to the office again. Miss Haregood was hot on familiarities. I imagined that quite a few young fellows had made excuses to call at that office.

"What's Miss Haregood like?" I said.

"Not bad," she told me. "A bit stuffy but quite decent—really."

The trolley came. Daisy was a bit too dainty about filling her plate. A little encouragement from me and she ended up with a real plateful. She said she'd never be able to eat it all, but she did. We didn't do much talking till the wait between courses.

"We didn't decide what we were going to talk about," I said. "What do you suggest?"

She said she'd leave it to me. I said that was risky. I might start asking questions, like Mr. Winter.

"By the way, what sort of questions was he asking? Things like whether you had a boyfriend?"

"Stuffy questions," she said. "It was horrid—really. All about Mr. Ramplock's murder."

The main course arrived and somehow I was glad of it.

But I didn't plan an inquisitorial campaign or marshal any thoughts. I hoped she'd go on talking without any leads from me. And she did. Boiled chicken is a much handier conversational accessory than *hors d'oeuvres*. *Hors d'oeuvres* are awkward to manipulate. They demand attention.

"Naturally you're all interested," I said. "But what particular side of it was he interested in?"

"That man Prince who's supposed to have done it," she said. "We were all asked if we knew him. You see, I did sort of know him."

If I gave a start I think I concealed it and she was concentrating in any case on the wing bone of her chicken. But I needn't have pricked my ears. In a way it was only a false alarm.

CHAPTER VII
QUESTION OF MOTIVES

THIS WAS Daisy's version of what had happened on that Friday morning, September the 30th. She had been alone in the office when Drale came in. He'd lifted his eyebrows and nodded towards Ramplock's room, and she had nodded to imply that he was in. Drale went through.

She thought it funny that he should have come back almost at once, for he had been carrying quite a sheaf of papers, but between doors, so to speak, she had heard him say he'd come back later. He was frowning to himself as he went by her and then she remembered a Ministry of Food questionnaire about which he'd asked her that morning. He had a look at it and pointed out that everything had been pencilled in and it needed only Mr. Ramplock's signature.

"Buzz through in about a quarter of an hour if he's free," he told her. So in approximately fifteen minutes she rang through but Ramplock had gone out. She buzzed Drale's office but his secretary said he was out too. He'd been gone some minutes.

That was all but Winter had been so interested that he'd made her try to recall each detail, which was why she remembered it so well with me. Winter had excused himself about that questioning, or it might be truer to say he had found an excellent excuse.

All the staff—a shrewd limitation to Daisy and himself—were in duty bound to help the police catch the man Prince. They owed it to justice and they owed it to Ramplocks. That last bit, I thought, was a queer mouthful for a man like Winter.

"What'd *you* think about it?" I said.

"I thought he was silly," she told me with a pout. "I didn't even see him, so how could he expect me to help? I don't see how any of us could help except Mr. Drale. If you've never seen or heard anybody you can't do anything really." I agreed. Then I was asking her what she would like next. What about the blackberry and apple tart? She gave a smile of happy repletion and said she really couldn't eat another thing, but she didn't turn down the suggestion of an ice.

"How did Ramplock and Winter get on together, Daisy?"

"I wouldn't like to say," she told me. "They didn't always agree, though. Relations don't, do they?"

For some reason or other that was amusing her. I said I hadn't any, so I didn't know. In any case Ramplock and Winter were only second or third cousins or something like that.

"All I know is they were having a real proper row one afternoon," she told me. "You could hear right in our office: not what they said but just the row. Miss Haregood sent me out on some excuse so I shouldn't hear."

The recollection of that was amusing her too. I was thinking that Winter and Ramplock must have been doing a bit of bellowing to have been heard through old Sam's soundproof doors.

The ices came, and went, and the questions had to be more subtle. But she was too much of a subordinate to have been aware of the bad feeling, or its undercurrent, though she did say that Miss Haregood had sometimes been most exasperated.

"By the way," I said, and made myself amused at the idea, "did Mr. Winter ask you not to mention yesterday's lunch to her?"

"He didn't actually say the lunch," she said. "He said I oughtn't to tell anyone we'd been talking about the man in Mr. Ramplock's room."

"Prince?"

"Yes, Prince. I thought it was silly. As if I should!"

The ice had gone, as I said, and she was saying she'd simply have to fly. But I had to wait for the bill and it was then that I thought of something.

"Where'd you go for your holiday, Daisy?"

"Shanklin," she said, and her blue eyes lighted. "It was lovely. Lovely weather too."

"Where did Mr. Ramplock go?"

She didn't know. And yet she was frowning.

"No idea whatever?"

Well, she said, "I remember there was a folder on his desk one day when I had to go in. He'd been marking something on it and he put it in the drawer ever so quickly when I came in. It was about Northern Ireland. I remembered it because my married sister's gone to live there. In Londonderry, she is, and the folder had something about Londonderry on it."

I paid the bill just then and it helped to take the emphasis from what I'd been asking. Then I walked with her to the bus stop and waited till it came. She gave me quite a hilarious wave as it moved off. A nice girl, Daisy. Sort of fluffy, but far from fluffy minded. She'd had no illusions about why I asked her to lunch. And the mere presence of her had been good company. She hadn't even asked me if I was married. Or had she looked that up somewhere too?

I took a taxi to the Yard. Wharton was in his room, eating a frugal something off a tray, and he greeted me with almost a pathetic anxiety. He asked if I'd got anything. I said I'd got a devil of a lot, though it'd be up to him to assess its value. He called in the stenographer and I dictated the morning's adventures. It took me over an hour, but you know the details and I give merely my own conclusions.

I began with that private meeting with Charles Downe and gave it as my opinion that his alibi, even if it depended only on his wife's word, was quite unbreakable. My idea was that he not only loathed Ramplock but had no great affection for his colleagues. Carefully handled he might reveal all sorts of things about Warbeck House, but I doubted if they'd be more than what one might call scandal.

Richard Winter was almost certainly in love with Jane Ramplock, and that gave him two motives, the second of which he shared with the other two disgruntled heads of departments. His alibi wasn't worth the name, but the intriguing thing was that he'd been more cock-a-hoop than disturbed when I'd pointed out the fact. Maybe if we didn't soon get our hands on Prince, Winter might be the one on whom to concentrate, for there were not only things which I suspected he knew, but he was also mightily pleased with himself about knowing them.

Henry Drale had an unbreakable alibi, and he had been the stickiest in the matter of giving evidence about the utter dislike of Ramplock. But he'd been talking in the presence of a subordinate—Susan Haregood—and he might speak his mind more freely when alone.

Susan Haregood had no real alibi, unless it was the time taken between flat and office. Only her aunt, who might have been got at, could state the time of leaving the flat. Not that I suggested further enquiry, for Haregood could be disregarded as far as committing a murder was concerned. Put a gun in her hand and she'd probably scream. And that brought me to the lunch with Daisy, whom I called Miss Purkes. Two highly interesting things had emerged from it: one to do with Winter and the other with Drale. There was also a third thing to which I'd refer later.

I took Drale first. In my judgment, and in spite of what he'd assured us, he must have known something about Prince. Either that or he was phenomenally inquisitive. He'd asked Miss Purkes to tell him when Ramplock was free. Then he'd changed his mind and had probably nipped downstairs. Mightn't it have been because he was sufficiently interested in Ramplock's caller to have kept a look-out on that private door that led from Ramplock's lift to the entrance hall? I added that it was a pity we didn't know when Drale had come back to his room again.

Winter was at once more obvious and more complex. The name of Prince had conveyed something to him, and, as he couldn't question Miss Haregood, he had tried the typist. That was the measure of his anxiety to get by hook or crook more information about Prince. There seemed in fact, taking Winter and Drale together, a conspiracy of silence about Prince. I'm no great hand in creating atmosphere, but I did say that in that building I could feel disquiet, hatred and suspicion. Something big—even bigger maybe than the general loathing of Ramplock—was still heavily and oppressively in the air of Warbeck House. *And yet it oughtn't to be.* Ramplock was dead and everyone should have been happy—even if in a discreet sort of way. For there they all were, back in those halcyon days of old Sam Ramplock: days which by Winter, Downe and Drale were never mentioned but as the good old times that had ineluctably gone.

That was that. George said I certainly hadn't wasted my time. He even forced a chuckle about the expense account, and altogether he went to his limit by way of commendation. I reminded him there was still something else—that holiday folder of Northern Ireland which Ramplock had been studying. He didn't see it.

"Wouldn't he have taken the lady?" I asked archly.

That shot him into action. Matthews was brought in, and I had to go over the very little that I'd learned from Daisy.

"If he went there we'll soon find out," George said. "What's the number of his garage?"

Ramplock's sports Rolls had been garaged at Jopps in Keen Street, not two hundred yards from the flats. Matthews had been over the car for prints, but had found none of the lady's. George got on the telephone, and he seemed pleased with what he heard.

"He was away for just over three weeks," he said. "Left in the car on Wednesday the 13th of July and came back on Thursday the 3rd of August."

A quarter of an hour later he was still doing fine. He'd rung Fanum House about the shipping of Ramplock's car over to Ireland. Ramplock, as he knew, was an A.A. member, and they'd handled the car. Ramplock had crossed from Stranraer to Larne on the night of the 17th of July.

"It's looking prettier," I said. "Bet you both a new hat the lady was with him. That's why he went from Stranraer. The most unlikely spot to meet anyone who might recognise him. The Liverpool-Belfast crossing might have been different. It's the devil of a long drive from here right round to Stranraer so he spent the night somewhere. We might find out where."

"Couldn't we get a list of all the women passengers on the boat?"

That was Matthews' idea.

"Try the short cut first," Wharton said. "Let's go right to the place where he stayed. Or one of the places where he's likely to have stayed. A place with a golf course."

"You're right," I said. "And it wouldn't be one of the famous courses, like Newcastle, County Down. It'd be some quiet little course near the sea."

"There you are," George told Matthews. "Take a man with you and find out where he stayed. Get everything you can on the lady. You'd better fly to Belfast. There should be a plane some time handy."

Matthews stood by for another quarter of an hour. There was a plane that left at six-thirty. George and I had tea brought up and we were sitting back and feeling comfortable. Too comfortable, maybe, and only by contrast with the fact that hitherto we'd unearthed precious little. Now we could hope. If nothing turned up about Prince we had in our hands a few levers to prize up information. And the black-haired lady seemed a good bet. Matthews was a good man, and there was no telling what he'd unearth.

George said there was nothing for me at the moment. I was saying I'd report in the morning if I didn't hear from him before, when there was a tap at the door and old Sergeant Thoms came in. He had a slight grin on his face as he gave Wharton the letter.

"Came a few minutes ago, sir. No prints on it."

Wharton had a look, gave a contemptuous grunt and more or less threw that letter my way. It was on ordinary paper and bore neither date nor address.

"Heard your broadcast. Sorry we shan't be able to meet.

A.W. PRINCE."

I had a look at the envelope. It was commonplace and plain like the paper which it matched. It had an E.C. postmark and the time was 11.30.

"St. Paul's is E.C.," I said.

"So is Liverpool Street," he told me.

It took a moment or two to think that out.

"You mean he might have gone to Harwich? Taken a boat from there to somewhere?"

"He might. But it wouldn't have been under the name of Prince."

"But what about his passport?"

"What about his name?" George said, and grunted. "Any guarantee that Prince is his real name?"

I thought he was being awkward for the sake of it. Prince, whatever his real name, had written that letter. The neat printing was that of the visiting card.

"Might be a blind in any case," George said. "What's it tell us? Just dam' all."

I had an early dinner at my club and then went home in case there should be any letters. There was one from my wife, and as I didn't know when the Case would give me as certain a leisure, I began answering it. Then the telephone went. Charles Downe was on the line.

"I was hardly expecting to find you in, he said. Are you busy?"

I said it depended.

"I've been wondering all day if I ought to tell you something," he said. "Now I think it's my duty."

"Yes?" I said, expecting him to come out with it.

"Could you possibly run out here?" he said. "My wife and I would be very pleased to see you?"

I gave it a quick thought. Maybe it mightn't do any harm to see Downe in his *milieu.* He gave me the briefest directions. It was only five minutes from the station.

I went out to the nippy night air from the comfort of the flat and I wasn't feeling too happy. I took the Underground at Leicester Square and finally got out to Willesden Green, and I had no difficulty about finding the house. It was perfect suburbia: a between-wars detached villa in a typical residential road. You know the kind of thing: each house with its garage at the side; its almond trees and lilacs and laburnums; its crazy-paving to the front door and the rose-beds in the neat lawns, and the trimmed hedges that ranged the whole gamut from lonicera to privet.

But there weren't any lace curtains, and Mrs. Downe was a quiet but pleasant little woman with whom her hubby—she did allude to him as that—came first and last. She seemed quite upset that I had already eaten. But I did have a whisky.

"You leave us now, my dear," Downe told her. "We shan't be long and then perhaps Mr. Travers will change his mind about having something."

The short time turned out to be an hour and a half. It may not read like it and because I'll keep to the main facts. It actually took ten minutes before Downe even touched the fringes.

"You see it's largely surmise," he said. "But I put you down as a shrewd man, Mr. Travers. You've had business experience?"

I acknowledged that I had. I added that all the same I wasn't in his class. The compliment was wasted.

"I'll put things as simply as I can," he said. "About three months ago Ramplock approached me very confidentially as to what my attitude would be if there was a question of making Ramplocks a public company or selling out. Mind you, Mr. Travers, he was very cautious, and he insisted on the most implicit confidence. He almost made me swear on the Bible. But you see the point?"

"I think so," I said. "If a directors' meeting was called, he wanted to know which way the votes would go. Yours and, say, Winter's, would make a tie. He could then give the chairman's casting vote. Did he approach Winter, do you know?"

"I'm practically sure he did, but I don't actually know."

"What did you tell him?"

"I temporised. I said I'd have to use my judgment when the situation arose."

"And what would Winter say?"

"If he was approached, then I'm practically sure he'd be hostile."

"On account of Mrs. Ramplock?"

"Well, yes. And I don't think he'd have viewed the prospect with any favour."

I didn't ask why. I said what about Drale. He said Drale was a Ramplocks man. Ramplocks was his father and mother, so to speak.

"And Mrs. Ramplock?"

"Ah!" he said, and showed his yellowing teeth. "That's where Ramplock made his mistake. They say he'd left her for another woman. He didn't think that the time might come when he might need to use her votes."

Things were getting clearer: remarkably clearer.

"Tell me something," I said. "Something that's at the core of all this. *Why* should he want to make Ramplocks a public company, or sell out?"

"Simple, my dear sir. I think he was getting tired of business. You know his record? Never could stick to anything long. All enthusiasm for this, and then getting bored and trying something else. I'd say he had some sporting idea or other in his mind. That old road-racing idea, or big game hunting. That's why he'd want money."

"Either I'm dense or misinformed," I said. "How *could* he need money? He had plenty of money. What about Sam Ramplock's money?"

"Not what you'd think after death duties," Downe told me knowingly. "I've been making a few private enquiries and I think I'm in a position to know things. Most of Sam's money went on death duties, and there were various Nonconformist charities. Sam Ramplock had a religious streak. He left a good slice to this and that."

"I know all about Sam," I said. "One eye on God and the other on the till. But it still doesn't say that his son needed money."

He smiled. It was almost a sneer.

"I've calculated what his income was. Don't forget that his wife's would be included in his for purposes of tax. I put it at a maximum of fifty thousand a year. What he kept, that is. Other money had to be placed to reserve."

"And you don't call fifty thousand pounds money?"

"After paying tax he'd have under five thousand left," he told me. "Out of that would be the upkeep of the Fareholt place, and pretty big expenses. Not much left for road-racing or big game hunting?"

"Carry on," I said. "I think I see what you're driving at."

"Sell out," he said, "or realise on a block of shares and he'd have anything up to half a million."

"I see. He could live on his capital at the rate of another ten thousand a year and still have plenty, even if he lived to be a centenarian. But what's your own idea about his intentions towards Ramplocks?"

"I don't know," he told me with a shake of the head. "Something tells me he'd have preferred to sell out. Don't ask me why I think so. Somewhere or other I got the impression that that's how things were. I've been trying to think where, and how, but for the life of me I can't place it."

"To whom might he sell out?"

"My dear sir, there'd be plenty of buyers. I could tell you a dozen concerns off-hand that'd be glad to get hold of Ramplocks."

"Well, tell me some."

"Well, there's London Provisions, Hallett and Coke, Herringwoods, Smith and Grover—and some of the big stores."

"Take it as read," I said. "And that, very confidentially, was the situation as you saw it at Warbeck House?"

That was the situation, he told me impressively. He added that there were scores of little happenings that had increased his own certainties and with which he wouldn't bother me.

"So we're back where we left off this morning in that tea-shop," I said. "Everything boils down to this. Did someone who knew his intentions feel so strongly about it all that they took the only way out? If so it could surely be only one of the directors."

"My dear sir, surely not! No end of our people have a very strong attachment to the firm. I don't know how they'd have felt if they'd thought the old name was going."

That seemed pretty feeble.

"Besides, Ramplock had a most regrettable manner," he was going on. "Don't tell *me*. I know all about the Ramplock charm. And he could be a perfect swine. I've heard him speak to a man as if he was dirt. People resent that sort of thing. It cuts deep, Mr. Travers. More than once he spoke to me in a very unmannerly fashion. I told him once to his face that I resented it. I wouldn't stand for it."

What could one do with a man like that? What did he expect? That we should place the hundreds of employees on the suspect list? Send round a questionnaire?

PRIVATE AND STRICTLY CONFIDENTIAL

Dear Sir or Madam,

1. How would you feel if there were no Ramplocks?
2. What did (do) you think of our Mr. Ramplock when

   a. Alive?

   b. Dead?

3. Did our Mr. Ramplock ever

   a. Dent your ego?

   b. Shatter it?

etc. etc.

I didn't try any ironies with him, of course. I just listened and nodded and let him run on with only an occasional prompting. Then the clock struck ten and Mrs. Downe looked in. I had to have coffee and sandwiches and cake, and it was eleven o'clock before I could get away, and by the time I got home I was torpid as a broody hen. But it had been worth it. And that's what I was telling Wharton next morning.

* * * * *

I haven't mentioned Owen Ramplock's will. It dated from soon after his father's death and everything was left to his wife, with a considerable sum to the boy on coming of age and the remainder on his mother's death. That's just a bare outline of what had been purely a stop-gap will, till Sam Ramplock's estate was finally settled. Then, of course, there'd been the trouble between husband and wife and Ramplock had deferred the making of another will till his private and domestic affairs had ceased to be in a state of flux. But the important thing about that will, and after what I'd heard from Downe, was that Mrs. Ramplock was now in complete control. Forty-five inherited shares added to her original forty-five gave her ninety per cent of the votes that might change the future of Ramplocks.

But there was something else. Immediately on learning of her husband's death, Jane Ramplock had rung the solicitors. That was natural. Her husband might have turned spiteful and she was anxious for the boy. Winter, as I guessed, would also have known the provisions of the will. He'd have rung Jane Ramplock or gone to see her, or maybe she had rung him. Drale also had rung the solicitors, and with every reason. A business like Ramplocks can't exist on a day to day basis, and the terms of that will might have demanded immediate changes in the conduct of the firm.

You see what I'm driving at? On the day of Ramplock's death it was probably gathered around Warbeck House that his wife was now in control. And, as I've argued before, the menace of Ramplock had gone and the clouds should have been lifted. But as far as I'd seen they weren't. And why not? Even the least informed must have known that Ramplocks could no longer be a private company. Death duties had to be paid. Were they pondering just what she would do? If Ramplocks was to be made a public company, wouldn't their jobs lie at the mercy of the shareholders? If she decided to sell, mightn't they be redundant?

It wasn't such a complicated situation as it seemed, as I told George, for the main outlines were clear. Everything had to be seen against the background of what is known as Big Business. Sam Ramplock might have died a millionaire several times over but his money had gone into expansion. Where some men collected race-horses or old silver or houses, Sam collected shops. They mightn't all be money spinners but taken by and large, the firm of Ramplocks meant very big money indeed. Even that two per cent holding, if realised, would bring Charles Downe a nice little sum. You see the beginnings of intrigue? Did he and Winter wish for a sale even when Ramplock was alive? People will do all sorts of things for money. It's still the best motive for murder.

If Downe had few loyalties where Ramplocks were concerned, what about Drale? Would money compensate in his case for the possible loss of his job? And the prestige, and the glow of satisfaction it must have brought to a man who had begun life as an errand boy under James Warbeck? And would all three of those directors be wondering now who was going to double-cross whom? Who might try to influence Jane Ramplock for his own ends? Might Winter, as a relation, hope to step into Ramplock's shoes? Would Drale expect it as a reward for a life's service?

"That's all very nice and technical," George told me. "But we're not concerned with what's going on now. We've got to know the situation when Jane Ramplock wasn't in control. Before her husband was killed. That's our object."

"You're wrong," I said. "People commit murder for reasons. Ramplock might have been murdered for something that's happening *now*. That's why it's important to know what's happening now."

"I want people's motives," he told me obstinately.

"Dammit, I'm trying to tell you the motives! The main motive was simply getting rid of Ramplock. You know what things are like in the provision trade. My wife says they're worse than during the war. So think of Ramplocks. Those directors at Warbeck House were harassed by shortages, by planning, by forms, by war damage claims, by changes of policy, by rising overheads, labour troubles and the devil knows what, and then they had to have Owen Ramplock wished on them by the terms of Sam's will. What would you think, George, if some whipper-snapper who'd never pounded a beat was set over you and started telling you your job, and then acted behind your back, perhaps, and bitched everything up and then proceeded to lay the blame on you? I tell you that Ramplock was driving people crazy. When they got the idea that he might be going to mess about with the firm itself, that was the last straw.

"Wait a minute," I said, as he began to interrupt me. "Something else occurs about motives. About Winter's motives. He had two reasons we agreed on for hating Ramplock. But something else arises out of what Downe told me. Take that attempted reconciliation business that Ramplock tried with his wife. It didn't come off. And why not? I say because Ramplock didn't want her. What he wanted was her votes. Once he'd got them he'd have left her flat on her feet. I'd say that Winter guessed that and he told Jane Ramplock so and she believed him. Mightn't that be the unpardonable offence that made her determined never to take him back again?"

"Maybe," George said. "But that line of argument says Ramplock was a fake. Doesn't that contradict the facts? Hadn't he broken with the lady-friend? She'd gone—lock, stock and barrel. There wasn't a thing of hers in that dressing-room."

"Couldn't that have been part of the fake? Didn't I say he was going to take the lady back?"

"Leave it," he told me exasperatedly. George hates you to buzz at him like a wasp. "Besides, you're forgetting one important thing."

"Probably several," I said. "Which one do you mean?"

"Prince," he said. "What about Prince? Or doesn't he come in?"

I ignored the irony. I said he certainly did. I said it merely got us back to where we started—at Big Business.

"I might even have a shot at where he fits in," I told him. "I think he's probably the contact man of some film who wanted to get its hands on Ramplocks. A contact man, George, like our old friend Stanley. Maybe he's now on his way to Tel-Aviv."

George gave a snort, derisory and contemptuous, and washed the whole thing out. He was going to the inquest, he said, and then he'd have another look round Ramplock's flat and have a talk with Goodge. I said that if nothing had turned up from Matthews I might do worse than see Drale again. If nothing emerged from that, it might pay me to call on Solversen.

As it happened I didn't see either. At least, not at first.

Chapter VIII
FINDING THE LADY

I WANTED to see Norris and I preferred to use the Agency telephone. And I hadn't mentioned the brain-wave to George because it had only reached me in that last minute when we had finished talking about Prince, and because George might have pooh-poohed the idea and told me to go and see Drale. You mightn't think it a brain-wave at all but more in the nature of a drowning man's straw, but I had a hunch there might be something in it. And it was this. Ramplock had been playing golf that March morning at Morecombe Hill with someone who to me was a stranger. And Ramplock by his own admission and from what I'd since heard, was a busy man. Why then had he taken a whole morning off? Was the answer in the man with whom he'd been playing?

I had a brief chat with Norris and then Bertha Munney had Morecombe Hill for me on the telephone. It was the steward who was speaking. He knew me well enough from the old days.

"You've heard about Owen Ramplock?" I said.

"I have, sir. A real tragedy, sir, if I may say so."

"Yes," I said. "He wasn't a member, was he?"

"Not a member, sir. I think I only remember him playing here twice since the war."

"Do you remember that time I was playing last myself, in March? He was playing too. Do you know with whom?"

"With a member, sir. Mr. Herringwood."

My free hand went to my glasses. Something had stirred in the depths of memory.

"You don't happen to know if he's connected with Herringwoods, the retail grocery people?"

"I believe, sir, he is."

"Could you give me his private address?"

"Just a minute, sir, and I'll find it for you."

It was The Firs, Wood Lane, Gainbury. I said it was a purely private enquiry and nothing to do with Owen Ramplock's death, which shows what fluency in lying an association with George Wharton had produced. Then I looked up *The Stock Exchange Year Book.* Herringwoods, with over a hundred shops in London and the Home Counties, could easily have gulped down even Ramplocks. Their head offices were at Stirling House, Kingsway.

A final word with Norris and I went along to see my brokers. I asked for a director whom I knew well but had to see a head clerk instead. That meant making the visit official.

"Herringwoods aren't doing so well," I said. "I know the market has taken the devil of a knock these last few months, but I'd have thought the shares wouldn't have dropped well below par. You got any private dope?"

After he'd made sure everything was strictly confidential, he told me quite a lot. The annual general meeting was due in November and it looked like being a lively one. Herringwoods had branched out into the hotel business and there'd been what he called a certain amount of jiggery-pokery about the recent acquisition of a big hotel at Bournemouth. One of the directors—Ralph Herringwood, son of Tom Herringwood, the chairman—had had an interest in that hotel—or so it was likely to be disclosed, and must have made a packet over the sale. Also the shareholders were dissatisfied with the Board and wanted new blood and less of the Herringwood monopoly.

I didn't get much more from him, but what I had seemed enough. The best way to draw a red herring across the trail of that Bournemouth hotel business would have been for the Herringwoods to have set it off against yet another acquisition, to be able to announce at that annual meeting that the firm were in a position to acquire the fine old business of Ramplocks. New blood on the board, a thriving new concern to pump life-blood into the old: a gain of face and the Herringwoods still in the saddle—and the little business of the Bournemouth deal still conveniently shelved.

But where did it all fit in? Ramplock was the last man Herringwoods wanted dead. If Prince had really been the contact man, then he too would have wanted Ramplock very much alive. And yet I couldn't dismiss the whole thing so easily from my mind. Instead the thoughts began whirling round. Money. Big money. Money talks. Ramplocks needing money, according to Downe. Herringwoods needing what Ramplock might want to sell. Downe knew more than he'd yet told. He'd mentioned Herringwoods as a possible buyer, but had it been too casually and obscured by those other names? And how did it fit in the jigsaw of Ramplock's murder? Maybe I'd better have another crack at Downe.

Then I changed my mind. I found a taxi and told the driver to drop me at Stirling House, Kingsway.

It was a huge modern building that seemed to be occupied entirely by Herringwoods. The inside was like an ants' nest. No bust of a founder in its entrance hall and no mahogany doors, but swing doors and beyond them an air of high-pressure, super-atomic business. Compared with its enquiry office, that at Warbeck House was only a kiosk. It took me five minutes to ask where I could find Mr. Ralph Herringwood, and then I was told to enquire again on the first floor.

I went up the rubber-covered stairs rather than in the lift and came out on a vast landing and the usual corridors and maze of rooms. Facing me was the second enquiry room. A showy blonde wanted to know if I had an appointment and shrugged her shoulders when I said I hadn't. She said she doubted if Mr. Herringwood could see me. He was very busy that morning. I almost asked if he were buying hotels.

She produced a kind of form and asked if I'd like to state my business and call again. I asked for an envelope, wrote something on the form, sealed the envelope and asked for it to be handed to him at once. She shrugged her shoulders again, but went out. Her colleague gave me a dirty look as if I ought to play the game. I took a seat.

It was ten minutes before I was disturbed and then another blonde looked in: a younger one with a first-class figure and a smart get-up. "Mr. Travers?"

The smile was formal. It seemed to be inviting me outside.

"You wished to see Mr. Ralph Herringwood?"

The question, and the smile, seemed slightly perplexed. I said it had all been on the chit I sent him. That rather flummoxed her.

"Will you wait just another minute? I'll see Mr. Herringwood again."

There were chairs along the wall. I took one and crossed my long legs. I studied the excised pattern on the wall facing me and doodled mentally with the shapes. Five minutes of that and she was back. Her smile had almost all she'd got. Mr. Herringwood would see me. She almost took my arm as we went along the corridor. She opened a door and announced me.

It was a fine, airy, handsome room, all chromium and glass. Herringwood sat at a long, stream-lined desk at the far end and it seemed a Sabbath day's journey till I got to the hand he was holding out.

"Take a seat, Mr. Travers." He frowned. "Haven't I seen you somewhere before?" I told him where and he wasn't tickled at the recollection. The look he gave me was queer. It was even suspicious. He gave a little involuntary grunt, then the face was once more a mixture of care and regret.

"Bad about old Owen," he told me. "A good chap. One of the best. Not that I knew him too well. An occasional game of golf, perhaps. But he was a nice chap. A pretty horrible business, the way he was done in. You people got any ideas, or aren't I supposed to ask?"

I thought he was sparring for time. I'd had time too—to have a good look at him. The same beefiness was there and the same sensual mouth. No pullover, of course, but about the brown suit there was a floridness, and too much colour in the yellow polka-dot tie.

"Nothing much yet," I said. "That's why we're looking around. Thought you might perhaps tell us something."

"Me? My dear fellow, I hardly knew him."

"You knew him well enough to allude to him as old Owen?"

"Just a friendly expression. Everybody does it."

I didn't relax. A definite astringency seemed the right attitude.

"Ever hear of a man named Prince? Or calling himself Prince?"

The surprise seemed genuine.

"Not to my knowledge. Why? Should I?" Then he gaped a bit. "Wasn't that the chap the police wanted to interview?"

"That's the chap. We thought you might know him."

He looked for a moment as if he were going to turn nasty. He forced a smile instead.

"Is this a joke, or what? Why the devil should I know him?"

"That's what we wondered," I said. "We thought he might be a contact man."

That shook him. He shifted uneasily in his seat. He pushed the silver cigarette box towards me. I said I'd rather not.

"A contact man," he said, and the lip drooped. "I still think it's a joke."

"Maybe," I said. "But there've been rumours. They haven't got far, as yet, but we've heard 'em."

He forced another smile.

"Look, my dear fellow, why can't you talk straight. I'm a business man and I like straight talk. You say there were rumours. What the devil you mean I don't know but at least you might tell me."

"That's only fair," I said. "The rumours were that you people were interested in Ramplocks."

His face flushed. He tried to get a grip of himself, but he was stammering.

"R-Ramplocks? Ri-ri-ridiculous, my dear chap. Why the devil should we want to acquire a firm like Ramplocks?"

"That's what we hoped you'd tell us. Naturally in strict confidence."

He got to his feet a bit heavily and with hands on his desk before he straightened himself.

"The whole thing's nonsense. Malicious nonsense. You can take my word for it, and I ought to know."

"You never were interested?" I asked, and sat on. "Never."

"And you wouldn't be interested now?"

The *no* shaped itself and didn't come. The look was all at once quizzical, then roguish and arch.

"Is that fair? Mightn't you have put ideas in my head?"

"It'd be a desirable acquisition?"

"It might. I've never thought about it. You heard something?"

"Nothing definite," I said, and got to my feet. "But we'll probably be hearing more."

"From whom? Or oughtn't I to ask?"

"A little bird."

"Cock or hen?"

"That'd be telling."

I allowed myself to smile. I followed up the smile as I shook hands.

"Talking of hens, that's a pleasing line you've got in secretaries?"

"Miss Williams?" The smile faded. "Quite a nice girl. What's your own taste, by the way?"

"I don't run to secretaries these days," I told him at the door. "When I did I never minded a little ornament with the proficiency. That's between ourselves."

On that flippant note we parted, though I did say I hoped I wouldn't be troubling him again. But I'd got only a few yards down the corridor when he was calling me back. His face was very straight.

"I don't know if you've got any inside knowledge"—there was almost a wink of secrecy—"but I'd be grateful if you'd let me know if there's any truth in what you hinted just now about Ramplocks. If there is and anything comes of it, we'd like to suggest a bit of commission."

"Nice of you," I said. "Money's always useful."

He put a finger to his lips, gave me a nod and turned back. I went on and down the stairs. I went into a shop a few doors on, showed my Warrant Card and asked to use the telephone. It was the Yard that I rang. Travers, I said, and the Ramplock Case.

I wanted a couple of men, Higson for one—if he was available—and in a private car. I wanted them at the double, and I'd contact them at the corner of Essex Street and the Strand. Then I made my way there and had only five minutes to wait.

I described Ralph Herringwood. The car could be drawn up on the opposite side from Stirling House and if Herringwood came out he was to be followed. My guess was that he'd go somewhere for lunch and there he'd meet someone. If so I was to be rung at the Yard. If he didn't leave the building till the afternoon, he was still to be followed and a report made on whatever he did. He could be left when Higson was of the opinion that he'd finally turned in for the night. I'd need a report in any case at eight o'clock in the morning.

I took a taxi to Warbeck House. I had to wait ten minutes before I was admitted to Drale's room, and the look he gave me asked if my call was really necessary.

"I know," I said. "You're up to your eyes, and I'm a pest. I want ten minutes. Not a second more."

"Take a seat," he told me a shade more genially. Then out went his palms. "How I keep my sanity I don't know. Sometimes I think I'm mad. I'm not here at all. I'm in a home. These are all delusions," and he swished a furious hand across the table and its piles of forms and documents.

"Of course you're mad," I told him soothingly. "I'm mad. We're all mad. That's why none of us know it. We won't admit we're just specks in space and eternity. So let's talk like a couple of lunatics who think they're sane. Just one subject and I'd like a straight answer. Was Owen Ramplock thinking of making tremendous changes here?"

His fingers went to his chin, and stayed there.

"What do you mean exactly?"

"Was he thinking of selling out, if he could get the necessary votes?"

The fingers moved gently.

"Where'd you hear that?"

"We get around," I said.

The fingers gripped the chin.

"Put your cards on the table," he told me. "Soon as yours go down, I'll lay down mine."

"Herringwoods were mentioned," I said. "I've just seen Ralph Herringwood. He says they've never been interested. That's all—except I think he's a liar. Between ourselves, of course."

"That's all your cards?"

"The whole pack."

He grunted. The hand went down. It went forward to the cigarette box and pushed it towards me.

"You know more than I do," he told me. "I only had suspicions. You may have facts. I know all about Herringwoods. They're in a bit of a jam. Too many irons in the fire and the wrong people handling 'em."

He got to his feet. He took his time about picking out a cigarette and lighting it.

"Yes," he said, and as if to himself. "I'm a man of my word, Mr. Travers. I said I'd put my cards on the table and I will. But it's going to sound nasty. I said I was opposed to change. I said Ramplocks was Ramplocks and his father would turn in his grave at any idea of change. Then we got to words and I told him I'd oppose him: fight him tooth and nail. He asked if I valued my job—that's all. That was his way. A sneer and a hint. If he'd been within reach of my fist I could have struck him."

"I know," I said. "I know a man to whom he once spoke in a similar way."

"Yes," he said heavily. "But it's worried me. A man doesn't like to be under the virtual threat of losing his job. It worried me more when he was killed. I doubt if you'd find a man with better grounds than I had. That's why I wanted you to test my alibi—not leave it to my word."

"Forget it," I said. "But just one other question. Do you think any of your fellow directors were in the same boat?"

"I don't know," he told me frankly. "There was something in the air but I couldn't quite put my finger on it."

"Well, I'll be moving," I said. "But no need now to let it get you down. You and Mrs. Ramplock can get together."

"I'll surprise you," he said. "If she wants to sell out, I shan't oppose her."

I stared.

"You don't understand," he said. "You don't know the strain we've been under here. This last business has just about finished me. I'm like a tyre with the wind out. I'm not so young as I was. Time I turned in my hand. Started spending my money."

"But suppose she sold to Herringwoods?"

"One cheque's as good as another—if it's right." He let out a breath. "Perhaps I'm talking a bit wildly, but there it is. Things don't matter the same as they did."

"I still think you're wrong to let it get you down," I said, and held out my hand. "Now I'll push off. You ought to have kicked me out before."

"Always glad to see you," he told me, even if it was a bit list-lessly, and out I went. I thought for a moment of looking in on Daisy, but I didn't. It was a quarter to twelve and I nipped down the stairs and began looking for a taxi to take me to the Yard.

It was five minutes before I halted one, and as I settled in the corner I was feeling sorry for Drale. I'd known what it was in my time to be driven almost crazy by a man set suddenly in authority, and once more I had my own private nausea where Owen Ramplock was concerned. And I'd never liked Drale so much as that morning. Big business, of what I'll call the bluff and beery type, never has appealed to me, but about Drale that morning there had been something to rouse a sympathy and a fellow-feeling and a liking. And then again I was thinking about Big Business. I thought about what people called the Stanley Case: how fantastic it had been, and even melodramatic. But that's what life always was, and is, and will be. All this Ram-plock-Herringwood business wasn't fantastic. It was Big Busi-ness. The contact men, the bluffs, the undercurrents, the rake-offs, pressure that was really blackmail, and vast sums juggled like billiard balls, only there weren't any balls. Nothing was real. Never a cheque or the sweet musical rustle of a stack of five-pound notes. Just a whispered word or a surreptitious meeting. And that last reminded me of Ralph Herringwood.

Wharton wasn't back but there was a telephone message from Matthews.

GOT SOME RESULTS STOP HOPE TO HAVE BETTER STOP RETURNING FIRST PLANE MORNING STOP.

Matthews seemed on to something which he wasn't too keen on disclosing till he'd got some confirmation and additional evidence. There was no point in my puzzling my wits over what it was, so I had a look at a couple of morning papers and tried to keep my mind off the Ramplock Case.

It was exactly a quarter to one when the buzzer went.

Higson was put through.

"That you, Mr. Travers? . . . He's just gone into the Worlington Hotel."

"Alone?"

"No, sir. He got there five minutes ago and stayed outside as if expecting someone. Then a taxi came up and a woman got out and he sort of bustled her inside before I could get a really good look."

"No idea what she was like?"

"Not much, sir. She had the big fur collar of her coat all turned up round her face as if she didn't want to be seen. He just sort of grabbed her arm and in they went."

"I'll be along," I said. "You stay put."

I had a car on tap and it wasn't more than three minutes before the driver was moving off. He dropped me opposite Swan and Edgar's in Piccadilly. I told him to wait.

I walked the short distance to where I saw Higson's car. He was reading the newspaper with his back to a door.

"Still inside," he told me.

"You go in," I said, "and don't look too much like a cop. Say you're looking for someone if a waiter taps you. Find out just where Herringwood's table is. Don't worry about the lady." I got into the car alongside Maltby. A copper came up to move us on, and I flashed my card at him. I watched the hotel door and my heart was beating quite a lot quicker than normal. I wondered if I were really going to see the black-haired lady friend, and what I should do when I did. Should Herringwood be given the go-by and we concentrate on following the lady? Ought I to nip back for my own car? I didn't know, and I hadn't time for any more worrying, for Higson was coming out. He waited for the traffic to thin.

"In the grill room, sir. Just round to the right as you go in. There's a waiter's screen you can have a squint round." A man was crossing the foyer and I guessed he was the manager. I stopped him and showed my Warrant Card. His eyebrows lifted.

"Nothing wrong," I said. "We're interested in someone who's just come in. I'd like to make sure. He's probably in the Grill Room."

He took me round by a different way: anxious for there to be no fuss and saying one couldn't be responsible for the clientele. I said I wanted a look, and no more.

We went through and round by a hundred yards of corridor. He stopped at a door with a glass upper half. I drew the flimsy curtain thing on one side and had my look. The room was large and it was packed. But I picked up Herringwood and when an intervening head was moved, I saw the lady. I didn't need to look twice. There wasn't any mistaking Susan Haregood.

CHAPTER IX
LITTLE BY LITTLE

I DIDN'T KNOW I'd pushed the curtain back. I didn't know I'd moved away till I heard the manager's voice behind me. I didn't even hear what he said, but I told him I'd identified the man and he wasn't the one we wanted. I was aware of his thanks, and even the relief in his tone, and then I pulled myself together and said I was grateful, and then I hurried out. The traffic had thinned and I crossed to the car. Higson slid into the back seat.

"Any luck, sir?"

"Too much," I said. "No need to follow the lady when she comes out. Pick up Herringwood and stick to his tail. If he goes back to Kingsway, stick around and follow him where he goes when the day's over. If he goes home get any dope on him you can. This is his address. Get a good idea of his domestic set-up. That all clear?"

He said it was. I got out of the car and stood irresolutely on the pavement. I moved out of the way of the surging people and stood with my back to the door where Higson had stood, and I was trying to get a shape and coherence into things. But I couldn't do any thinking there and I went on to my car.

That meeting of Susan Haregood and Herringwood had been a staggering thing for both my expectations and the way I had seemed at last to be discerning a pattern behind the killing of Owen Ramplock. Could there be two people more dissimilar? She, prim, austere, coldly competent, and with the sex appeal of a ledger: he the hard-bitten business man with a sex life—or so I'd summed him up—whose chastest page would bring a blush to Haregood's cheek. What in heaven's name had those two in common?

You see how the sight of those two in that grill room had knocked me off my mental perch? I should have seen the connection from the very first moment, and yet I was only seeing it as I asked myself that question. Business was the connection— Big Business. Maybe Herringwood had been right when he said he had never been interested in Ramplocks, and that my mention of the firm had given him ideas. If so, he had got hold of Haregood to try and worm out of her whether or not it was true that Ramplocks was likely to be in the market.

Then suddenly my brain was functioning normally again. Something was badly wrong about that theory. I thought back. I saw myself and Herringwood in his room at Stirling House, and I somehow knew that I'd made no mistake about his being a liar. He *had* been interested in Ramplocks. Under-the-surface negotiations had been going on with Owen Ramplock. Susan Haregood must have had some confidential knowledge of them. That then was why he had rung her up and made that urgent appointment for lunch.

"Cock or hen?"

That's what he had said. And why drag in a hen? It's the cocks who're behind the Big Business. And the question had been put, as I recalled, about how the news of Herringwood's interest in Ramplocks had got to my ears. Possibly then I ought to modify the theory. He wasn't seeing her about the prospects now of a sale of Ramplocks, but to find out how the leakage of information had occurred. Maybe he was seeing her for both reasons.

Then I thought of something else. Suppose everything was wrong. Suppose Herringwood was seeing her for none of those reasons. Suppose he was seeing her *because he was implicated in Ramplock's death*? Suppose they were both somehow in it! Merely suppose he wanted to question her about just how much we, the police, knew!

I liked the idea. I had jolted him badly in his room. I'd expected action, and quick action. And first things would come first. If I'd scared him, then the scare hadn't been about business. He was too old and slippery a hand for that. He could have wriggled out of that without being scared. But suppose it was a question of his neck. That'd scare him to action. And with whom could he talk? Only with Susan Haregood. And not at once with her. She couldn't risk leaving Warbeck House till her normal lunch hour. And so he'd have to wait, and all the time he'd be wondering and sweating about just how much we knew.

I liked that theory and it gave me a line on the next course of action. At Piccadilly Circus I found an empty kiosk and rang the Yard. Wharton was in. I told him I thought I was on to something and I'd be seeing him in half an hour. Then I moved on to Warbeck House. It was still not much after one o'clock and I hoped that Drale would be out. He was. It was a kind of secretary's secretary that I saw—an elderly bald-headed man who told me he'd been with the firm for years.

"You keep a staff record here?" I said.

There was a record duly filed. But it wasn't a dossier. It was the record of an employee's service with the firm from the time of entry and included promotions. There was also a copy of the original testimonials or a note of the recommendation that had led to the employment.

"Good enough," I said. "Mind if I have a look at it?"

He went across the corridor to another room and through it to a smaller room. Except for a table and chair under a window, a dozen tall filing cabinets were its only furnishings. He waved a hand at them. Everything was in alphabetical order, as he pointed out.

"Let me have the key," I said, "and leave me to it. I expect you're pretty busy."

He didn't seem to be happy about it even when I told him that there'd be no trouble with Drale. Then I stuck the chair against the door-knob in case of a sudden re-entry and got to work on the files that included Susan Haregood. I found plenty. If anything I found too much. That was when I found her age was thirty-four. I wouldn't have been too surprised if she'd been forty-four. I'd put her as very near forty. But let me give you the brief, relevant data.

> *Joined Ramplocks March 1949.*
> *Previously Secretary-Receptionist at the Avington Hotel, Southbeach.*
> *Testimonial from the management stated her tact, competence and unusual grasp.*
> *Testimonials from Herringwoods, Limited, reinforced the above.*

It added that they parted with her with regret but wished her well in her new appointment. It was actually signed by Tom Herringwood, their Chairman.

That was a staggerer. I locked the file, put the chair back, hollered for the clerk, told him I hadn't found what I wanted, and made my way out to the car. I stopped at the first post-office and rang my brokers and asked for the man I'd seen before. He wasn't there, but someone else gave me the information I wanted. The Avington at Southbeach was one of the Herringwood hotels.

A stenographer was called in and I dictated the morning's happenings at length. When it was all over, George was good enough to say there might be something in our idea of Big Business after all. *Our idea*, you'll have noticed. Then there was the old question of where it got us.

I said I thought I'd indicated that clearly enough. Was or was not Herringwood implicated in the murder of Ramplock? Personally I thought he was in it up to the neck. Then the buzzer went. Higson was on the line again.

"Thought I'd better report, sir, that our friend's back in Kingsway again. The lady went off first, separately."

"Thanks," I said. "Carry on as I told you. Don't ring here unless he goes out again."

"I think we should stick tight," I told George. "Higson may have some more on him before the day's out. His alibi, for instance. I don't think we ought to alarm his wife with an interview."

"All the same," George said, "I think I'd like to run my eye over that Harewood woman again. Think I'll drop in and have a friendly chat with all concerned. I don't know that I oughtn't to get a copy of what you saw in that file. Might worm out of Drale or someone the name of some employee or other with a grievance. Get at the files that way."

I wasn't worrying about how George would do it. Guile was never his short suit. And he'd had that Colosseum smile, which was always a good sign. It might even mean that he had some private ideas. If so I'd never know of them till he'd tried them out. And he was being rather too casual about the nothing he'd learned that morning. The inquest had been formal, as I knew, and afterwards Goodge, or so he said, hadn't been too helpful. Nor had anything new been gathered at the flats. Then he told me, just casually, that the cremation was in the morning. He didn't even seem too enthusiastic about that message from Matthews.

"I think I'll see Solversen again," I said. "I think he knows something."

George grunted.

"If he does, how're you going to get him to talk?"

"Ways and means," I said. I can be just as casual as George.

I left him there and went down to the car. The sun was shining and it was a bracing October afternoon. That made me remember something. Solversen would be out on his usual afternoon walk with the boy and his nurse, so I let the car dawdle and it was just short of four o'clock when I turned in at the drive. The front door of the Lodge was open. I think it was just as I noticed it that I suddenly thought I knew a way to make old Solversen open his mouth.

He may have heard my steps on the brick path for he was at the door before I had reached it. There was the ungainly and yet somehow friendly look of him. His eyes wrinkled up but he didn't say a word.

"Afternoon, Mr. Solversen," I said. "I won't disturb you but I'm paying an official call on Mrs. Ramplock. I saw your door open and I wondered if you could tell me whether she was in or not."

The eyes seemed to have narrowed at that word *official*.

"Let me see now. It's . . . ?"

"Travers," I said. "I was here with Superintendent Wharton."

"Sure, sure," he said, and took the Warrant Card. He looked at it. He even turned it over and looked at the back.

"We're supposed to show a card," I told him. "It's meant as a guarantee that we're genuine. Not that some people don't ring up Scotland Yard as well."

He gave me the card back. There was a wry smile and a shake of the head.

"Guess we didn't have doodads like them in my time. Mighty handy though."

I thought his hand was going out. I remembered his grip and kept my own back.

"And you're on your way to see Jane. I doubt if she's in."

I gave a Whartonian grunt.

"A pity," I said. "It's highly important. I'll have to wait till she gets back. Any idea where she's gone?"

He didn't answer that. He was saying I might as well come in for a minute. He might ring the house and make sure. So I went past him through the door and on to the living-room, and all at once I had the queerest feeling when the knowledge of him was behind me and almost the breath of him at my neck. A sort of shiver went through me as if his hands would suddenly come forward and close about my neck. That was why I moved suddenly left when I was in that room, and was in a chair. At once that queer feeling went. The same cat was on the same rug and the same kettle sang gently on the polished stove. The same telephone was on the desk. But he didn't make for it. He had taken the other chair, and his pouch was out and he was rolling himself a cigarette.

"So you're goin' to see Jane," he said reflectively. "It wouldn't be about tomorrow?"

"Tomorrow?" I remembered. "If you mean the cremation, that's not my business. That's private and personal. I have to see her officially."

"Officially, you say. You mean about Owen?"

The same quiet drawl, and yet there seemed a hint of anxiety.

"Yes," I said. "Murder's a nasty business, Mr. Solversen. It's our job to get at the truth."

"Sure," he said, and as he lighted the cigarette he was giving me a slow scrutiny from under the shaggy grey eyebrows.

"Curious what people tell you when you're after evidence," I said, and kept my eyes on his. "You warn them that the truth's bound sooner or later to come out, but they don't believe you. They keep things back or tell you lies. Then they don't like it when they're due for a shock."

"What sort of a shock, son?"

That should have flattered my age, but somehow I don't think he was talking altogether to me. It was as if the word slipped out and his thoughts had been elsewhere.

"They're made to testify in a coroner's court—in public," I told him with what I hoped was grimness. "Instead of everything being told us in confidence, it's all dragged out in open court. That's sometimes a happy event for the newspapers."

"Yes," he said. "And you think Jane's keeping something back?"

"I didn't say so," I told him coldly. "But there's no law against a man drawing his own conclusions. And now, if you'll let me use your phone, I'll find out if she's in."

"Why the hurry? Let you and me talk this over. Don't like worryin' Jane—not till after tomorrow."

"A murder enquiry doesn't wait. I don't say we like it, Mr. Solversen, but there're times when people's feelings can't be taken into account. This happens to be one of them."

He was worried. The cigarette was out but he hadn't noticed.

"It's not unlikely that I may have to ask you to come to the Yard yourself," I told him. "You may be asked to make a statement. You'd rather have that, wouldn't you, than appear in a coroner's court?"

"A statement?" There was a grimness about the quiet question. "Just what do you mean, young man?"

"What I said. We're not convinced that you've told us all you know about Owen Ramplock. We'd like to ask you a few more questions. Officially, this time. And now I come to think of it, you might save my going on to the house. You might prefer to answer some questions now instead of elsewhere. You might know what Mrs. Ramplock knows. We think you do."

He gave a sort of grunt. There'd been too much to answer. And he was aware that the cigarette was out, for his long arm went forward and he dropped the butt on the fire.

"You're not forced to do as I suggest," I said. "But here's the first question. Did you ever hear of a firm named Herringwoods?"

"The name again?"

"Herringwoods. They have a chain of shops—stores, if you like—in London and the suburbs."

"No," he said. "Never heard the name till now."

"Have you ever seen down here a Susan Haregood? She was Owen Ramplock's secretary."

"Can't say as I have."

I wondered why he answered that question so promptly.

"Ever heard of her?"

"I might have. I sort of seem to recollect the name. Not more than that, though."

"Now a question I'd have put to Mrs. Ramplock," I said.

"She hinted at some sort of unpardonable offence her husband had recently given her. A month ago, say, she'd have been prepared to take him back. Then just recently this thing happened. What was it? What did he do?"

He grunted. He fingered his chin, just as Ralph Herringwood had done. He grunted again.

"You say this is confidential?"

"If I'm convinced that what you tell me is the truth, the whole truth, and nothing but the truth."

"Sounds like your coroner's court," he told me with a sudden dry humour. "Well, I reckon I can tell you."

He told me. In a way it was fantastic, and yet I knew it was the truth. And it had happened in the August just after she turned down her husband's request for a divorce.

She had been to town and she'd suddenly been aware that a man was following her. She'd seen him at lunch and twice during the afternoon at two of the stores. She had gone from Watford by Underground, and she noticed him again at Baker Street Station and she had seen him when she got out at Watford. She told Solversen about him.

He thought it over and had a scheme. He induced her to go to town again. He managed a quick word with her on the train and she said a car had been behind her own and she thought she had seen the man again. He, by the way, had gone to the station by bus. The upshot was that when at last at the end of that afternoon the man left her at Watford Station, Solversen followed him back to town, and to Chancery Lane, where he went into the offices of a firm of private enquiry agents. Solversen waited a bit till the man came out again, then he went in and asked to see one of the principals. It was the part of his story that he seemed to enjoy most, for he'd told Howard Cleeve—I'd recognised him from his description—not only that he'd break the neck of any man who pestered Jane Ramplock again, but that he could tell Owen Ramplock, his client, the same thing. Then he'd marched out.

"It was a firm called the Metropolitan Enquiry Bureau?" I asked him.

He said it was. And that Jane Ramplock had had no more bother. And what he'd also done was to tell her she'd been mistaken. The man hadn't been following her after all. But when he got wind of the reconciliation, he too didn't trust Owen's deathbed repentance. So about a fortnight ago he had told her the truth about the man. She had been furiously angry, and with reason, and it didn't sound like a reading from a penny novelette the way he put it.

"There was him, Mr. Travers, in that prisoner-of-war camp and Jane just sittin' and waitin' for him. When he did get home, I reckon it was Jane who got him back into shape again. Then he goes and quits her for some other woman and when she won't give him a divorce, the dirty rat tries to frame her."

I thought that last a bit of an exaggeration. Or was it? Could she have been caught in some situation that was innocent enough but could still have been twisted and distorted to make a case?

"Who was the man he had in mind?" I said. "Was it Winter?"

He didn't know, he said, but from the look he gave me I thought I'd gone near the truth.

"I like Dick Winter," he said. "I used to reckon he was a mite too high-hat. But he's genuine, Mr. Travers. And he's mighty fond of Jane and the boy. Don't reckon it goes no further."

"Was what you've been telling me the sort of thing you were going to tell Owen Ramplock if he came down here again?"

For a moment I thought he was going to close up, as he had done with Wharton. Then he reckoned it was and it wasn't.

What had worried him was what was behind it all. There were things that puzzled him. Something wasn't in keeping. Owen Ramplock himself, for instance. He'd got to know him pretty well. Life had made him at least a judge of character and motive, and it bewildered him that Owen should have done the things that he did. Something must have been behind it all. Somewhere there must have been some extraordinary motive, and if he had come to Fareholt again, he'd made up his mind to corner him and try to worm out of him just what it was.

In my job one can miss a vital point, and I missed one then. Maybe there was a reluctance to accept what Solversen had just told me as being more than private suspicion. Solversen, I tacitly and airily assumed, knew less about Ramplock than I had come to know. I could account for practically all that he had done, and that was why I missed something that might have solved that case in a matter of hours.

"This may be repetition," I said, "but did he, to your knowledge, ever try to force his wife to do anything, one way or the other, with her shares? To use her votes the way he wanted?"

That was a bit out of his depth and I gathered that she'd never discussed the matter with him. But when I put the matter more clearly, he said he vaguely remembered something Jane had told him that she wanted Ramplocks to stay as it was. She had liked old Sam Ramplock and that would have been Sam's wish.

"I want to see you get the man who killed Owen," he told me. "But I'll be frank with you, Mr. Travers. If it's goin' to make trouble for Jane, I'd as soon he went unhung. Nothin' ain't goin' to worry Jane more'n she've been worried already. He's dead and she've got her life ahead of her, and she've got the boy. Don't want that boy to grow up with nothin' stickin' to his name."

I accepted that attitude. I even respected it, and I wasn't prepared to be a special pleader on behalf of what we call justice.

"Just one last question," I said, "and I'm finished. You mentioned another woman. Everybody assumes there was another woman. You told Superintendent Wharton that there always was. But have you any private knowledge?"

The lips clamped tight. There was a dour shake of the head before he opened them again.

"No, sir, I guess I haven't. But I still hold there was a woman. Nothin' else could have gotten him in that mess."

There wasn't a doubt that he was keeping something back. I got to my feet, not because I'd finished with him, but because I thought I could handle him another way.

"I shan't need to see Mrs. Ramplock," I told him. "You've been frank with me and that's good enough. Now I want to put a proposition up to you."

"What sort of proposition, son?"

"This," I said. "I hope you know me better than when I first came into this room. I know you better, or I think I do. That's why I've decided not to see Mrs. Ramplock. And I'll surprise you by saying that I've her interests at heart as much as you have. I don't want her name to be smirched, or the boy's. I'm going to do my best from now on to keep her out of things. *If* you'll help me. As far as she's concerned, why shouldn't you and I form a sort of partnership? You help in any way you can to find Owen Ramplock's murderer and I do my damnedest to keep her clear of everything. What do you say?"

I didn't smile and I didn't pose. I just looked him straight in the eye.

"I trust you," I said. "The question is, are you prepared to trust me?"

His eyes shifted first.

"I reckon I am," he told me simply. "I might have to think things over. All the same I guess you and me can sort of work together."

"I know we can. That was a smart job you did over that detective agency. You keep your eyes and ears open. Think back and see if you can remember anything that has a bearing, then let me know. Not at the Yard. Ring me late in the evening—any evening—at this number instead. Or come and see me."

He said he would. And he had the last question. Was he free to tell Jane what we'd been talking about?

"Use your own judgment," I said as I held out my hand. "No use being in partnership if one partner doesn't trust the other. Tell her just as much as you like."

He watched from the door as I reversed the car and drove through the gates. I took it steady on the way back through Fareholt, for I was doing a lot of thinking about Solversen. Maybe he was a bit of an exhibitionist as Winter had suggested. Maybe his life in Canada and the States had been pretty humdrum, and those experiences of his were only the product of an imaginative mind. I doubted if he'd ever had a job with a detective agency, for instance, in Canada or the States, for there'd been that business of my Warrant Card which he'd claimed was something new to him. Yet every private eye had something similar, or was I wrong. Maybe it was fifty years ago when he had had the experience he'd claimed, and how things had been then I didn't know.

That he was very much of a paradox I was well aware. That drawling, soothing, almost hypnotic voice of his could make most men believe him. That, and his homely face, gave a verisimilitude. But somehow I couldn't make a final summing-up. All I could do was hope. That he knew more than he'd told me was almost certain. The only doubt was whether or not I'd convinced him that he might safely tell me that more.

My car was running out of petrol and I pulled up at a garage on the by-pass. I told the man to look at the tyres for one had seemed a shade flat, and while I stood there waiting for change for the pound note I'd given him, a car came slowly by. Had there not been a street lamp and if that car had not been crawling behind a huge lorry I should never have seen its driver so clearly, but as it was there was no mistake. It was Winter.

So Winter was running down to Timbers. A longish journey, that, in the dark and with a threat of fog. Maybe he was going to settle some final arrangements about the next day's cremation. I wouldn't know, but there was something that came to me as I took my change from the garage hand. Winter was a man who'd been neglected. True, we'd had little time, and the enquiry, for that matter, had hardly begun. And yet something was telling me that we ought to have found time to spare for Winter. I was to blame. I was the one who'd assured Wharton that Winter not only knew things but was highly complacent about knowing them.

It brought on a despondency. Winter, for all his motives, didn't seem to me the sort of man who'd resort to murder, even on some mad, quixotic impulse and for something that had seemed to him to be threatening Jane Ramplock. And nothing was more certain, or so it seemed in the light of that interview with Solversen, than that Solversen himself had had no hand in the killing. And Ralph Herringwood was surely not so desperate as to have thought murder the only way out. Or was he? Would that hotel scandal be sufficient to land him in jail? I didn't know, and somehow I didn't care. All I knew was that the fog was gathering and it was a raw night, and I had to concentrate on driving that car. I wasn't feeling any happier when at last I drew in at the Yard.

Chapter X

THE LADY FOUND

GEORGE HAD just got back. He said it was a dirty night and would I like a cup of tea. He'd just rung down for one, and I made it two.

Perhaps it was because I was looking a bit frayed that he didn't begin pestering me about my afternoon. He'd spent his time at Warbeck House, he said. He'd seen the Haregood file and had talks with Drale and Downe and Winter.

"Winter," I said. "I passed him about a mile along the by-pass. I'd say he was going to see Jane Ramplock. Why? Because of anything you happened to say to him?"

He began a slow prowl round the room. A pot of tea came in but he was still trying to think things out.

"Can't see the connection," he told me at last. "I went into his alibi, the same as you did. Nothing in that unless they were in it together. Then I asked him about Prince and whether he'd kept anything back."

He gave me a queer, sideways, peering sort of look.

"Now *there* was something queer. There was a bit of smugness about him. He said there *was* something he thought he knew about Prince. You know: on the tip of his tongue but he couldn't just remember it. When he did he'd let us know."

"Still the same old secretiveness," I said. "Downe was the same. He thought he knew something if he could only remember. But what about Jane Ramplock? Did you mention her to Winter?"

Just skirted round the subject, he said. Winter seemed a bit touchy when she was mentioned.

"I don't like the chap a lot. He's a queer sort of bird. Too lah-di-dah, for my liking."

I asked what he meant.

"Well, that plummy sort of voice of his. When he gets excited you can hardly make out what he says."

"A nervous complaint or something due to the war," I said. "But what did you make him excited about?"

George looked a bit sheepish. It was when he tried to put on a bit of pressure and hinted about having to ask him to make an official statement. I gathered that Winter had told him to go to blazes, and George had had to laugh it off.

I got to work on my own statement. That cup of tea had cleared my thinking ducts and I'd known I was going to interest him in what had passed between me and Solversen. There wasn't even a superciliousness when I came to that bit about the private detective.

"Might do worse than check up," he said. "If he was serious about breaking that detective's neck why couldn't he have shot Ramplock? If he's spent the kind of life he says he has, using a gun wouldn't worry him."

I told him I was rather heavily discounting a good deal of that wild and woolly life of Solversen's. But maybe he was the kind who could easily come to credit his own illusions, and if so it wasn't our policy to shatter them. I wanted him on my side, at least as long as I suspected there was something he might have to tell me.

"Let's hope Matthews has something for us in the morning," I said. "If only he can prove that Ramplock had his lady-friend with him on that holiday, then, with what I learned from Solversen, we'll be sure of at least the sequence of events. That holiday must have made Ramplock so finally infatuated with the lady that he came back and asked for a divorce. He'd even got it so badly that he employed an agency to try to get enough on his wife—say with Winter—to use for pressure. When Solversen exposed all that, then he thought of a fake reconciliation."

George agreed that it fitted in, but it didn't get us any farther towards finding Ramplock's killer—or Prince. That was when he let out that ports and airports had been on the look-out for Prince ever since we'd had his description. Before I could even hint at a resentment at that bit of secretiveness, he was telling me with an ersatz regard that I was looking as if I'd had a long day. I didn't protest. All I knew was that I wanted a good meal inside me, and then just one pipe, maybe, and bed.

I slept like a log. I was at the Yard before the eight o'clock when Higson was due, and I'd gone into his report before George arrived.

Herringwood hadn't left the office till just short of five o'clock and had driven that big Buick straight to Gainsford, which is one of the newer suburbs. He had a big house there, facing the golf course, but was now living at a large private hotel called Warndon House. The reason apparently was that he'd had bad luck with his two marriages—each wife had divorced him—and domestic help was hard to get.

Higson described Warndon House as a swagger place with its own swimming pool and tennis courts, and regular nights for dancing. Herringwood hadn't left the place that night. He'd spent an hour in the cocktail bar, had had dinner and then had danced. The dance closed down at midnight and then presumably he had gone to bed. Higson had stayed around for a further half-hour but Warndon House had seemed dead to the world.

The little else he'd been able to gather about Herringwood was that he was a good spender and popular enough with the staff. The second divorce had been only a year previously and he had been at the hotel for the last eight months. No new special lady friends were known. As for Herringwood's alibi for the murder morning, he hadn't been able to check up. He and his colleague had taken risks to get what they had, and he was afraid of anything getting to Herringwood's ears. All he had learned was that he usually left the hotel at just after nine o'clock.

I said he'd done a good job and he'd better keep Stirling House under observation during the day. George arrived in time to get the gist of things and agree. The lunch hour was the vital time, I said, but he needn't ring the Yard if Herringwood lunched alone.

"And what now?" I asked George.

He didn't know. He was at a loose end, as I was, till Matthews arrived, and that wouldn't be till near midday. But George isn't one to make work for the sake of it. He'd think things over quietly, he said, and apparently I could do the same. I didn't fancy the fug there'd be in his room, so I went down to the Embankment. I'd thought of taking a walk along to the Tate, and then I changed my mind. On that morning of Ramplock's funeral rites there might be little doing at Warbeck House. Maybe I could glean a few things from Daisy.

I picked up a taxi in Whitehall and it was just short of ten o'clock when I took a peep into that annexe room. Daisy was sitting there, engrossed in a magazine. She was wearing a black skirt and a white blouse with a large black bow. She was looking fine and I—well I just couldn't help looking.

"Morning, Daisy."

A conjuror couldn't have had that book more quickly out of sight, but the smile was a bit breathless.

"You frightened me," she said.

"Anyone in there?"

"No," she said. "Everyone's gone to the funeral. We're supposed to be closed down, really, as a mark of respect."

"Well, you needn't be funereal with me," I told her, and took a handy seat. "Even if you *are* running the firm."

She giggled at that.

"Not even our Miss Haregood," I went on. "She gone too?"

"Yes," she said, and gave a little frown. "I don't think she was too keen."

"Don't blame her," I said. "There's not much fun at funerals. Or wasn't she partial to fun?"

"She liked a joke sometimes."

"Good," I said. "And talking of fun, did Winter take you to lunch yesterday?"

"Of course he didn't."

"That's not so good," I said. "You're losing your touch, Daisy. But what about slipping out for coffee with me?"

"Oh, I daren't," she told me quickly. "Somebody might turn up who didn't know about the funeral."

"That's all right," I said. "We'll put a notice on the door—'Back in twenty minutes. Gone to Scotland Yard.'"

She giggled again but she hardly knew what to make of me away from a lunch table. I tried to look serious.

"Something you can do for me," I said. "Strictly between ourselves. Heard anybody mention Prince lately?"

She hadn't, beyond general speculation.

"Ever heard of a man named Ralph Herringwood?"

She hadn't.

I gave her a description but it didn't help.

"Ever hear of Herringwoods, the grocery people?"

"Of course," she said. "We deal at one of their shops. It's nearer than the Ramplock one."

"I'll keep it dark," I said. "And you've never heard the firm mentioned in this office?"

She said, and her little pug nose wrinkled delightfully, that she had. All sorts of firms trading like Ramplocks had to be mentioned from time to time. Consignments went astray, and invoices got mixed. There was business to do with the Retail Traders' Association, and all sorts of things.

"Leave it," I said. "You're too smart for me when you talk business. But something else in strict confidence. Who was here before Miss Haregood?"

"A Miss Collies. She was ever so nice. She left to get married."

"Know where she's living?"

She didn't. She believed it was somewhere in Scotland but she wasn't certain even of that. Which was a pity. Had she been living in London I might have slipped along for a chat with her. Maybe Herringwoods had been angling for Ramplocks even before the arrival of Susan Haregood. There were a whole lot of things I could think of which she might have told me.

"Heard of any other changes that might be happening around here now Mr. Ramplock's dead?"

She hesitated. That was curious. She was always as quick on a question as a kitten on a paper ball.

"Just between ourselves," I said.

"Well," she said, and there still seemed a reluctance, "I did hear something about Mr. Drale going to retire."

"That's interesting. Just how did you hear it, Daisy?"

It took quite a bit of coaxing to get the picture and when it came it didn't fit. Drale had been a bit snappy one afternoon with Miss Haregood when he had come out of Ramplock's office. She had been terse in return. Daisy had said that Mr. Drale oughtn't to speak to people like that. Susan, I gathered, had given a thin-lipped smile. The actual words she had used were these, or as near as Daisy remembered them, and they had been spoken with definite venom.

"I think he's just having a last fling."

Daisy hadn't understood, but Susan Haregood had let out too much.

"I shouldn't have said that," she told Daisy, "and you're not to repeat it. You understand that?"

Well, there it was. But rumours about Drale's retirement had only begun a day or two ago, and, if Drale had spoken to others as he had spoken to me, I saw every reason for them. But that remark of Susan Haregood's had been made about a fortnight ago. Which meant that she had had inside knowledge.

I didn't stay much longer with Daisy. I'd exhausted my questions and I didn't want that chat to look too much like an enquiry. I did say that we must have lunch together soon, and I asked her if she'd change her mind about coffee. But she sat tight, which was no great tribute to my charm. She smiled so cutely as I went through the door that I wished I were twenty years younger. Then I'd have gone back.

I went round to that tea-shop where I'd met Downe and had coffee and a cake, and I was thinking about what I'd learned. Drale had put Ramplock's back up about that matter of votes, and Ramplock had turned nasty. He had hinted at dismissal. But that shouldn't have worried Drale. The value of his holding would have put him in clover for the rest of his days, but the loss of the job and the prestige it carried must have been a hateful prospect. And it must have been maddening to know that a comparative tyro like Ramplock had the power to carry out his hinted threats.

But that, according to Drale's story to me, had been about a month ago. Susan Haregood's sneer had been a fortnight ago, and there had seemed a discrepancy. But now it seemed there wasn't. During the fortnight that had elapsed till she let slip that remark to Daisy, she might still have been aware of the situation between Drale and Ramplock. It was just that no occasion had arisen to provoke the remark.

But thinking of that made me go back to what would happen now to Ramplocks. Something obviously would have to be done. Old Sam might have amassed or secreted enough to stand the shock of death duties, but now there would be the new impact of a second death within a year. The firm would simply have to become a public company or sell out. Money, and a tremendous deal of it, would have to be raised. That was something that Herringwood too must have foreseen. But had he only seen after his angling for Ramplocks had failed? For apparently it *had* failed. Had I been wrong when I'd thought that Ramplock was the last person whom Ralph Herringwood wanted dead? If Herringwood was desperate, wouldn't he regard Ramplock as more useful dead than alive?

Somewhere there was a pattern. Could I prove that Ralph Herringwood's scheming had failed? I thought it was a question of simple arithmetic. Ramplock—to be absolutely free—had to get fifty-one votes, and when Drale turned him down and

Winter, and even Downe wasn't amenable either, they just weren't forthcoming. So Ramplock was no longer of any use alive; in Herringwood's plan, that is. And what use would he be when dead? I didn't know, but I did see again—as Herringwood must have seen—that impact of death duties. Maybe when a directors' meeting was held—and it would have to be soon—an offer from Herringwoods would be laid before the Board. And if so, I should hear the result from Charles Downe.

I made my way back to the Yard. Matthews was earlier than we'd thought and he and George were somewhere downstairs. In about ten minutes they came back.

Matthews had not had too much trouble in picking up Ramplock's trail from Stranraer for he had asked about the roads to Ballyminch. That was where Matthews found the end of the trail. A Major and Mrs. Ramplock had spent all their time there at the Ulster Hotel, which was what Matthews described as a posh place. The couple spent their time on the little beach or playing golf on a nearby course. Once or twice they spent the whole day somewhere in the car.

His description of the lady was that she must have been a stunner. Handsome, gorgeous and beautiful were adjectives he'd heard. Very much of the lady too, and a perfect complement for the charm of Ramplock. That was what he had when he sent his wire. But possibilities had turned up. A Mrs. McClure, who had been staying at the hotel, had been a photographic fiend, and there was just the possibility that she might have taken something that had included the lady. But she lived at Clonore in County Donegal and the visit to her had accounted for the delay. But he'd had the luck to get the negative of a picture of the open verandah at breakfast, with a view of the sea and the rocks beyond. Ramplock was plainly recognisable at a table at the far end, but the lady unfortunately had her back to the camera. Wharton had been getting an enlargement rushed through.

"No gossip at all?" I asked Matthews. "The lady hadn't let drop any clues?"

If so, as he said, it had been to guests who had long since gone. At the hotel Ramplock registered as from simply London, and the proprietor and the secretary had recalled nothing that might help. But Matthews had a list of the guests who had been at the hotel during the three weeks. It wasn't a hilarious prospect but they might be questioned. Wharton didn't like it, nor did I.

"What did he call her?" I asked.

"No one ever heard a Christian name," he told me. "It was always *darling* and that sort of thing."

Then the enlargement came up. It showed Ramplock in the act of eating something: elbows well out and eyes on his plate. That was why he hadn't been aware of the camera, or probably he'd have concealed his face. It must have been a hot day for he was wearing no coat and the sleeves of the sports shirt were rolled up to his elbows. The lady was only a tiny portion of what seemed to be a bathing costume; a piece of bare back, a slim neck and a head bent forward and slightly foreshortened. The hair was very dark and the curved visible arm seemed sun tanned.

That was that. Maybe it would be a help and more likely it wouldn't. There even seemed a chance that Matthews might have to go back to Ireland and begin looking up that list of guests. George still didn't like it. He was hoping for a short cut. Matthews, he said, had better read up the notes on the case and report in the morning. I didn't report anything. George can have a nasty mind, and I didn't want to drag in Daisy. Besides, or so I told myself, I'd learned so little that it wasn't worth the telling.

I did duty till he came back from a meal, but nothing had come from Higson. Then I rang Charles Downe with the hope that he might be back in harness, and he was. He actually volunteered the information that he was back because of a directors' meeting at Warbeck House the very next afternoon at two o clock. I said I'd only rung to see if he had anything new for me, but I'd be uncommonly obliged if he'd let me know in confidence what transpired at that meeting.

"Everything go off all right at the cremation?" I added politely.

He said there'd been a short service, thoroughly representative and remarkably well attended before the actual cremation. Jane Ramplock hadn't been there and Solversen had apparently represented her. I said something fatuous about the end of an epoch and rang off.

George didn't seem too interested in all that. He was being rather scornful again about Big Business. He said he didn't give a Shinwell what happened to Ramplocks or Herringwoods, and added as an afterthought that he himself was registered as a customer at the Home and Colonial. There was something about shutting the stable door after the horse was gone. Our job was the horse. Something that had happened at nine-twenty on the Tuesday morning.

You can't argue with him when he's in a mood like that. I said I'd get lunch out and report back. And then the buzzer went. George dealt with it. He gave a kind of start.

"Yes, he's here."

He was staring at me as he passed me the receiver. My eyebrows lifted too. Solversen was the last person I expected on the line.

"How are you, Mr. Solversen?" I said.

He didn't answer that one. He'd been in town on account of that memorial service, he said, and he'd thought he'd like a word with me. He was speaking from a call-box at Baker Street. He'd tried the private number I'd given him but I hadn't been in.

"Why not come along here?" I told him. "Have a look round the Yard. Get a taxi and charge it to us."

Some other time, he said. Just a word was all he wanted.

"Then why not tell it now?" I said. "Everything here is strictly confidential."

"Well," he said, "you remember when you and that Superintendent What's-his-name were down at Timbers? How I called you back and gave you some advice?"

"You did," I said. "You suggested we might do worse than go to Warbeck House. And we've been."

"Depends on what you're looking for."

"See anything?"

"Did you run your eye over that secretary of Owen's?"

"We did," I said. "Why?"

"I saw her this mornin'," he said. "Only seen her once before. Strikes me you might do a lot worse than have another look."

Then he rang off. I stood with the receiver in my hand. I slowly put it back. My fingers went to my glasses.

"What'd he want?" George was asking sharply.

"Tell you in a minute," I said, and was buzzing through and asking for Warbeck House. Enquiries answered me and I asked to be put through to Miss Purkes.

"That you, Daisy? This is You-know-who who dropped in this morning. You alone?"

She said she was. S.H. wouldn't be in again till the morning. It was she who used the initials.

"Tell me something rather important," I said. "How did you people—Mr. Ramplock's private staff—have your holidays?"

"Well," she said, "Mr. Ramplock went when I told you and Miss H. went the same time because we couldn't both get away. Mr. McGraw from Mr. Drale's department acted for Mr. Ramplock, and then when the other got back I had my holiday like I told you. Why did you want to know?"

"Just to make sure about Mr. Ramplock," I said. "Thanks a lot and don't forget that lunch."

I hung up. George was looking like a shipwrecked sailor with smoke on the skyline.

"There we are, George," I said. "No more looking for the dark-haired lady. She was right under our noses all the time."

"You don't mean that secretary!"

"Looks like it," I said. "That was Solversen's tip when he advised us to have a look at Warbeck House. If he could follow that detective who was watching Jane Ramplock, why couldn't he have done some sleuthing around Ramplock's flat?"

"But it's dam' nonsense!" He gave a snort. "That Haregood woman's got a face that'd . . ."

"I know," I said. "A face that'd sink a thousand ships. Or has she? Did you ever have a real good look at her, George? Did you ever think what her eyes'd be like if she weren't wearing those glasses? Or her hair if she didn't have it drawn back? See her in your mind's eye. Shorten the skirt a bit and think of her legs. Add some make-up and stick her in an evening gown. Put her in a bathing costume if you like, but you'll have something."

"Oh?" he said. "But why all the hocus-pocus?"

"To keep Jane Ramplock off the scent," I said. "Maybe she was wished on Ramplock by Ralph Herringwood. I don't know. Ramplock might have picked her himself. But there's a simple way to find out."

"And how's that?"

I told him. I was feeling so pleased that I thought him curiously obtuse for not having thought of it himself.

CHAPTER XI

NOTHING BUT THE TRUTH?

OPERATION SUSAN was timed for four o'clock at the Tellier Park flat. George, who boasts of his ability to extract the truth from a woman, was in charge. He would do the talking and I the observation.

That boast is something which I have seen him many a time make good, and maybe it was all a question of his mental make-up. It's folly, in my submission, to argue that women's brains are better or worse than men's. The only difference is that they're different. We may have the logic but they've the agility, and under that term I include such things as bland ignorance, a shifting of issues, the sudden counter-charge and an insistence on the irrelevant. If you're a married man it's not unlikely that you'll agree. But those things are part of George's own technique and armoury, and he has the logic as well. If necessary I believe he could even resort to tears.

Tellier Park was a tree-lined avenue: secluded, quiet and with an air of the expensive. That flat wasn't one of a block, but half of a converted detached house in Edwardian Tudor. It even had a garage built into its outer wall, and its small front garden was still colourful and trim. But the doors of the garage were open and it was empty. I nudged George and nodded that way. He gave a grunt and continued his way along the crazy-paving path. He pushed the bell and craned forward to listen. The door was opened before he needed to push a second time.

A woman of about sixty-five was standing there: thin, tallish, and with a homely, not unfriendly kind of air.

"Miss Haregood at home?" Wharton said.

"I'm afraid she isn't." She'd a quiet, pleasant voice. "I'm expecting her back at any minute."

Wharton gave our names and we showed Warrant Cards. It was something to do with Mr. Ramplock's death he said.

Just some information we'd hoped Miss Haregood might give us.

Oh dear, she said, and as if she'd hoped there was an end to Owen Ramplock. "Perhaps you'd better come in. Susan's had trouble with her car and has just taken it round to the garage. This is the lounge. I'm afraid it's not very tidy."

"Nothing like tidiness to spoil a living-room," Wharton told her.

But it didn't look untidy to me. I saw only a mixture of the bourgeois and the tasteful: a showy radiogram, an old-fashioned gramophone, a settee and chairs that held one suspended, as it were, in air; meretricious pictures and then a girl's head over the fireplace that looked like an Augustus John; a superb walnut knee-hole writing desk, and not far off it a Victorian what-not, its shelves crammed with trinkets and oddments.

"I think you're right," she was telling Wharton. "My name, by the way, is Harless. Mrs. Harless. I'm Miss Haregood's aunt."

"She's had a trying day?"

"Yes," she said. "Funerals are always trying, don't you think? And, of course, she was particularly upset, being his private secretary. A very charming man. But I expect you knew him?"

"Yes," Wharton said. "A very charming man, as you say. Your niece liked her work, Mrs. Harless?"

"Very much," she said, and smiled. "She used to grumble sometimes, of course. Who doesn't?"

"The travelling?" I said.

"Yes," she said. "Everywhere he went, she had to go too. Sometimes it meant being away two whole nights."

"But you weren't scared of being alone?"

"Good gracious, no!" she told us. "I've got neighbours and a telephone. And there's the dog. He's with Susan in the car.

"Perhaps you'd like a cup of tea," she said. "It won't take a—"

She broke off. There was the bark of a dog, and a sound at the outer door.

"There's Susan now. Perhaps I'd better leave you alone."

"Just one moment," Wharton said. He had got to his feet as I had, and somehow he was between her and the door. Then the door opened. A dog—a cairn—came barking in, even if the barking was bluster, for its tail was wagging and it was sidling towards me, asking for a pat. But I was looking at Susan Haregood. The eyes had opened at the sight of us and then the lips had clamped together. But there was colour on the lips. There were no glasses. The hair was brought fetchingly forward. The chrysalis was almost a butterfly.

"Down, Sandy, down!" the aunt was saying. "These gentlemen came to see you, dear. It's about poor Mr. Ramplock."

"Sorry to be a nuisance," Wharton said. "Just something that came up at the last moment, Miss Haregood. We shan't keep you long."

The room was all movement. Mrs. Harless was gathering up the dog in her arms, and we were moving back for Susan Haregood to make a choice of seats. I'd looked at the dog and when I looked at Susan Haregood again she was wearing glasses. She must have taken them from her bag. Wharton and I had the settee. She took a chair, and she sat primly, legs crossed but the tweed skirt decorously down. And she'd said never a word.

"We'd have preferred to see you at Warbeck House," Wharton was telling her, "but you weren't available. That's why we had to bother you here."

"Is it all that urgent?" The voice was level but the fingers were fidgeting with the clasp of the bag.

"We think so," he said, and opened with his smaller artillery. "Considering the special relationship between yourself and Mr. Ramplock."

"I don't know," she said. "I knew very little of anything except what you might call business, and I think we've gone into all that. . . . Won't you have a cigarette? And you, Mr. Travers? It is Mr. Travers, isn't it?"

I smiled a reply and I said I'd been smoking far too much. George said we wouldn't be staying that long.

"You just give us a straight answer or two and we'll be away and gone. You and Mr. Ramplock, for instance, were on friendly terms?"

"I suppose we were," she told him coldly. "As much as an employer and his secretary usually are."

"You wouldn't say you were on specially good terms?" The eyes narrowed.

"Just what do you mean?"

He shrugged his shoulders.

"I hoped you'd know. But let's go further. You weren't by any chance on highly intimate terms?"

She drew herself up. The gesture, the words, were straight from melodrama.

"Is it part of your business to come here and insult me?"

"If necessary, yes," he told her coolly. "In so far as the truth can be insulting. Or do you prefer to tell us the truth?"

"I refuse to say anything. I refuse to sit here and be insulted."

"She refuses to be insulted," Wharton told me with heavy irony. "She'd rather come along to the Yard and make a statement there. This isn't quiet and confidential enough for her. Or perhaps she'd prefer to attend the inquest and answer questions there."

She was moistening her lips. The look in her eyes wasn't pleasant, but behind the stimulated anger was an uneasiness. You could see her brain working. What did we know? What could be explained?

"Perhaps you'd rather I told you the truth," Wharton said grimly. "You were his mistress. Blunt, but true. You used to sleep at that flat of his. Your aunt was told you were accompanying him here and there on business. We have hairs from your head, found in that room you used as a dressing-room. We have your finger-prints. Anything to add to that?"

"It's all a lie. I did use that room. Mr. Ramplock used to have me there to take notes. I often used to go in the evenings."

"Notes after business hours," he told me with a lifting of eyebrows. "And a special room rigged up for it. What was he doing? Making counterfeit money? Or writing a book?"

"He *was* writing a book." She fairly snatched at that. "He wanted to write a history of the firm. We were getting some notes together."

"I see. Notes which weren't found in his room and which I'm pretty sure you can't produce."

"Then you don't believe me?"

"You let me ask a question first. Take particular notice of it, Mr. Travers, and of the answer. Did or did not intimacy ever take place between you and Mr. Ramplock?"

"I've told you already. And I object to such vulgarity."

"So now we're vulgar," Wharton told me. "Sex is vulgar."

He shrugged his shoulders and then began feeling for his wallet. He brought out that photograph and held it so that she could barely see.

"Major and Mrs. Ramplock having a hearty meal at the Ulster Hotel, Ballyminch. Absolutely unaware that Mrs. McClure was taking photographs again. And Mrs. McClure just as unaware that Mrs. Ramplock wasn't Mrs. Ramplock."

A violent red flooded her face. Then all at once she was crying. For a moment I couldn't believe. So deftly had she merged with us back into that office chrysalis that the Camberwell Beauty of Ballyminch had seemed a something preposterous after all. But she was crying. Susan Haregood was crying. They were tears. Sobbing that came from somewhere deep: not for herself, or so it seemed, but for something that had gone.

Wharton was leaning forward. Between sobs his voice was quiet, persuasive. We weren't concerned with morals. All we wanted was to get at the truth. Not the truth about the private life of her and Ramplock if it had no connection with his murder. The truth about who killed him. Surely she wanted that truth as well?

The sobbing slowly died away. She dried her eyes for the last time, but the lip still quivered.

"That's all right," Wharton told her. "We won't refer to it again. But why didn't you tell us the truth from the first? We're not judges of morals."

There was a tap at the door. I nipped towards it and peered through. It was Mrs. Harless, wondering if we'd like a cup of tea. I said we were grateful but just hadn't the time. We hoped to be away in a very few minutes. Then the cairn edged its way in and made for Susan Haregood. I told Mrs. Harless to let him stay. I was glad I did. When I came back the dog was on Susan's lap and she was holding it as if it were something tangible in a once accepted order of things that had suddenly and poignantly ceased to exist.

"I'm sorry," she said, and the lip quivered for a moment again. "But I simply daren't tell you the truth—not after what happened."

"Let's talk it over quietly," he told her, "like sensible people. Later on you'll be asked to make an official statement. It depends on you whether anything ever becomes public. So tell us the truth now. About that office camouflage. About everything. Don't distress yourself. And take your time."

She began to talk. There were things which it seemed to me she was still keeping back, but on the whole I thought that what she told us was the truth. She had met Ramplock at that South-beach hotel in the autumn before his father died. They had been attracted to each other and she had lunched once or twice with him in town. Then in the March they had spent a week-end together. Soon afterwards he had needed a new private secretary and it had apparently been what is known as an awfully big adventure for her to take the job and assume that business camouflage. And if he had got his divorce he was going to marry her.

It was when we began probing into the Herringwood business that I was sure she was keeping something back. She said the testimonials were unprompted and wholly genuine, and she really had done an enormous lot towards the prosperity of the Avington.

"Did Ralph Herringwood approach you subsequently?" Wharton wanted to know.

"But why should he?"

"We're asking you," he said. "After all, he did have lunch with you yesterday. Probably rang you up after Mr. Travers had seen him. What did you talk about then?"

He'd heard rumours that Ramplocks was likely to be in the market, she said. But she'd known nothing for certain. All she could tell him was that something would have to be done on account of death duties. She couldn't say a word when I pointed out that Herringwood knew that much in any case.

"Now a business question," Wharton said. "Did Ramplock himself ever have any ideas about parting with the business or making it into a public company?"

"I know he was very disturbed about it," she said. "He told me so."

She didn't look at us when she mentioned Jane Ramplock. On account of herself he'd as good as broken with his wife, and she thought she might do something out of spite: join forces with Drale and Winter, for instance, and take the control from his hands. But he'd been most secretive about it. His excuse had been that he had a private scheme of his own and he wanted it to be a surprise.

"Let me tell you something," she said, and her hands went together with a kind of intensity. "I was getting so that I didn't care about business. It was him I was thinking of. Business just didn't seem to matter. You won't understand but . . ."

I thought she was going to cry again. She just shook her head and for the first time she even tried to smile.

"We understand all right," Wharton told her. "We can be human, you know, as well as most people. But about removing your things from his flat. Just what was the idea behind that?"

It was his idea, she said, and part of the secret—or so she'd subsequently thought. Everything was in a highly sensitive state, was what he'd told her. If the truth about her were known or even suspected, everything, including their future, might be imperilled. So one afternoon when her aunt was out he'd personally brought her things to Tellier Park.

"And when was that exactly?" Wharton wanted to know. It was about a fortnight before his death.

"It worried me in a way," she said. "I wondered if he was tired of me and that was a way of getting rid of me. He never would let me talk to him alone—not after that. He kept saying it was too dangerous."

"He had an obstinate streak?"

"Very much so. He always hated being crossed."

"Ever hear anything about him falling out with Drale?"

"He didn't like him," she said. "Drale was too old-fashioned. He resented Owen. I'm practically sure that Owen was going to get rid of him. He hinted as much."

"What about his holdings in the firm? He'd have had to be bought out."

"Owen could have managed it," she told us confidently. "He didn't like Winter either. I think he'd have had to go too."

"When?"

She didn't know but she thought it was all tied up with that mysterious scheme.

"One last question," he said, "and it's a blunt one. You give us a blunt answer. Could his surprise for you have been this? That he was disposing of the business himself or making it into a public company and realising his own handsome share of things and then you and he going off somewhere to spend the rest of your lives?"

She stared. It was something that was suddenly coming to her. She was trying to believe it. That was why the lip quivered again.

Wharton got quickly to his feet. The cairn jumped from her lap. Maybe that brief distraction stayed the tears.

"Let me put something to you," Wharton said. "You won't want your aunt to see you like this. You nip upstairs and tidy up and we'll go along to the Yard. I'd like to get all this down while it's fresh in your mind. I'll make an excuse to your aunt. Tell her there's something in the office you want to show us."

I thought she'd object, but she didn't. She even didn't seem to notice when Wharton took her arm and they went towards the door.

It was half-past five when we got to the Yard and after eight o'clock when she left it, with me driving her home. We'd rung the aunt to say she'd been delayed.

There'd been nothing alarming about the taking of that statement; if anything it was informal, on the surface of it—to the point of cosiness. Wharton had even had tea sent up, and we might have been three old friends reconstructing some family happening, with the stenographer unobtrusively in the background. But we learned precious little more than she'd told us at Tellier Park.

Ramplock emerged, perhaps, a bit more clearly: self-assured, obstinate, a good friend and a bad enemy. Being head of Ramplocks had inflated his ego. He'd become impatient of advice and contemptuous of protests, and had liked secretiveness because it gave him a sense of power. The old charm was still obvious, if only as a necessary veneer. As a lover he had probably been superb, and yet I doubted if he had loved anyone quite as much as himself. That she had been deeply in love with him was beyond all question.

He had been generous enough. The car had been a present, and he had helped furnish the flat which was larger than the one that her aunt had occupied at Southbeach. Her official salary was ten pounds a week, but that had been rather an amusing oddment than a necessary income, for his gifts in the course of their relationship had amounted to many times that salary. But there was one other interesting thing about that official job. He had wished to establish her in her own apartment in town, but she would have none of it. What she gave, she gave, and she was not prepared to be a paid woman with life no more interesting than as a one-woman harem. She had been trained for the work she'd done at Southbeach and she liked doing it. There was, as

I said, a kind of romance and delightful intimacy about being, on the face of it, merely the private secretary of a man who was infinitely more than an employer.

She showed no signs of anger or even disappointment when we told her that she would receive no benefit from Ramplock's will. She hadn't expected it, she said, and it was purely voluntarily that she told us he'd intended to make a new will as soon as his private affairs were in final order, and that again now seemed to her to be connected with that mysterious scheme of his, at the nature of which he'd refused even to hint.

An idea had come to me and I asked her about it. Did she know anyone whose nickname was Prince? She said she didn't.

"Ralph Herringwood," I said. "You must have been in contact pretty often. Did anyone ever call him, or allude to him as, Prince?"

She said she didn't even know if he had a nickname, and I didn't press the point, for it had seemed to me that the mention of Herringwood's name had brought an uneasiness. He was someone she didn't care to have mentioned, and that seemed a something which it might not be unfruitful to explore. And that was practically at the end of that long interview. Wharton thanked her warmly—too warmly I thought—and said I should be driving her home. As it was the first indication he had given me, I gathered that I was expected to carry on the enquiries in a more subtle kind of way.

But possibly there was something I had missed, for I could find never a question to ask her. She sat there beside me and was saying never a word. I made a remark or two about traffic lights and the absence of fog, but she merely shifted on her seat and went back to her thoughts. It was not till we were in the Edgware Road that I put a direct question.

"What about your work, Miss Haregood? Will you be giving it up?"

"Yes," she said. "I shall never go back again—not after to-night."

There was nothing else till we were nearing Tellier Park. Then she asked if she might be set down at the end of the road and not at the flat. I drew the car in at the kerb.

"I wonder if I might say something purely in a private capacity."

She didn't speak.

"About what you've said tonight," I went on. "I'd like you to think things over. Wharton was nice up there in his room, but he can be pretty ruthless with a witness who's let him down. So think things over. If you still think there's anything you've left out, ring him first thing in the morning and let him know."

"Haven't you heard enough?" she told me bitterly.

"Maybe. I hope so. Tearing private lives apart isn't our idea of fun, but we've got to get at the truth somehow."

The sententiousness was wasted. She was already out of the car. I watched her hurrying almost blindly along that road. I saw her enter her gate and then I moved the car back and round.

Wharton was still in his room when I got there.

"Get anything else out of her?" was the first thing he wanted to know.

"Should I?" I said.

"Thought you might think of something," he told me off-handedly. Then he was giving me that peering look. "You didn't fall for all that yarn of hers, did you?"

I said I didn't know. That's the trouble with me: the reason why I'll never make a ruthless kind of sleuth. You remember the man who couldn't be a good philosopher because cheerfulness was always breaking in? Well, with me it's sentiment. I get sneaking sympathies and let them bias cold judgment. At that moment I was still hearing the bitterness in the voice of a woman who had been on the rack.

"One thing I did get," I said. "She's quitting her job—at once."

"What else could she do?" he told me. "The game was up, wasn't it?"

He took a turn about the room, then he told me *we'd* been right from the start. There'd always been something fishy about that woman.

"A showy bit of goods she'll be when she's rigged up," he said. "I'd rather like to have a look at her, just to see how she struck Ramplock. I'm having a man on her tail."

"Why?"

He looked as if he couldn't credit his ears.

"Why? You don't think she told us the truth, do you? I wouldn't be surprised if she killed Ramplock. He turned her down, didn't he? Didn't she as good as tell us so?"

I said that was one way of looking at it. But when did she kill him? It must have been after nine-twenty, and after the man Prince had left the flat. And Daisy Purkes could substantiate her alibi for that.

"We've busted better alibis than that," he told me. "Best thing you can do in the morning is go over all those alibis again. And that reminds me. Not a bad idea that of yours, about Prince being a nickname. You might look into that too."

I went back to my empty flat, rang downstairs and got some sort of a cold and not too palatable meal, then drew my chair to the electric fire and stoked my pipe. But I was too tired to think. Thoughts swirled and merged into each other and refused to isolate themselves. I kept seeing Susan Haregood and hating myself somehow for the numb tragedy in her face and it was no consolation that I knew why she had fainted that morning at that short conference at Warbeck House. It had been the accumulation of shock at Ramplock's death, and not the mention of Prince's name. And then I wondered what it was that she was keeping back. Then I shifted to those alibis I had to probe in the morning, and even there I kept moving from this suspect to that. I even went back to Goodge and wondered if Wharton was keeping him up his sleeve. Maybe Ramplock had sacked Goodge and because Goodge knew too much about Susan Haregood. Maybe that was why Ramplock had closed down that liaison and brought her belongings to Tellier Park. And so to Susan Haregood again, and the same old circling, till I gave it up for good and made my way to bed.

Chapter XII
THUNDERBOLT

I HATED that day's work. It seemed footling and aimless and I could put no heart into it. George boasts that he can smell a liar a mile off. There may be some truth in it, even if the distance is exaggerated, and I'm just as entitled to claim that I can discern anything that's fishy about an alibi. Alibis have been, in a way, my speciality, but these seemed to me to be fool-proof and Travers-proof, with that last sounding rather like tautology.

For I had to look a bit of a fool. I had to tell yarns which no one could believe, about the red-tape specialists not being satisfied with the way we'd reported on those alibis. I had to gush charm and ooze regrets and all the time I was feeling like a mountebank. Even with Mrs. Downe. She looked as if she didn't believe a word of it.

"Seems funny to me they want to know what my hubby was doing. Why don't they come here and ask me themselves?"

I said that was bureaucracy all over. And surely she'd heard Mr. Downe fulminate against it? Bureaucracy-ridden and bureaucracy mad, that's what we were.

That appeased her.

"A pity they haven't something better to do," she told me. "No wonder taxes are what they are. But about my hubby. He's what they call a creature of habit, Mr. Travers. Always off in the morning to the very dot. That's why it upset him because we overslept. Usually he'd be away at a quarter to nine but he didn't leave here till just on half-past."

I said that was all I needed, and jotted down a simple statement and got her to sign. I was fool enough to say how I'd liked that cake of hers and that my wife might like the recipe some time, and then she asked me if I'd any children and that made her tell me about her own, and bang went another twenty minutes of the tax-payer's money. When she gave me a wave as I moved the car on, I felt as if I was coming up to breathe.

From Willesden Green I drove to St. John's Wood and there I picked up Matthews. He'd been there for the last two hours making general enquiries about Winter, and he had something for me. A newspaper man with a pitch just outside Kewper Court claimed that Winter had left his flat that morning soon after half-past eight. My eyes popped a bit at that.

"Winter told me it was about nine o'clock. Just before nine. Got the newspaper man's name and address?"

He had. And the man was sure because Winter always bought *The Times* from him. A rare punctual gentleman, was what he said. So near to nine o'clock that you could almost set your watch by him. And there'd been another thing. Usually Winter took a bus from the station from that same corner, but that morning he'd crossed the road and had disappeared round the corner of Umberstone Street as if he were making for the Park.

"Good lord!" I said, and my fingers went to my glasses. "Wonder if Winter's nickname was Prince!"

He didn't follow me, so I explained. He thought we were on to something. I was sure of it; something that at least would help us to put the screw on Winter.

"I'll leave the car here," I said, then changed my mind "No. You take the time by your watch and walk at a moderate pace to Ramplock's flat, and I'll come behind in the car."

It took seven minutes exactly. And so Winter could have been at that flat long long before the nine o'clock he'd mentioned in his alibi. But why the wait? If he'd killed Ramplock, that is. Forty minutes after the time of arrival. A forty minute wait till the time of Ramplock's death.

"Was he keeping this place under observation?" Matthews said.

"But why that particular morning?"

"Perhaps he had an idea that Prince was coming."

"Good God," I said blasphemously. "And I was wondering if he *was* Prince."

But that was absurd. Why should Winter have disguised himself to call secretly on Ramplock that morning when Drale saw him in the room? It was lunacy, and in spite of it I still had the remnants of a hunch.

"You stay here," I told Matthews. "I'll be back in a couple of minutes."

My old friend was at the bureau. He greeted me quite respectfully. He even withdrew while I was using the telephone.

"Morning, Mr. Solversen," I said. "Just ringing up to thank you for that tip of yours about the lady. We're much obliged. It turned out rather well."

The uneasiness turned out to be for Jane Ramplock. I said she'd never know—at least from us.

"Some time you must tell me how you got on to her," I told him. "Meanwhile, there's something else you can tell me. Strictly in confidence, of course. It's about Winter. Did he have a nickname?"

I heard a slight grunt at the other end of the line.

"Can't say as I know," he said. "Jane always called him Dick."

"Nothing else?"

"Not as I know."

"And you? What did you call him?"

"Guess I called him Dick." He gave a bit of a chuckle. "Seemed a bit familiar but I reckoned I was a sort of relation."

"Well, thanks a lot," I said. "Hope you'll slip up here and have lunch with me one of these times."

So that was that. The hunch hadn't been a hunch at all, but merely a desperate thrashing of the waters with a hope of landing any kind of fish.

"Where now, sir?" Matthews asked when we got back into the car. "Going to put the screw on Winter?"

I said he could keep. Maybe he hadn't come to the flats at all. Maybe he'd taken a stroll in the Park. Even if he hadn't, there was nothing we could prove. And he wasn't the kind to crack up with questioning.

So we went to that Holborn warehouse and he and I saw Harmer, the manager. I had to reel off the same old string of excuses. But he didn't seem to mind. He even took a sardonic joy in meeting someone who shared his own views on bureaucracy.

"Exactly as I told you on the telephone," he said. "Mr. Drale got here just before nine and him and me was together best part of another couple of hours."

I made another précis and he signed it. I asked him to have a drink and he and I and Matthews slipped into the Saracen's Head and disposed of two beers apiece. He winked when I told him as we were parting that there wasn't any need to let Drale know about that statement.

"Now where? sir?" Matthews asked me with a grin. I said frankly that I didn't know. Then something came to me—something about combining business with pleasure—and I made for Ludgate Hill and round to Warbeck House. I left Matthews in the car and slipped up the stairs. Saturday was a half-day and I hoped I'd be in time. Daisy's door wasn't locked but she wasn't in the room. I stepped inside and gave a call. She popped out of the little cloakroom like a Jack-in-the-box, only it wasn't a Jack but a fluffy rabbit. There was a white blouse with little blue spots and frilly stuff round the neck, and the browny-gold hair was all fluffed up round her ears.

I put a finger to my lips.

"Some news for you. Just popped in to tell you. Miss Haregood's quit. She isn't coming back."

"I know, she said. Mr. Drale told me this morning."

I refused to be deflated.

"Get your testimonials ready," I said. "Why shouldn't you get her job?"

The pretty little mouth gaped a bit.

"Oh, but I couldn't," she said, and that was the first time she'd smiled, even if the smile was just a mite forlorn.

"Where's your ambition?" I asked her sternly. "Of course you can do the job. Think it over. Then roll up your sleeves and wade in. I might be able to help."

"You really think you could?"

"Sure of it," I said handsomely.

"You're a dear," she said.

I didn't like the way she was coming towards me. And it had been dear—not *old* dear.

"Well, you do as I say," I told her, and backed towards the door. "By the way, it's the directors' meeting this afternoon?"

"Uh-huh."

"Behind closed doors, eh?"

"Uh-huh."

"All the more reason why you'll have to think quick," I said. "But something I was forgetting. Something I've got to do."

The same spiel and this time not so ready an acceptance. Or was that roguish look in her eye something quite different from her views, if any, on bureaucrats? I didn't know, but I wasn't taking chances.

"That morning when Mr. Ramplock was killed," I said. "You and Miss Haregood got here together?"

She couldn't help giggling at that. She was supposed to be in at nine, but that morning it had been a quarter-past. She'd expected what she called a Haregood ticking off, but she'd chatted away and put on such an innocent sort of act that Miss Haregood had forgotten all about it.

"But trust her not to forget anything! And fancy her telling you!"

"Only because I had to ask her."

"Why's she leaving?"

I looked surprised. I had to. There wasn't an answer ready.

"What'd Mr. Drale tell you?"

"Well, that she'd been taken unwell. The doctor said she had to have a long holiday."

"That's right," I said, and made for the door. I turned as I went through and she was standing there like a magazine-cover Mona Lisa.

"Lunch some time next week?" I said.

"Uh-huh."

"On you, if you get the job?"

"Uh-huh."

In her own way she was as hypnotic as old Solversen. I gave a nod, forgot the smile, and gently closed the door. I went down the stairs as if I'd a bomb in my hand and the fuse was burning.

Matthews and I had lunch at a pub and then went back to the Yard. George had eaten but he wasn't looking any too pleased. Maybe there'd been ground glass in the stew. But the news about Winter's alibi cheered him. And then it didn't. He didn't see any more clearly than we what use to make of what we'd learned. Then he shifted ground.

"You think Drale will be back in the office?"

I said that directors' meeting was almost due.

"Might be interesting to know what happens," he told me.

"I've arranged to hear from Downe," I reminded him.

"Better to hear two sides. You get Downe's version and I'll get Drale's."

He pushed the buzzer and in a couple of minutes had Drale on the line. From what he was saying I thought he was being just a bit too specious, especially that bit about having some money to invest and wanting to get in on the ground floor in the new company—if there was to be one. One or two other things, too, to talk over.

"He'll be here at as near six-fifteen as he can make it," he told me. "Maybe a bit later on account of that meeting."

I said Downe would probably ring me and suggest our meeting, and later Wharton and I could compare notes. That afternoon I was proposing to have another word with Ralph Herringwood. There might be something to be made out of letting him know just a little of what we'd learned about Susan Haregood. I might try a bluff and hint that she'd incriminated him. George didn't like it. When he finally consented it was after he'd virtually composed the whole scenario, including the answers that Herringwood would optimistically make. Matthews, he said, had better get back to St. John's Wood. Winter would be at the directors' meeting and the coast would be clear. What he suggested, in fact, was everything short of breaking and entering.

I was late starting. The midday forecast had mentioned fog in London and the Home Counties and there was already a bit of a mist. When I got to Herringwood's hotel it was rather clearer and I hoped I'd get back before it thickened again. But Herringwood wasn't in. I talked about urgency and made myself a bit of a nuisance, but the fact remained that his Buick wasn't there and no one had seen him. Someone suggested he might be playing golf.

I drove the six miles round the outer suburban fringe to Morecombe Hill, but the pro said he wasn't on the course, unless he was walking round with friends. The steward knew nothing and there wasn't a sign of the Buick in the park. So I drove back to town again, and I just made Kingsway in time, for the mist was definitely becoming a fog.

Stirling House was open and no more. A stray telephonist told me no one was there and she was certain that Herringwood was not in the building. I waited while his room was rung but there wasn't any answer. I asked where people on the staff parked their cars and she thought it was in the square beyond Portugal Street. The fog was swirling about but I drove slowly round and still there was no sign of that Buick. It was then nearer six o'clock than five and I made an adventurous way to the Yard. The fog was so dense down by the Embankment that the last couple of hundred yards took me ten minutes.

George's room was a not unpleasant fug after the raw dampness of outdoors and he looked comfortable and full of tea. I told him about the wasted afternoon. He thought Herringwood had stayed in town to go to a matinée.

"I'm wondering something else," I said. "Why shouldn't he be staying on to hear what's happened at that directors meeting?"

"We don't even know if he's interested," he told me. "And he could get the news just as well at his hotel if he was. There're such things as telephones, aren't there?"

I said I believed so.

"He hasn't by any chance been to see Susan Haregood?"

She'd not stirred out of the house, he said, and the only callers had been a couple of tradesmen. I couldn't help thinking it a pity he'd taken Higson off Herringwood's tail and transferred him to Tellier Park. A gloom was settling on me, in fact, something like the gloom outside. Even George said he was glad Drale was coming to the Yard instead of having to be seen at Warbeck House.

I had a cup of tea and felt better when I'd lighted my pipe. He told me Matthews hadn't had any more luck round Winter's flat. It was exactly twenty minutes past six and I was saying that Drale was bound to be a bit late. Then the buzzer went.

"That'll be him now," George said. "Probably telling us he won't be here for a bit."

I wasn't looking his way. What startled me was what he suddenly said, and how he said it.

"What's that? . . . Go over it again."

He was staring beyond that receiver as if he was seeing a cobra.

"Right!" he said. "I'll be down straightaway. Keep him there."

He flicked the receiver back and was making for his hat and overcoat.

"Don't stand gawking there!" He snapped that at me. "Get your coat and let's go."

He went lumbering down the stairs and I at his heels. Something had happened and what I couldn't even begin to guess—except maybe that Drale was waiting for us with urgent news. But it wasn't that. Drale wasn't there. Chief-Inspector Yule was there and another man with him.

"Well, let's have it!" Wharton said.

The man—Flint was his name—had taken the message: not a 999 but a message in the ordinary way. These were the exact words as taken down.

"That Scotland Yard? This is a Mr. Winter of Kewper Court, St. John's Wood—"

"Just a moment, sir, will you. Now do you mind repeating?"

"Winter's the name, of Kewper Court, St. John's Wood. Is Superintendent Wharton or Mr. Travers about?"

"I can find out, sir, if you'll hold the line. But can't you give me some idea—"

"Good God, man! there mayn't be time. Tell them that I'm expecting Prince—you know, Prince who the police wanted to get hold of. I expect him here at any time—"

That was all. The voice definitely broke off. There was a queer noise just before it was lost in air—a noise like a plop. Then there was a louder noise as if the telephone had fallen from Winter's hand.

"You there, sir!"

But there wasn't a sound. A second or two and there was the faint tooting of a motor horn and then silence again. The time then was just on six-twenty.

"A plop," Wharton said, and licked his lips. "A noise like the popping of a cork. Was that it?"

"Yes, sir," and he frowned. "But a bit duller."

"Anything gone out?"

"Not yet, sir," Yule told him. "We were waiting for you."

"For me," Wharton said slowly. Then he exploded. "Dammit, don't stand there! Get a car round here at once. Rush a car round here for me. Then stand by till I ring."

He tossed his head exasperatedly. Then there were steps in the corridor. A sergeant looked in. Drale was with him.

"Sorry I'm a bit late, Superintendent. It was this dam' fog—"

His face was wet and his hat and coat dripping. George wasn't looking at him. Then he whipped round.

"You'd better come with us, Mr. Drale—"

"With you?"

"No time for argument," Wharton told him. "Looks like something's happened to Winter. We're going round to see."

"Winter? Why, I saw him not an hour ago! I gathered he was having tea in town with someone."

"Tell us later," George told him as our car came up. "Hop in at the back with Mr. Travers."

"But I can't. I've got an appointment."

"Plenty of time for that. Maybe we shan't have to keep you more'n a few minutes."

Drale let out a breath, shrugged his shoulders resignedly, and gave me a look. I shrugged my shoulders too and gently urged him inside. The car moved off.

"You know exactly where his place is?" Wharton was hollering back. Drale said he'd been there only twice at the most, and he doubted if he'd find it again in that fog.

We got there. On a clear night we'd have made it in twenty minutes and without sirens. That night it took us three quarters of an hour, and George was worse than a hungry man kept from his meal. And, except to curse the fog and blast the almost invisible traffic, he said never a word. Drale whispered a question or two but I had to whisper back that we'd know when we got there.

It was not till the morning that I really saw the lay-out of Winter's flat. It wasn't one of a block and the only reason, or so I thought, why it was called a flat was either that part of it went over an archway that led into a bombed area that had once been a large yard—that yard was the court—or that before the war the ground floor had been a greengrocer's shop. Tum an L on its back and you'll have a good idea. The long stroke went right through with its right-hand half above the archway. The short stroke made an entrance hall, small kitchen and a tiny scullery with a tradesmen's door. A flight of iron stairs led up from near that back door to a landing where a door admitted to Winter's bedroom, and a bathroom and lavatory. They were above the archway. All the rest of that first floor was a big room, long and with only a ten-foot width, that was used as a lounge.

But we saw little of that then. A police car was already in the yard. A man named Wright reported that the front door was locked but an entry might be made through the scullery window. He'd been told to expect us and had waited from minute to minute.

"No one about?"

"No, sir."

"No sound from inside?"

"Nothing, sir."

"Right," said Wharton. "Let's see that window."

Two minutes later we were in that scullery. Brushes and pails stood about as if a woman came in to clean. We went through the entrance hall, a small room with a lavatory cunningly placed under the stairs. Its flooring was coconut matting and there didn't seem a trace of foot-prints.

Wharton went up the carpeted stairs. Each tread was scrutinised before he moved upwards, and then he trod carefully at the side. We stayed in the hall and watched till he turned right on the little landing. Two or three minutes and we heard his voice as if he were telephoning. Then it seemed an age before he appeared again.

"Mr. Travers? Mr. Drale? And mind how you come up the stairs."

We went carefully up. We skirted the wall round the landing and were at once at an open door. I went in and Drale was just behind me.

Through the legs of the old gate-legged table I could see half of a man. I moved slowly round towards the open desk by which George was standing, and then I saw the upper half. Winter was lying with his head towards that desk. The top of that head was as much a mess as Ramplock's had been. A pipe lay quite near the hand with its open palm. Some of its ash had spilled on the oriental rug and there was a burn as big as a shilling where it had smouldered.

"There we are," Wharton said grimly. "Another visit from our friend Mr. Prince. And you still know nothing about him, Mr. Drale?"

Drale shook his head as if he hadn't heard or just didn't care. He kept snapping his eyes as if the soft light was a glare. The fingers that held the hat were shaking. What lay there was something beyond his surmise. At that moment I doubt if he'd have heard Gabriel's horn.

Chapter XIII

NO DAYLIGHT

"Never seen a dead man before?"

Drale seemed to shake himself like a horse when it gets to its feet.

"Yes," he said. "I mean, no. . . . Not like that. It's incredible. You can't believe it."

"Stay here a minute," Wharton told him. "And keep those gloves on. Don't want the place messed up with prints."

He went down the stairs and I could just hear him talking when my eyes began running round that room. It was a bachelor's room: the room of a man with taste. The prints were good, the desk and the walnut marquetry clock were right, and the Dresden group on the mantelpiece looked pre-Marcolini. A long, low Georgian bookcase was filled with books—first editions probably, from the heterogeneous bindings—and the two rugs had quality all over them. There was a rack of expensive-looking pipes and a pair of old leather slippers by a chair that faced the electric fire. On the desk was the telephone. The receiver lay on the fawn carpet where it had fallen from the hand.

Wharton came back.

"Just a minute or two, Mr. Drale, and you may as well go. You say you saw him about an hour before you got to the Yard?"

"Yes," he said. "I thought he might be going with Mrs. Ramplock but he said something about having tea with someone in town."

"Mrs. Ramplock went straight back to Fareholt?"

"I think so—yes. She said she wanted to get there before the fog."

"Well, tell us what happened. What time was it over?"

Drale said he couldn't be sure but it would be at about a quarter to five. He had stayed behind with Downe for about ten minutes and then Downe had gone. Drale had thought the meeting might be even more protracted so he had slipped out to a Lyons for a cup of tea and to kill time till he was due at the

Yard. Then he remembered something he ought to do—get the notes for a proposed circular to the shops—so he'd gone back to the office and taken the notes so as to have that circular ready for the Monday. Then he'd waited for a bus but the fog was thick and he thought he could do the journey more quickly on foot. So he'd walked the Embankment way and had got to the Yard practically on time.

"I see. And what happened at the meeting?"

Drale shrugged his shoulders. There'd been a lot of talk. A representative of the Bank had been there, and Harold Quimper, the firm's solicitor. The ground had been explored. The chances were that Ramplocks would become a public company.

"Anything mentioned about. Herringwoods?" I asked him.

"Yes," he said. "An official letter from their directors, pointing out the advantages of an amalgamation and wanting our views."

"You people rejected it?"

"It's like everything else—in the air," he told me. "I'm not worrying. I'm resigning. They didn't want me to but I don't think I'll change my mind."

"Isn't all this going to make a difference?" Wharton said and waved a hand at the body. "Only you and Downe and Mrs. Ramplock left? Who's going to run things?"

"We've got people coming on," Drale told him. "If the worse comes to the worst I might stay in harness myself for a bit."

"You'll probably have to," George said. "And you can't give us any more help about this business?"

"None at all. I don't know a thing beyond what I've just said."

"You never had any reason to suspect that Winter had some private knowledge about Prince?"

Drale shot him a look.

"I don't get you."

Wharton told him about that telephone call to the Yard. Drale just couldn't believe it.

"I didn't know his private affairs but—well, who *is* Prince? I mean—I know nothing about him. Why should Winter know anything about him? Surely if he did he'd have come forward when you people sent out that broadcast?"

"I'll tell you something," Wharton said. "Winter hinted to me that he did have ideas about Prince. He said when he knew more he'd let me know. What do you make of that?"

"Don't know," Drale told him. "It's beyond me."

Then his eyes narrowed.

"What sort of game do you think he was playing?"

Wharton shrugged his shoulders and left it at that. He wouldn't keep Drale any longer, he said. Our car would take him wherever he wanted to go. Drale said it was too late now for that appointment, and he'd be going home. The Underground would be quickest if the car could take him to the station.

Wharton went down with him. I heard the car move off. Another minute, and another car. Anders had arrived, and Matthews and the circus.

"A hell of a night to bring anyone out," Anders said, and his eyes were already on the body.

"Grumble at him, not me," Wharton told him. "Seen anything like him before?"

Anders squatted down beside the body. He thought so, he said.

"Not another Ramplock?"

"Director of the same firm."

Anders looked interested. He let the head fall back.

"What's the idea? Socialists on the job? Polishing off the capitalists?"

"You tell me how long he's been dead."

"Don't know," Anders said. "One and a half to two hours."

"Round about six-twenty?"

"Might be. Know when he had his last meal?"

"Round about five o'clock. I'm not certain but I think he had tea. With someone in town."

"The room's devilish hot," Anders told me. "What about turning off one of the bars?"

I switched one off. Anders was saying the wound was much like Ramplock's. A bit nearer the left temple, perhaps.

"How near was the gun?"

"Pretty close," Anders said. "The hair here's been singed."

He let the head fall again and got to his feet. Wharton ran the chalk line round. He went out to the landing and called down to Matthews.

"Get to work on the stair carpet and hand-rails. Work your way up. And get the camera up here."

I went through the door in the corner by the bookcase. It opened into Winter's bedroom. I went through a door beyond and into the bathroom. I saw nothing except that Winter had washed when he came back from town, for a towel on the rod was still wet and rumpled. I went back to the bedroom and ran an eye over it from the door.

It had an almost new Indian carpet that exactly covered the floor, and little more than the necessary furnishings. The bed was a double one, nicely sprung, and with one central pillow. Above it was a reading lamp with the switch-cord hanging down. On one side of the bed was a small bookcase and on the other a table. A photograph in a handsome silver frame seemed familiar and I saw it was Jane Ramplock, and taken apparently some few years before.

With my gloved hands I went through the drawers of chest, dressing-table and wardrobe. I was looking for a gun but there wasn't one, or a single round of ammunition. I went back to the lounge. The camera had finished and the body was on the table. Wharton was just going through the pockets. It was the waist-coat he tried first but Prince hadn't left a visiting-card.

There was nothing of importance, as he said. Anders could get him away when he liked.

"Soon as you can, let me know about the bullet. I want to know if it was the same gun as was used on Ramplock."

The body, and Anders, went down the stairs. The fingerprint men moved in. George and I went through the bedroom. I said I'd found nothing but his eyes were roving round. He squinted down for a look at that photograph. He didn't say a word.

That second murder was connected with the first. There wasn't a shadow of doubt of it, in our minds. Such things had happened before and we hadn't been unduly disturbed. Sometimes, professionally, we'd even been glad at new sets of clues and a tying up of motives. Maybe the depression came from the chill of that room: a chill that made one shiver and hunch up shoulders in a heavy overcoat.

"This shouldn't have happened," George told me quietly. "I feel sort of responsible. Somewhere or other we've slipped up."

That was how I'd been feeling myself. Winter was almost the last man we wanted dead.

"What do you make of it?" he said.

"What *can* we make of it?" I said. "What he told you must have been right. He did have a line on Prince. It may have been Prince he was meeting at tea. He got him to come round here and Prince shot him with the same gun and the same silencer he'd used on Ramplock."

"How'd he get in?"

"The back door was locked and bolted but the front door wasn't bolted. Anyone with the trick of it could have that door open in two or three minutes. Coconut matting on the hall floor and carpet on the stairs. Almost certainly the lounge door was open because Winter would have been listening for him. And Winter was busy telephoning. Prince could have been right on him before he knew. There isn't a mirror in the room."

"A silencer's a clumsy thing," George said. "Wonder why Winter didn't duck?" He shook his head. "Probably what you say. Prince was on him too quick. He was actually speaking when he was shot."

He shuffled quietly in the cold of that room. Thoughts were heavy, like the cold air.

"I don't like it," I said. "Everything seems too pat. It almost looks as if Winter asked to be killed."

"How do you mean?"

"Don't know," I said. "Everything's too muddled at the moment. But let's think it over. Let's assume both deaths were tied up with the affairs of Ramplocks and start from there. For the sake of simplicity let's call it Big Business."

"Pretty obvious, isn't it?"

"All the better," I said. "We've something to start on. So Ramplock was killed to prevent something happening. You agree?"

He nodded.

"But it didn't stop it happening. So Winter had to be killed to stop it happening."

"Yes?"

"This particular thing—let's call it simply The Motive—must have been tied up with that directors' meeting this afternoon. You still agree?"

"I'm ahead of you," he told me grimly. "Winter had an appointment with someone after it to tell that someone the outcome. That someone may or may not have been Prince. Whoever it was, he knew that meeting hadn't turned out the way he wanted it. The Motive, as you call it, was still there. So Winter had to be killed."

"That's it exactly," I said. "But what about this. I said things had been too pat. How did X know it was going to be foggy? Surely it'd have been pretty dangerous to do what he did on a perfectly clear night, like last night?"

"There was the weather report."

"Wasn't that cutting things rather fine? Was this a spur-of-the-moment job? Or was it planned ahead to meet all the eventualities of that directors' meeting?"

"Don't know," he said. "What I want to know is this. If Winter had tea in town with Prince, why did he ask him here?"

"Maybe to show him something. Or to go more fully into the details of that meeting. But that brings me to something else: about Winter asking to be killed. Surely he must have known that we had Prince as principal suspect for the Ramplock killing, and yet he asked Prince to come here. And he hadn't a gun. I went through everywhere here and there wasn't one in the lounge."

"He didn't expect Prince so soon," George said. "That's why he rang us. We were to take the place of a gun."

"Yet he was in a hell of a hurry. He wanted us here at the double. Didn't he know it was a foggy night? How the devil *could* we get here at the double?"

George let out a breath. He took a turn about the room. He stopped before the table and picked up the photograph of Jane Ramplock. He put it down again.

"Where was Herringwood this afternoon?" he said. "Why shouldn't it have been him that Winter was meeting in town?"

"I wasn't expecting that," I said. "But Herringwood's alibi can be tested in the morning."

"Alibis," he said. "Where've they got us? Someone's lying. Lying like hell. The whole case is cluttered with lies."

"You can eliminate Drale and Downe. Winter's eliminated himself. That leaves Herringwood—"

"And Mrs. Ramplock, and your pal Solversen, and that Haregood woman. Maybe Goodge too. And Prince."

"Well, back to the treadmill," I said. "If the same person did both jobs, there's nothing for it but to test the alibis for six-twenty tonight. Then put the two sets together."

He let out a breath. I wondered what he was going to say, but he didn't say a word. He just moved off to the door and through to the lounge.

There were no prints but Winter's and an unknown set which turned out later to be the woman's who kept the place clean. The circus moved through the bedroom and bathroom.

"No point in us hanging about here," George said gloomily. "What about getting hold of your pal Downe?"

I rang Downe while George was having a conference back in the bedroom. Mrs. Downe was first on the line. She said her hubby had been trying to get me. I said if it wasn't too late, I'd come out to Willesden Green. Then Downe was speaking. He said it wasn't a fit night to be out, but it had begun to rain and the fog shouldn't be so dense. He offered to meet me at the station but I told him I'd find my way.

Kewper Court was nearer Baker Street than St. John's Wood Station, but the latter was on my way. It was raining, as Downe had said, and the fog was already thinner. When I got out at Willesden Green it was little more than a raw mist. It was well after nine o'clock when I got to Marion Road and Sunnymead. Mrs. Downe had hot coffee ready for me, and as soon as she'd poured it she told us archly that she'd leave us alone.

"Well, how did things go?" I asked Downe.

The question wasn't necessary, for he'd been itching to tell me. All gabble and hot air, he said, and wasn't it remarkable how when people got round a table they could never stick to a point. He'd had the facts and figures ready but could they come to any decision? Not a bit of it. The Bank representative had to consult Higher-ups, and Quimper advised waiting for the Bank. It was a case of everyone in the battalion out of step except Charles Downe.

"There was a Herringwood offer?" I asked him.

"Only a feeler," he said. "A rather wordy effusion about the benefits of amalgamation and suggesting we meet them."

"What were the meeting's reactions?"

"Well, Drale was in the chair," he said. "Mrs. Ramplock insisted on that. She's a very charming lady but obviously quite ignorant about business. Drale thought there'd be no harm in seeing them. I think it was Quimper who moved an amendment that it stand over till we'd heard again from the Bank. That was agreed."

"Anyone support Drale?"

"As a matter of fact, I did," he said. "Always be friendly with the mammon of unrighteousness, Mr. Travers. It won't cost us anything to hear what Herringwoods have to propose. We shan't be committed."

I said he was only too right. But what, in his view, were the chances? He said he thought Ramplocks would be a public company. He had no doubt that Stock Exchange permission would be given to deal in shares.

"Any other business?"

"Nothing particular," he said. "We're sending a circular to all the shops in connection with Mr. Ramplock's death. Just hinting at changes and calling for the same efficiency and so on. Oh, and Drale mentioned his resignation. Mrs. Ramplock was very disturbed about it. She literally begged him to stay on."

"And you thought, what?"

"About Drale?" He frowned a bit magisterially. The aura of that meeting was still around him. "I think he ought to stay on. When everything's settled—well, perhaps that might be different. He has the business at his finger tips. No doubt whatever about that. We simply can't carry anything without him. And we're still short, as you might say, of Sam Ramplock. His son never replaced him. Quite the contrary."

"And now you'll also be short of Winter."

His little eyes goggled.

"Winter? You've heard something?"

"You tell me," I said. "What should I have heard?"

"Well"—he gave a simpering sort of smile—"I did think he might be marrying Mrs. Ramplock; I mean after a decent interval, if you know what I mean."

"He won't," I said bluntly. "He's dead."

His hands dropped and his mouth gaped.

"Dead! My dear sir, I can't . . . you must be joking."

"No," I said. "Why do you think I came out here at this time of night? He's dead. He was murdered tonight in his flat. Soon after six o'clock."

He went back and down in his chair like a punctured tyre. The cheap pomposity had gone. He was just a bewildered, almost frightened little man.

"We're after people's alibis again," I told him. "You tell me how that meeting broke up and when, and all you know about what people were going to do."

"Let me see," he said, and was sitting up in his chair again, even if every now and again he'd give me a look as if he still couldn't credit what I'd said. "We finished about a quarter to five. Everyone left except me and Drale. I stayed with him for about a quarter of an hour going over some figures that the bank had questioned. Then I took a train at St. Paul's and came straight here."

"Your alibi doesn't worry me," I told him. "Your wife will confirm that you were here from soon after six."

The simper was telling me that some thing was wrong. "Well, actually she couldn't. I mean, she wasn't here. She was spending the afternoon with her mother at Pinner. She didn't get back till about half-past seven."

"See anyone you knew at Willesden Green Station?"

His eyes screwed up as he said he didn't. But someone might have seen *him*.

"Leave it," I said. "Tell me about the others. Mrs. Ramplock, for instance."

He seemed to remember hearing her say she was going straight back to Fareholt before the fog got bad. He remembered more. Mr. Arnoldson of the Bank had asked her to have tea with him, and she'd said she'd have to get back. She'd driven her own car to town, he knew that much.

"And Winter?"

There he knew nothing and had heard nothing. The last he'd seen of Winter was when he was leaving the room with Quimper, and that was after Mrs. Ramplock had gone out with Arnoldson.

"Drale say anything about where he was going?"

"Yes," he said. "I believe he mentioned an appointment at six o'clock or thereabouts. I left him in the room. We'd agreed on a letter he was to write to the Bank."

"Well, that seems to be all," I said, and got to my feet. "If you mention this to your wife, simply say it was a sudden death."

"But the murder," he said, and was hard at my heels like a boy chasing a circus, as I moved to the door. "How was he murdered? Not like Ramplock?"

"Too early to say," I told him. "And if I were you, I shouldn't speculate. Sorry to have to rush away like this. Thanks for the coffee, and the information. By the way, you don't happen to know if Solversen accompanied Mrs. Ramplock to town?"

"I don't," he said, and the foxy face was all questions.

"Just wondered," I said. "Thanks again. Apologise to your wife, for me, and thank her."

It was raining hard when I stepped outside. He went with me, hatless, to the gate. I looked back from fifty yards on but it was too dark to see. All the same I'd have bet that he was still there.

It was well after eleven when I got to the Yard. George had something brought up on a tray and while I was eating I told him about Downe and the Downe version of the meeting. We began hunting for that connecting link—the thing I'd called The Motive.

"All I can see is Herringwoods," he said. "They wanted Ramplocks badly. They still do. Ramplock fell down on the job of selling out so he was got rid of. Someone reported that that directors' meeting today hadn't been any more favourable, so Winter was wiped out. That doesn't make sense."

I agreed. There was, of course, the chance that Winter had been playing a double game: that he'd been in favour of selling to Herringwoods and had been prepared to use his influence with Jane Ramplock. But she'd been opposed to any change whatever till her husband's death forced it on her. She wanted to keep the old Ramplock name and traditions. She hadn't yielded to her husband so why should she give way to Winter?

"Yet there's something in it," George said stubbornly. "Winter hinted he knew Prince. Prince, or so we've thought, was Herringwood's contact man. And Prince knew his way to Winter's flat on a foggy night."

I gave it up. You can't play concentrated chess beyond a certain time if you're only an amateur. I said I'd sleep on it and hope the morning would bring some sort of clarity. Not that I was hoping too much. With Winter gone there was one less to question.

"If anything happens before morning I'll let you know," George said. "If not, you go and see Herringwood. Catch him bright and early in case he's playing golf. And use your own judgment."

No scenario. That showed George was just a bit rattled.

"By the way, I rang Mrs. Ramplock," he said at the door. "She said she was home before six."

"She didn't happen to mention if old Solversen was with her?"

He looked at me as if I'd given him a new idea.

CHAPTER XIV

BEAUTY AND THE BEAST

I LOOKED at my watch, decided I could have another quarter of an hour, and then the telephone went.

"Yes?" I said drowsily.

"Thought you might be up," Wharton said. "Our lady friend's hopped it and her aunt as well."

"Good lord!" I said. "When'd it happen?"

"Last night. They slipped away round the back in the fog. I'm just off there with a search warrant."

"You want me there?"

"You carry on," he told me. "Thought you'd better know. Might change the way you tackle our other friend. Higson heard a car at the back, by the way. Could have been his."

I got up and had my breakfast and it was then only just after eight o'clock. It was raining and there'd be no need to worry about Herringwood's golf unless it suddenly cleared. So I dotted down a few notes: questions I ought to put to Herringwood and methods of applying a little pressure. As for that business of Susan Haregood and her aunt, it had me beaten. I thought I'd read her pretty correctly, but apparently it was Wharton who'd been right.

And yet I didn't know. My information was that she'd been warned not to leave town. When I'd last seen her she'd been pretty badly shaken. That Ramplock business and the way she'd had to keep things to herself must have left her near a nervous breakdown. Why shouldn't she have wanted to get away from everything? I thought she'd every reason, but there again Wharton might know far more than he'd divulged to me.

The streets were bare of traffic and it was just after nine o'clock when I got to that hotel. The girl at the desk told me she hadn't seen anything of Herringwood but he was definitely in. I said I'd go up to him and she gave me the number of his room. It was on the first floor looking out over a couple of hard tennis-courts.

There was a sort of a growl when I tapped at the door, so I walked in. He was still in bed but he blinked a bit and sat up when he saw me: not me, but a someone. It took him some seconds to recognise me. The light wasn't too good and the curtains weren't drawn, but to me he looked rather a horrible sight. No doubt I'm none too presentable myself when yawning and bleary-eyed, but at least I don't show an acreage of fat belly and I haven't a beard that blues my jowl. His eyes were puffy too, and his lower denture was still in a tumbler of water on the bed-side-table.

"Sorry to rout you out like this," I said. "But it happens to be important."

"What's that?" He peered at me. "Good God! What're you doing here?"

"On an official visit," I said. "Would you rather talk to me now or wait till after breakfast?"

"Oh my God!" He slid sideways out of bed, grabbed the tumbler and shambled across to a door. "Give me a minute and I'll hear what it's about."

He left that bathroom door open. I couldn't see him but there were the sounds of sluicing and gargling. When he came in again he was almost presentable. But his temper hadn't improved.

"Well, what is it now?"

"Shan't keep you long," I said. "And hadn't you better sit down."

"Mind if I start getting some clothes on? I'm supposed to be playing golf at ten."

"You can shave as well if you like," I said. "I don't give a damn what you do so long as you answer my questions."

"What questions?"

"All sorts," I said. "Where you were from six o'clock onwards yesterday, for instance."

"Where *I* was?" He glowered. "What the hell is that to do with you?"

"Plenty," I said. "Just a little matter of murder."

"I've told you all I know." He spread his palms. "My dear fellow, why can't you go away and leave me alone? I've got nothing to tell you. If Ramplock goes and gets himself killed, that's his business. I know nothing—"

"Not Ramplock," I said. "Another murder. Yesterday evening. A man named Winter. Know him?"

"Winter?" That was steadying him. "You don't mean that chap at Ramplocks?"

"You knew him?"

"By name, yes," he said. "I rather think I met him somewhere once. He was at Repton. Tallish chap with a moustache."

"And that's all you know?"

"Every word."

"Well, he was murdered in his flat at round about six o'clock last night," I said. "We're checking on alibis. We'd like to know, just for the records, where you were from lunch-time onwards."

"Why pick on me?"

"Look," I said. "I ask the questions. You answer them. This is official. You either answer them here or at the Yard. Take your choice. Now tell me where you were."

He gave me a dirty look but he did sit down on the bed.

"Well, if you must know, I went to a movie. That new musical at the Collodeon. What's it called, now? *Love on the Loose*—that's it."

"And then?"

"Then I went to my club—the Wanderers—and had tea. Then I came back here. Got here about half-past six. Fred at the garage knows that. I asked him to give the car a rub down."

"Clear enough," I said. "You may be asked to go over it again some time. This is only preliminary. Mind talking business for a minute instead?"

"For God's sake hurry up and get it over," he told me irritably. That was a bad sign from my point of view. He didn't seem to be interested even faintly in Winter.

"Shan't be long," I told him amiably. "You people would like a merger with Ramplocks. That's so, isn't it?"

"Haven't we gone into all that?"

"We didn't get as far as your letter that was laid before their directors yesterday afternoon. I suppose, by the way, you didn't stay on in town in order to hear the reception the letter got?"

"Look, my dear fellow," he told me with what was meant to be patience. "What's that got to do with murder?"

"We're trying to find out," I said. "But answer the question."

"I tell you I went to that movie. I'd been told it was good. I had tea at—"

"I know," I said. "And when did you hear what reception that letter had got?"

"Who says I've heard?"

"I say I'm pretty sure you've heard."

He shrugged his fat shoulders.

"Very well. Then I've heard."

I shook a worried head at him.

"Aren't you being stupid? If you're in the clear about both those murders, why sheer away from perfectly simple questions? I don't care if you heard or not. What I do want to know is this. If someone told you what happened about that letter, who was it, and when."

"Nobody told me."

He was lying. I let out a breath.

"You're making it awkward for yourself. Do you know what happened to that letter or don't you?"

"If it eases your mind, I don't."

I couldn't call him a liar to his face. I made play with jotting down a note, then shifted ground.

"When did you last see Susan Haregood?"

"Who?" he said, but he had given just a bit of a start.

"Susan Haregood. She was Ramplock's private secretary. Used to be employed by you people before she got that job last March."

"Susan Haregood," he said, forehead like the ribbed sea sand. Then he smiled. "But of course. She used to be at the Avington. A damn competent woman."

"So I'd say," I told him. "And you saw her last—when?" His eyes were narrowing.

"When did I see her last? . . . Don't know. Must have been a devil of a long time ago."

"Remember that morning I saw you in your office?"

He was too quick for me. He knew that I knew. His face was suddenly beaming.

"Sorry, and all that. I remember now. I ran into her that morning and I got her to have lunch with me." The look was almost salacious. "A charming woman, really, you know."

"I don't doubt it," I said. "When she isn't wearing horn-rims that are just plain glass, and has a hair-do and loosens up a bit. Which reminds me. Just how friendly were you with her in the old Avington days?"

"Just what are you suggesting?"

"What you're thinking," I said. "Loosen up yourself. I know the facts of life. You mightn't think it but I've been around."

He got to his feet.

"You're wrong, my dear fellow. She wasn't that sort of a girl."

"You should know," I said. "But a private tip. Two, in fact. We've had a long talk with her. She's done quite a lot of talking herself. In fact, you'd be surprised. She even mentioned you."

"Me?"

"Yes, you. You don't feel like having a guess at what she told us?"

"Sorry. I'm not interested."

"A pity. It's going to be awkward. Suppose we have you at Ramplock's inquest when it's reopened. Mightn't a whole lot of unpleasant questions have to be answered in open court?"

He whipped round on me. That belly of his was so near I could see the hair begin and cone upwards to his chest. The smell of bed was still on him.

"What game're you trying? Blackmail?"

"Just being nice and friendly," I said. "Giving you a tip. And the second tip's this. Don't try and get in touch with her. You'll be wasting your time. She just doesn't happen to be available."

He gave me a long, steady look. That last bit was news to him. I could see that.

"Look," he said. "Why shouldn't you do some opening up. You mean she's under arrest?"

"Sorry, but I can't tell you that."

He moved slowly off to the window. He began drawing the curtain and I don't think he even knew he was doing it.

"One last question and I'll be going," I said. "After you got here yesterday evening, did you stay here?"

"I did," he said, and it was uncommonly mildly. "I had a drink or two and had dinner and danced till midnight. Probably had a few more drinks than usual. That's why I was a bit rattled."

"No need to apologise," I told him. "Guess I've been that way myself. Still time for your golf if you get busy."

He was at my elbow when I reached the door.

"Look," he said. "We don't want to get under each other's skin about all this. What about having lunch with me tomorrow?"

"I doubt it," I said. "Never know where I'll be. If it comes to that, you don't know where you'll be yourself."

The laugh wasn't any too hearty.

"I'll risk it. Some other time then. Give me a ring and I'll fix it."

"Very nice of you," I said. "But we may be seeing each other before."

As I drove back I was thinking that I hadn't put up too good a show. Or had I? I didn't know his golf handicap— mine was eight—but even if he was plus two I'd have played him that morning on level terms for a pound a hole. I'd rattled him badly. I'd left him with the devil knows what on his mind, and if George thought the occasion ripe, then Herringwood might crack up when George himself had him at the Yard. And yet somehow that wasn't more than a general consolation. Herringwood hadn't killed Winter. His alibi seemed too foolproof for that.

And yet somewhere Herringwood must fit in. I didn't disbelieve his story of having been at a movie, but I was dead sure he'd been killing time till he learned what reception that letter from his firm had received at that directors' meeting. And I was as certain that the information had been given him. And by whom? By Drale, who'd been unwilling to have that letter more or less ignored? By Downe, who'd supported him? By the now dead Winter? Had old Solversen taken a hand? Was there even a possibility that Jane Ramplock and Herringwood knew each other better than we'd even dreamed? Beauty and the Beast? I didn't know. I didn't know anything. That's why I toyed with the fantastic.

And I spilled it all to George. He was alone in his room. Matthews was out trying to trace Susan Haregood. George didn't commit himself but at least he didn't think I'd gone too far wrong. I'd had to bluff and skirt over remarkably thin ice, and he knew it.

I asked him how Susan Haregood had got away and he said the fog was to blame, though the getaway must have been planned before. The aunt had been out on the Saturday morning and had probably done the planning.

Higson's car had been across the road when the fog came down and he'd hardly been able to see across. Every now and again he'd cross the road and have a look round, and the other man would slip through a nearby cutting and have a look in Roland Street which ran along the back. The two were together when Higson, on one of his looks, realised the light in the lounge was out. When they got round to the back they were just in time to hear a car changing gear as it moved away. Higson had knocked at the back door and then rung the front door bell and made a din to rouse the dead, but there'd been no answer. Then he'd gone to the Tube station and made enquiries but had got nothing. A report hadn't reached George till after I'd left the Yard.

"If they left as late as that, then they probably spent last night at a hotel in town," I said.

"I know," George said. "Only a few thousands to enquire at. We're trying to find the taxi, or the private-hire car."

"Anything from Anders?"

There was plenty. The bullet was from the same gun that had killed Ramplock. Winter had had tea—tea with milk, and probably a bun. If he had had them at just after five o'clock, then the time of death fitted exactly in.

"Tomorrow we might try that tea-shop where Downe took me," I said. "He didn't have that meal at home or the time wouldn't have fitted. We might even learn whom he had tea with."

I guessed he'd found nothing at Susan Haregood's flat or he'd have told me, but I asked him all the same. He was asking how he could know what had been taken when he didn't know what had been there? But the place was tidy, he said, which was another indication that the bags had been packed well beforehand.

I was wondering where the two would go after they left a London hotel. It wouldn't be Ballyminch for that would bring back too much of Ramplock. For the same reason I thought they wouldn't be at the seaside.

"No good arguing the toss," he told me. "They may be abroad by now for all we know. Better put your coat on again. We're going down to Fareholt."

He'd rung Mrs. Ramplock, he said, and arranged to see her at half-past eleven, and he'd heard that Solversen hadn't gone with her to town.

"No reason why he shouldn't have gone up on his own, though. All alone at that Lodge place. No one to check up on his movements. What we'll do is to see her first and then him."

But it didn't quite pan out that way. The road—little more than a lane—ran straight for quite a way past the Lodge. As we came slowly up I saw something about two hundred yards on. I pulled up the car.

"Look, George; isn't that Solversen?"

It was. What looked like the young nurse was pushing a low perambulator or push-car and Solversen was with her. We couldn't see the boy for the nurse masked him.

"A boy of two and a half," George said. "Why take him out in a pram?"

"Because they're going for a longish walk," I said. "A boy of that age couldn't walk far."

"Stop just inside," he told me.

He was ready to hop out before I drew the car up again.

"You keep a look-out," he said. "If his door's open I'm going inside."

The door was open. He took a quick look round and went in. I nipped back to the lane. Solversen and the nurse were just moving out of sight round the distant bend. But I waited there: one eye on the bend and the other on the Lodge. Five minutes went by and I couldn't help thinking George was taking the devil of a risk. But three more minutes passed before he came out. He gave another quick look round and was in that car again as soon as I.

"Find anything?"

"Not a lot," he said. "Better get a move on. We're a bit late."

A watery sun was breaking through as we drew up at the house. Jane Ramplock must have been waiting for us, for she was at the door when we got out.

I'd only to see her again to know the absurdity of that idea that she and Herringwood might have had something in common. I thought, too, that she was looking better than when I had seen her last, with more colour in her cheeks and—for her— almost a vivacity in how she moved and spoke.

"Not at all," she said, when Wharton began apologising for troubling her. "Do come in. It's quite cold out of the sun."

She had given him a smile and she gave me one too. It was as if we were old friends.

"I think we'll go to the morning room," she told us. "It's much more warm in there."

It was a snug little room that looked as if it might once have been her husband's den, for a faint and not unpleasant smell of tobacco still lingered about it. I drew a chair up for her to the fire. She smiled quietly at us, hands motionless in her lap.

"You wish to ask me some questions?"

It was unexpectedly direct. Wharton was hardly ready for it.

"Well, yes," he said. "I may have to reopen things, if you know what I mean. I hope it won't cause you distress."

"I'm not easily distressed," she told him quietly. "Ask me what you like, if it's necessary."

"Well, about your husband's death, Mrs. Ramplock. We've come to the conclusion that it was bound up with business. What my colleague, Mr. Travers, calls Big Business. I ought to say, too, that we're on very delicate ground, and I must ask you to treat what we say in very strict confidence."

"Of course—yes."

I may have to go over some old ground too. For instance, did your husband ever mention the firm of Herringwoods?

The hands went together and she was looking across the room. The long sensitive fingers were perfectly still.

"Never. But we rarely talked business. And, of course, he was here only a very few months after he took over the chairmanship."

"He never mentioned Mr. Ralph Herringwood? As a personal friend or a business acquaintance?"

"Never. In fact I'd hardly heard the name of Herringwoods till a proposition of theirs came before a directors' meeting which we held yesterday afternoon."

"Then what would you say if I suggested that your husband wanted to dispose of the business to Herringwoods?"

"I don't think I'd believe it."

It was a plain statement of fact and she was looking straight at him.

"Would you object to telling us why?"

"Why should I object?" She smiled as if the question was almost too considerate. "I had the idea that my husband had got bound up with Ramplocks, if you know what I mean. I don't think he'd ever have sold to anybody."

Wharton gave me a look.

"That's contrary to our information—not that I'm questioning what you say. But couldn't your husband have been playing some sort of double game? Couldn't he have deliberately deceived you—say, after he had a promise from you about your votes?"

She looked away and she was biting her lip.

"Yes," she said. "There's a possibility. I'll grant you that."

"Thank you," he said. "But to go back. Did anyone at all ever mention Herringwoods in your hearing? Any of the other directors, for instance?"

"I don't think so," she said. "Unless it was Mr. Drale."

"Drale?" said Wharton and leaned forward.

"I'm not certain," she said. "He did mention quite a number of firms who were competitors of ours, you might say."

"Tell us about it. Was it here or in London? If here, why did he come here? And when?"

"You must let me think," she said. "It was at the end of August when my husband had asked for a divorce. Mr. Drale asked if he might see me and I was very glad to see him. He came here, of course, and he was most anxious about the business. He wanted me to promise him the use of my votes."

"Really? And why?"

"He was afraid my husband might try to secure a majority vote and dispose of the business. I'll be frank with you. He knew about the proposed divorce. It seemed to be common knowledge"—there was hardly a trace of bitterness as she said that—"and it wasn't unlikely that my husband would give up everything on account of the woman—if there was a woman."

Wharton smiled with a patient amusement.

"But isn't that just a bit at variance with what you told us about your husband being bound up with the firm?"

"I don't think so," she told him gently. "I told Mr. Drale what I've told you, that I was sure my husband would never break with the firm. And so, you see, the question of the use of my votes didn't arise."

"You convinced Drale?"

"There was no need," she said. "It was he who came here to convince me."

"I see. And I'm much obliged for the frankness. And what're your own views now about Herringwoods, after that letter of theirs you saw yesterday?"

"I didn't commit myself at the meeting," she said. "I preferred to listen to people more experienced than myself. But since you ask me, I'll admit that I'm strongly opposed. I've thought a good deal about things since my husband's death and even to me it was obvious at once that a very large sum would have to be provided to cover death duties. I knew there'd have to be big changes and I was resigned to them. But only to Ramplocks becoming a public company. I had no thought of a sale or merger or whatever you business people call it."

Wharton gave a chuckle.

"I don't know. It strikes me, madam, that if you haven't got business sense you've plenty of common-sense. In the long run there oughtn't to be a lot of difference. But to come to something unpleasant. I hope you'll forgive us for having to ask it. Did your husband ever try to apply any pressure so as to acquire your voting powers?"

"I couldn't say," she said, and was looking once more across the room. The fingers twined and intertwined in her lap.

"I'll be frank with you," she said again. "My husband had a vindictive streak. Don't mistake me. He had many, many good qualities: more than I could tell you, but he also had this other quality: a hateful quality. I hardly know how to describe it to you. It was a kind of implied threat. He would say something and leave it in the air, and only a minute or two later you would realise that he'd been making a threat."

"We know about it, Mrs. Ramplock," I said. "We've come across instances of it. But would you mind giving us the exact context?"

"Yes," she said. "He wrote me first and asked to see me. I met him in town and we had lunch together. It was in August and he'd just got back from his holiday. He said he was anxious about me and Peter. That was rather stupid. It was he who'd caused the anxiety—to me, I mean—and I said so. Then he asked me to promise I'd never use my votes against him. I said I should have to use my judgment when any situation arose. Then he asked if I realised that he might have to ask me for a divorce. That was just as we parted, as it were."

"I see," Wharton said. "The implied threat. If you gave him your votes, then no divorce, and vice versa. Pretty cool of him, wasn't it?"

"I can't explain it to you. You wouldn't understand. We'd been virtually divorced since the March. Everything at that lunch was stilted and unnatural. It was hateful."

"It must have been," I said. "But hadn't it struck you that you could talk in the same terms? *You* could get a divorce and still have absolute control over your voting rights?"

"Yes," she said, and the fingers were very still. "I said you wouldn't understand. Perhaps he knew."

"Yes," I said, and as gently. "Undoubtedly he knew, or there'd have been no force in the threat. But he didn't guess the time would come when you no longer wanted him back. And that reminds me. What were his proposals when he came down here to see you that last week-end?"

"There were none. He began by asking what my attitude would be if he did come back. I refused to discuss it—I mean any haggling or arguing. It was hateful enough as it was. After all, it was he who was in the wrong. I was supposed to be the patient Penelope. I told him frankly that the role didn't suit me. Perhaps I was angry. I think I was. I only know that we weren't together more than ten minutes. It was in this room that we were talking, and I left him here, and that was the last I saw of him."

"Well, I think that clears things up," Wharton said, and got to his feet.

"Just a question of my own," she said. "Perhaps you won't see your way clear to answering it but it's about Big Business, as you called it. Why should Big Business have killed my husband? Business hadn't affected his health, or I should have heard of it."

Wharton slowly shook his head.

"Perhaps I was vague for a reason. You believe in coincidences Mrs. Ramplock?"

"But naturally. Aren't there such things?"

"Undoubtedly. Sometimes they're so much so—in our job at least—that we have to wonder if they're quite the pure coincidence they seem. For instance, your husband was a director—more than a director, if you like—of Ramplocks. And he, to put it bluntly, was murdered."

She frowned. The eyes went enquiringly to his, and with a faint fear.

"But suppose a second director of Ramplocks was murdered. Would that be coincidence?"

"You're not trying to tell me . . . ?"

"Yes," he said. "This time it was Winter. Last night he was murdered in his flat."

"No! . . . No! . . ."

Her face was suddenly a dull white. I was as quickly behind her, but she didn't faint.

"No," she said again. "I'm all right. . . . But don't tell me anything else—not now."

CHAPTER XV

MOST OF THE TRUTH

I HAD NIPPED out to the hall and through to what I happily guessed was the kitchen, and had found that elderly maid. Five minutes later Wharton and I had left. Some of Jane Ramplock's colour had come again but we had no more talk, except when Wharton apologised for his clumsiness or lack of tact. All she told him was that it was better, perhaps, that she should have heard things that way.

Just as we turned out of the drive, Wharton looked back, and he told me to stop. Coming towards us not fifty yards away were Solversen and the nurse. The boy was walking and Solversen was holding his hand.

"Morning, Wharton told them generally. "Been out for a walk?"

"Some of us," Solversen said dryly. "Guess this young feller's been doin' more ridin' than walkin'."

He was a nice-looking, sturdy boy and his big eyes were full on me. He didn't seem too keen on Wharton's pat on the head.

"You're Peter Ramplock?" I asked him with an avuncular smile.

He nodded, eyes still on me. Perhaps it was the horn-rims that fascinated him.

"Come on now, Master Peter," the nurse told him, and had him back in the push-car before you could say knife. She gave us a shy sort of look just before she moved off.

"Guess I'll be around later, Betty, if it's fine," Solversen told her.

"A nice-looking boy," Wharton said. "But where were you yesterday evening, Mr. Solversen? I tried to get hold of you round about six o'clock and couldn't get anything out of that telephone of yours."

"You heard it?"

"Of course I heard it. Apparently you didn't."

"Must be something wrong," he said. "About six o'clock, you say?"

"About that."

"That's mighty queer," he said. "I was here. Matter of fact I rang Jane round about then. Thought I heard her car come home and couldn't be sure, so I rang her and there she was."

"You'd better let the telephone people know and have a check-up," Wharton told him. "Some nasty news for you, by the way. We've just had to tell it to Mrs. Ramplock. About Winter."

"Winter? What's wrong with him?"

"Dead. Killed last evening in his flat."

That took him clean in the wind. It was a moment or two before he could open his mouth.

"You're not . . . ?"

"Oh, no," Wharton said. "I'm serious enough. He was shot—the same way as Owen Ramplock was."

"Well, well." He was shaking his head as if he still wasn't sure. "You say you told Jane?"

"We had to. And she was pretty upset. I told that maid of hers we'd be ringing up to see how she was feeling."

"Guess I'll go along myself if you folks'll excuse me." He didn't say goodbye but just moved off. We watched him for fifty yards, perhaps, but he didn't look back.

"Well, that's his alibi," I told George as I moved the car on again.

"Might be," George said gruffly, "if he isn't nipping along there to fix up about that telephone call of his."

"He seemed a mightily surprised man to me," I said. "But about Jane Ramplock. Get any ideas?"

He said what I'd have said, that all we'd got was confirmation of what we'd long since known. I mentioned the undercurrents: the jockeying for position and the moves and counter-moves. Drale trying to get Jane Ramplock's votes so that Ramplock couldn't monkey with the business. Ramplock with those implied threats. Winter in the background with his three votes and his hatred of Ramplock. Foxy-faced Downe picking up information here and there and nosing for more. Susan Haregood, goggle-eyed for Ramplock and desperately anxious about that mysterious scheme.

"What *was* the scheme?" George fired at me.

"What we thought," I said. "When he met his wife at that lunch in August and he saw very well that she was aching to have him back. That was the game he played that last week-end. He thought she'd be still of the same mind. If she knew about a woman, maybe he'd have told her it was all off—if it had ever been on. That's why he'd temporarily got rid of Haregood. You must have some truth to bolster a lie. In so many words he was just after her votes, then he'd have left her again. And Winter knew it."

"Then who killed Winter?"

"Is thy servant as one of the prophets?" I told him. "Ostensibly Prince did. How that ties up with what we've just been saying, I haven't the foggiest idea."

We left it at that till we got to the Yard. He said he hadn't been able to get Quimper but was seeing him that afternoon.

Nothing had come in, and that made him say I might go round to Kewper Court where Higson was ferreting about. I was saying I'd nip along first to the club and get a quick meal, and that was when the buzzer went. Matthews was on the line.

I'll give George his due. I honestly believe he'd been going to show me, before I left, just what it was he'd found in Solversen's room, but Matthews put it out of his mind.

"Think I'm on to something, sir," Matthews was saying.

He'd found the private-hire car that had come for the two women, and it had taken them straight to Liverpool Street There he had had no luck. But each of the women had a biggish bag and it looked as if they were going somewhere to stay. So he tried a short cut instead of beginning enquiries from porters and staff, and he'd been lucky. The occupants of the adjacent flat—a couple of maiden ladies—had heard the aunt mention a relation of some sort—they thought it was a brother—in Lowestoft.

"Where you ringing from?" Wharton asked him.

"From the flat," he said. "I've only just left the two old ladies."

Wharton told him to report at the double. Then we looked up trains. There was one at four-thirty which would give me plenty of time.

"Wait a minute," Wharton said. "Let's see what train those women might have taken."

Apparently they could have caught the nine o'clock. It didn't reach Lowestoft till eleven-thirty-five.

"Pretty late, that, to arrive," he said. "They'd have had to fix something up by telephone. You can't dump yourself at that time of night, even on a brother, without letting him know."

But it was a Sunday and he doubted if he could get into touch with the telephone people and trace a call. We left it that I should report to the local police. By that time he might have something for me, and he'd get them to arrange about a hotel.

It wasn't too tedious a journey considering it was a Sunday. Matthews and I read the papers and yarned about this and that, and it wasn't till we were through Ipswich that we really began arguing about the case. But he hadn't any profitable ideas. He was a cheery, optimistic sort of chap, and pretty positive that we'd know a lot more when we'd got our hands on those two women. I wasn't so sure.

We had a look round outside the railway station but it didn't do us any good. There were taxis and buses and the women might have taken either, according to where they had to go. So we reported to the local police, and that wasn't very helpful either. Wharton wouldn't have anything till mid-morning about that telephone call. I asked how late the buses ran and was told it depended. A few ran till midnight but the majority only till eleven, and as we had no idea where the women had gone, it was a question wasted. We weren't even sure that they had come to Lowestoft. As I told Matthews when we were on the way to our hotel, we'd only a chance mention of a brother and the memory of two old ladies to go on.

We had dinner, we went for a walk in the cold, bracing air and we went to bed early. After breakfast we hung about and when we got to the police-station we still had to wait. Then something came through. A telephone call had been booked from Tellier Park to Horley, Suffolk, on the Friday night at nine-fifteen. The number of the receiving subscriber was Horley 221 and the name Mr. H. Zimmers, Homelands, Horley.

"Know anything about him?" I said.

The sergeant didn't. But he rang the Horley policeman and he was out. I said it didn't matter. And I wouldn't use one of their cars. We weren't in a hurry and there was a bus stop within fifty yards.

We got a bus in twenty minutes. Horley was under four miles off and when we were out of the cramped main street we bowled along over open heath country that ran back from the shore. It was a bracing, dry morning with a sun that shone quite warmly through the upstair window where I sat. Matthews was downstairs, getting information about Homelands.

It couldn't have been more than a quarter of an hour when the bus reached the tiny straggling village. It went on to a pub and turned. Matthews told me that Homelands lay back from the road along a lane to the right and that Zimmers was a retired schoolmaster, and a widower. We found the lane and spoke to a small boy. He showed us the cottage which lay to the right and had a small back garden that looked over the low cliffs to the sea.

Matthews went on to reconnoitre and I sat on a piece of dry driftwood in the sun and lighted my pipe. It was ten minutes before he was back. There was a shelter, he said, facing the sea and Susan Haregood was sitting there in a deck chair knitting. But it'd be hard to approach without alarming her, and I was the danger there.

"Carry your note-book in your hand and be making enquiries about something or other," I said. "Say you're getting up a petition to have later buses. Anything'll do. Just keep her busy till I can come up. See her back's to the gate."

We went over the lie of the land. He went off and I was well behind. I saw him go through the side gate and heard a dog bark, and I guessed it was the cairn. I went past the gate myself, coat collar tucked up and with a stoop to hide my height, and then came back and through the same gate. I could hear Matthews talking, and I went on by the side of the cottage. There was the shelter at the garden end. I had it in profile and I had been too quick. The cairn had got the smell of me and was coming towards me and barking. That was when she spotted me.

I went straight on. I lifted my hat to her and said good-morning. I had to talk quickly.

"Miss Haregood, we're here to talk. Either you talk or you come with us back to town. If you don't want any scandal with that uncle of yours, or whoever he is, you'll sit here and talk to us now. And it'll be officially. That or town. Take your choice."

No glasses; reasonable lipstick and nails painted; hair fluffy at the ears and gathered to a bun at the back of neck: a skin-tight red jumper and a brown tweed skirt. She looked emancipated, and somehow I didn't like her so well. She was biting her lip but her eyes were hard on mine.

"Explain us how you like," I said. "Friends from town. Anything you like."

Matthews nudged me. The aunt was coming. I took whatever words there were out of the niece's mouth.

"Morning, Mrs. Harless. Sorry to have had to come all this way to disturb you again, but something's cropped up. We think Miss Haregood can help us."

She didn't look too surprised.

"Susan badly needed a rest," she said, "so we thought we'd come here for a day or two with my brother. He's out at the moment."

"Then we'll just have a talk with your niece and get it over quickly," I said. "A nuisance but it just can't be helped."

She took the cue and went back to the cottage and the cairn went with her. There were three more folding chairs. I took one and placed it so that I'd hide her from the house. Matthews took one on the other side of her and opened his note-book.

"Now let's talk," I said. "And this time I want the truth about you and Ralph Herringwood."

It wasn't so easy or so fluent as that. We heard evasions and protestations. I had to get to my feet at last and tell Matthews to ring for a police car. Then I had to give implicit assurances about secrecy, and when all that was settled I had to rely on a bluff.

"I've seen Herringwood," I told her. "I've got his statement. I'm not telling you what he said about you. All I want is your version. He may be a liar; I don't know. It won't take us long to check up."

That was when she began talking. I leave out the preliminaries—the apologetics, the self-justification and the rest of it—and give you the bird's-eye view.

What she'd told us about getting the Ramplocks job had been implicitly true, she said. She and Ramplock were already in love with each other and there had to be all that secrecy and mumbo-jumbo because of his wife and her Ramplock shares. But before she'd been at Warbeck House more than a few days, Ralph Herringwood rang her and asked how she was liking the job. That was when I had to interrupt her.

"Get this straight," I said. "We're not interested in morals. You've been told that before. What had Herringwood been to you before you met Ramplock?"

"Well, I thought at one time I was going to marry him."

"Let me put it more frankly," I said. "You were his mistress but he'd talked about marriage when he could get a divorce. Then he changed his mind. Isn't that it?"

"There're things you've got to do sometimes."

"Granted," I said. "But what I said was roughly right?"

"Yes," she said, "but it was hateful of you to—"

"Forget it," I said. "And now go on from there. To when he began applying the pressure."

That was what he'd done. He got her to arrange a meeting with Ramplock and the outcome was that golf game at More-combe Hill. And somehow he found out about the relationship between her and Ramplock. I should say it rather amused him. In any case it gave him another lever. This time he wanted her to induce Ramplock to consider a merger with Herringwoods. She was to sound him and get his views.

"A tall order, wasn't it?"

She answered the question even if she didn't quite get the drift of it. It was something she just couldn't do, so she made up things and fobbed him off with lies. That was up to the time of the Ballyminch holiday. When she came back he was at her again. This time he showed his hand more plainly. He could tell Ramplock that she was his discarded mistress; or he could tell Jane Ramplock what was going on. But he couldn't be fobbed off any longer with lies and she had to think up something to tell Ramplock.

What she said was that she'd naturally known Ralph Her-ringwood when she was at the Avington and she'd met him recently and he'd been wanting to know how she liked her work. They'd got to talking about business generally and he'd said an extraordinary thing—that it mightn't be a bad idea for Ramplocks and Herringwoods to amalgamate. Ramplock had merely laughed at it.

Then she'd tried something else. She said a man had been following her and she wondered why. That made him think and for a week or two he insisted on their taking extra precautions. Then, with Herringwood still applying the pressure, she said she'd seen the man again and she thought he was someone she'd once seen at the Avington. She even put forward the preposterous theory that Herringwood might be trying to get something he could use to induce Ramplock to consider that merger. Ramplock didn't think it preposterous. He took it seriously enough. He asked his wife to lunch—to find out, he said, if there was anything she knew—and after that he made up his mind to get a divorce.

She reported to Herringwood and he changed his mind. A divorce would play right into his hands. It'd be easier to deal with an antagonised wife than with Ramplock. And just after that, Ramplock began going all over mysterious. And Herringwood didn't worry her again. Not till after the murder. Then he rang her and arranged for that lunch.

What he told her was to keep her mouth shut about everything and he'd keep quiet too. He also wanted to know what the police were doing and she told him the precious little that she knew. His last words were a last pressure. If she knew which side her bread was buttered, she'd tell the police just nothing at all. It should be easy to act dumb.

That was all, except that when she left me that night at Tellier Park she was near the breaking point. Even before she reached her door she knew she must get away. She didn't trust herself any longer, and she didn't trust Herringwood. She was frightened of us and of what we might discover.

"So you hid your head in the sand," I told her.

Recriminations were no use: they never are. I said we'd go back to the Martindale Hotel and type out a proper statement. That afternoon she would call there at about four o'clock—she could say I'd asked her to tea—and then she could read the statement and sign it. I added that I was almost certain no public use would have to be made of it. And just when I'd finished telling her that, the uncle turned up. That made things easier for her. I mentioned the tea and then he and I talked for a minute or two about Ramplock's murder. I said we hadn't got far but we'd have got far less but for the help of Susan Haregood. We were quite a sociable party by the time we left. There wasn't much sign of strain about Susan Haregood. Maybe she was feeling all the better for having made a clean breast of things. She showed the loveliest teeth when I said I'd be seeing her at four.

That was a pretty good act. There wasn't much cheerfulness about her when she turned up at the hotel. We'd spent the whole afternoon on that statement and when she'd got half-way through she was saying there was something we'd left out. It was her omission, not ours, even if it was something we might have deduced.

It was about the pressure Herringwood had tried to apply to induce her to use her influence with Ramplock about a merger. The line he suggested was that she should ask him whether he preferred her or the business. If the former, why not throw everything up and go away with her, and at the same time force his wife to take action herself about a divorce. She'd tried something of the sort when she'd thought Ramplock was in the mood—it was one night at his flat—and he'd taken it rather badly. He'd his own way of doing things, he said, and he seemed curiously suspicious about how the idea had come into her head. She had had to report to Herringwood that what he'd suggested was too dangerous.

"Pardon me," I said, "but why did it seem so important to you to add all that?"

"Because I wanted to tell you everything," she said. "I want to go out of here and never have anyone question me again. It's been horrible. All of it. Horrible!"

I shrugged my shoulders. I said it was something that had to be done.

"Not you," she said. "You've been awfully decent—in a way. But you don't know how horrible it's been. No one would know."

I said she'd feel happier about things when she'd signed and was free to go. That was not till a goodish time later. I told her again that I hoped the whole business would be kept private but that might depend on Herringwood.

"He's a rat," she told us. "Just a dirty common rat. I hope he did it. I hope you get him and he hangs for it."

Then she broke down. Matthews and I stood around like a couple of gawks till the crying stopped, then she let me show her the nearest bathroom. I thought she was a long time tidying up, and when I went to see what had happened to her, she had gone. They told me downstairs that she'd been gone a good ten minutes.

We had over an hour to wait for a train. I rang the Yard and said I'd be reporting at about half-past nine, then we had a drink or two. The train was already late but it had a restaurant car, and the meal helped to pass the time. At Liverpool Street we were a quarter of an hour late and it was nearly ten o'clock when we got to the Yard. George was in. He looked as if he'd have liked to ask us where the devil we'd been dallying.

"A bit late, aren't you?" was what he said.

I let it go at that and gave him the statement.

"Stop Press," I said. "All the latest."

"I'll look at it later," he said. "You give me a quick précis."

I gave him one. He actually didn't say a thing till I'd finished it.

"Doesn't seem to get us much further forward," was what he said. "Unless you've got any ideas yourself."

I said he couldn't deny that things looked pretty bad for Herringwood. He mightn't have done the murder but at least we had enough on him to make him tell what he knew. Even if that didn't tell us the identity of the murderer—the identity of Prince if he preferred it that way—it ought at least to give us a lead. Herringwood, I said, was in everything up to the neck, and there wasn't a doubt in my mind about it.

"He's got an unbreakable alibi for both murders," George said. "I know. I've been at that hotel today."

He was going across to the tall corner cupboard and fetching something, or so I thought. But he came back empty-handed, or so I thought again.

"Besides," he said, and afterwards I knew he had staged a first-class act, "this wouldn't have been any good to Herringwood. It'd have taken more'n this to make him into Prince." He opened his hand and there was something black on the palm.

From where it stood it looked like some monstrous hairy caterpillar. I went nearer. It was a thick, black, false moustache.

CHAPTER XVI
SESSION AT THE YARD

I STARED at it. I couldn't help smiling: it looked so curious in the palm of his hand.

"Where'd you get it?"

"In that desk of Solversen's," he told me. "In a drawer. There was a little bottle of spirit gum with it."

"Amusing, that," I said. "I'd like to have seen him with it on."

"Amusing?" His tone was oddly quiet. "Why amusing?"

"Well, his sticking it on and fooling a professional detective. Beating him at his own game, so to speak."

"You think that's all it was for?"

"What else?"

"He couldn't have been Prince?"

That pulled me up short. Solversen: plumpers in his cheeks, glasses on, and that moustache. He was the right height for the man Drale had seen, and that chambermaid. The right girth too, if he'd fixed a pillow across his belly. But there was still the one insuperable thing against it.

"It's a pleasant thought," I said, "but why should Solversen disguise himself to see Ramplock? Even with all the accessories he'd have been spotted in a flash. I doubt if he could have disguised his voice, for instance."

"Mightn't he have been disguised so he shouldn't be recognised by the staff at Warbeck House?"

"With a private lift and a private door to Ramplock's room? And that room private, too?"

"Drale went in."

"Maybe," I said. "But that was a hundred to one chance. Those two women wouldn't have let anyone in if they'd known Ramplock had a caller. Drale was an exception, and even then

Miss Purkes was sure Ramplock was alone. And there's something else. Why did Ramplock call him Prince?"

"Because either his nickname or some assumed name was Prince."

I said I didn't quite get it.

"Ramplock might have had enquiries made about him," he said.

I had to smile.

"Don't tell me he's an impostor!"

"We've known one or two in our time," he told me dourly.

"Listen, George," I said. "I'm not trying to be awkward. I'm like you—hunting round for the truth, and hunting hard as hell's pavement. What I say is this. Solversen's alibis can be tested. I don't think Jane Ramplock would lie, even if she thought he was trying to use her and however much she may like him. And if you're not satisfied with what she tells you, you can always apply to Canada or the States and get a line on Solversen."

"Too late to worry her now," he said. "I'd thought of it and then I left it till I'd seen you. But get one thing out of your mind. Solversen claimed he'd rung her on the Saturday night at round about six o'clock, and she answered him. That's no alibi. *How do we know where he was ringing from?*"

That was good, and I told him so. For all we, or she knew, he might have been ringing from the neighbourhood of Winter's flat. But we left it there. I'd had a fairly long day and I wasn't feeling like concentrated thought. I did ask him if anything else had happened while I was away. There'd been nothing, he said, that he hadn't told me, except, perhaps that he'd seen Quimper, the man who, as far as we knew, had been the last one to see Winter alive. Quimper said he had left Winter in the entrance hall. He himself had waited for a word with Arnoldson, the Bank representative.

"So Winter just walked out of the door and into the fog, and that was that," I said. "But he did have tea. It wasn't at that place where I saw Downe that morning?"

Wharton said he hadn't had time to find out. But he now had photographs of Winter. Matthews could tackle the job in the morning.

I woke next morning with something at the back of my mind. I ran it to earth while I was shaving—that my wife was due back on the Thursday night and I ought to give her a ring. Then I remembered something else—that it was exactly a week since Ramplock's death. I wondered how long it might still be before we got Ramplock's murderer. I didn't think somehow it would be long, or was I being buoyed up by the day ahead? All sorts of things ought to happen. There'd be Herringwood to see, and Solversen's alibis to test. We might have to go to Fareholt again. Matthews might get something, and it mightn't be a bad idea to see the Metropolitan Enquiry Bureau and check up on Solversen's yarn.

Perhaps it was the same buoyancy that had me at the Yard well before the orthodox eight o'clock. But George was already there.

"Something missing in that Haregood statement," he said. "She doesn't explain why she sneaked away in the fog. Why didn't she go during the day and get to that Horley place at a reasonable time?"

"The overnight weather report promised fog," I said. "And she knew she wouldn't be expected to leave town, even if she hadn't been warned. And she didn't want to risk anyone knowing where she was. But you can ring her up and ask her?"

"Yes," he said, "and hear some more lies."

I didn't answer that. I thought it was rather funny. The telephone was more marvellous than I'd thought. It even extended his smelling-out range to far beyond the usual mile.

"What's the day's programme?" I asked him.

"I'm having Herringwood here at ten-thirty," he said. "I'll be ringing him in a few minutes' time. If he cuts up rough, we'll have him brought in."

"Too early to ring Mrs. Ramplock?"

"Shouldn't be. We'll give her a minute or two."

He went on with his notes and I had a pipe and looked through a couple of newspapers. It was nearly half-past eight when he got the Fareholt number.

His voice would have thawed out an igloo. He asked after her health. He apologised for the unpardonable abruptness of that announcement of Winter's death. He trotted out his own version of the red-tape bureaucracy hokum and oozed out still more apologies. Then he did some listening. He'd mentioned the vital times but I couldn't gather what was coming from the other end. I did know it was being rather hard to keep up the breeziness and charm.

"Well, that's that," he said. "I'm positive we shan't have to worry you again. And, by the way, it must be nice for you having Solversen down there."

He said he was a father himself. He asked, far too casually, if Solversen had had any children. He said, "Really?" and "You're right," and "I'm sure," and a few other things and then it was as if he had to drag himself away. But the receiver went down with a peevish smack.

"Everything water-tight," he said, "and I'm damned if we can make it otherwise. He *was* with her at the time of Ramplock's murder and he did ring from the Lodge on Saturday night. She asked him to come to dinner and he was there at half-past six."

But he had a pencil and paper and was jotting something down.

"You didn't give her any ideas on that impostor business?"

"Oh yes," he said. "I kept it pretty smooth. He was in touch with her late father for years. Wrote to him from all over the place at odd times. And then to her."

"And you've got a line on him?"

"Just going to get a cable off," he told me. "He was married years ago. Had no children and lost his wife a few years after marriage in a railway accident. His last port of stay was Montreal."

"His job?"

"Didn't ask her and she didn't say. Sort of hinted he was living on his savings, same as he is now."

I stopped him as he was going out of the room. He thought it might be a good idea if I saw that Enquiry Bureau. I said I'd be back before Herringwood's arrival at ten-thirty.

There was plenty of time and I didn't bother about a car. It was just short of nine-thirty when I was shown into Howard Cleeve's office. We'd had dealings with his firm and knew each other slightly. He didn't like it so much when I showed him my Warrant Card and mentioned the Ramplock Case. He had quite a lot of objections to talking.

"Let's keep that for the customers," I told him. "You and I ought to understand each other. Besides, your client's dead. And you have my word that nothing will come out about your people."

I didn't like Cleeve and I didn't like his agency, but he was straight enough with me. He even had a hearty laugh over his interview with Solversen. It had been a great joke, he said, but I didn't tell him to keep that too for the customers.

"What about Ramplock? Did he think it a joke as well?"

"Not by a long chalk," he told me. "Called the whole thing off. He paid up though. Didn't quibble or anything."

"Well, that's the lot," I said. "Don't expect to have to bother you any more. Keep it well under your toupée but it was Solversen we were interested in, not Ramplock."

His eyebrows lifted.

"I don't expect you to believe it," I said, "but it's true. If a man had his wife watched—"

"Wait a minute. Who gave you that idea?"

"Solversen," I said, and sat down again. "Didn't he make that clear to you?"

"I was having a quiet laugh behind his back," he said. "Mind you, the wife was involved but it wasn't her we were watching. It was—"

He broke off to consult his books again.

"That's right," he said. "He wanted us to find out if she contacted—personally, that is, and not by telephone—a man named Drale and another named Downe. He was particularly hot on Drale."

"And did you?"

"We didn't. We picked her up twice and followed her to town and she didn't meet either. And neither of them went down to her place. We had descriptions and men at both ends."

Drale and Downe—that brought another idea. There was something we'd been forgetting—the reason why Ramplock had called the Broad Street Detective Agency that morning. We don't handle divorce stuff, so it couldn't have been to watch his wife. Had he decided then, after some weeks of thought, to let us handle that watching of Drale and Downe? And if so, why the urgency? Why did he want a man at once? He knew where both were, at least during the daytime, and, if necessary, he could give them orders that would keep them both under his eye. So where was the urgency? It just didn't make sense.

"Interesting," I said, and frowned, "but it doesn't help *us*."

I thanked him again, told him to keep himself out of jail and then walked through to Fleet Street. I hopped a bus at the Law Courts and it was a quarter-past ten when I got back to the Yard. George said that Herringwood had blustered a bit but he was coming. I told him what I'd learned from Cleeve.

"That's interesting," he said. "What was his idea? Thought they'd be double-crossing him?"

"That's it," I said. "Their share, plus hers, could have ousted him. Or blocked any little game to tamper with Ramplocks."

"And Solversen's yarn was O.K.," he said. "He must have bought that moustache in town. Funny sort of capers for a man of his age?"

"In some ways he's very much of a boy," I said. "And everyone likes playing at Indians. Even I—"

The buzzer went. Matthews was on the line.

He had something. Winter *had* gone round to St. Paul's Churchyard to that tea-shop. He'd unearthed a waitress who'd served him with a pot of tea and a toasted bun. She spotted him from the photograph and because of the fog, and because the bill had come to one and three and he'd given her the balance of a florin as tip. *But Winter had been absolutely alone.*

"Not so good," Wharton told me. "He must have gone straight back to his flat. Plenty of time to get there soon after six if he took the Underground. But how the devil did he contact Prince?"

We didn't argue it. The buzzer went again. Herringwood had arrived. Wharton said he was to be brought straight up.

If I'd passed him in the street I don't think I'd have turned my head, he was so different. Nothing gaudy or garish about him: just the quiet man of affairs, pin-stripe pants and black coat and all. The belly had been girdled well in and the dark blue and black tie was a nice touch. The slightly blue jowl was there, of course, and the tooth-brush moustache—clipped closer than my own—and the sensual mouth, but all softened down and etherealised as it were by the careful get-up. I don't say he cooed like a sucking dove but even his tone had a gentleness—the sort one uses, for instance, when reluctantly forced to part with an old retainer.

Wharton was suavity itself. He talked almost poetically about the weather. When he adjusted those ancient spectacles and peered over their tops, Herringwood was startled at what came next. It was spoken so mildly.

"Well, Mr. Herringwood, you appear to be in Queer Street. In fact I should be extremely uncomfortable if I were in your shoes at this moment."

Herringwood stared.

"In fact," Wharton was going on, "your only chance is to come clean. If I'm not convinced of the absolute truth of what you have to say, you'll be cooling your heels in a mightily uncomfortable place—and don't think that's a bluff. So get going. Tell us everything that transpired between you and Susan Haregood from the first time you clapped eyes on her." He opened that statement of hers with an obvious ostentation. He leaned forward, peering over the spectacle tops again.

"Well, Mr. Herringwood?"

"I still don't see—"

"Of course you don't," Wharton told him. "You're not supposed to see. Your job is to talk. I'm a busy man. Talk now, or I'll have the inquest on Ramplock reopened tomorrow and you'll talk in open court. And I'll see the Press is there."

Herringwood shifted uneasily.

"Look Superintendent, can't we treat this confidentially?" The smile was a bit sheepish. "Of course it depends on what you want to know. I realise that."

"He realises it," Wharton told me. "It depends on what we want to know. If it isn't fit for clean ears, then he isn't going to tell us."

He let out a breath. He leaned forward. The little veins by his temple looked like whip-cord.

"Talk, Mr. Herringwood. Get talking! Tell us when you first ran across Susan Haregood."

It was like working with broken forceps on stubborn teeth. This came out and had to be checked with that. This was a lie and that was a lie and something else was being held back. It was cutting steps up a cliff face with a kitchen knife, but we got there. At least we got to something that didn't deviate too much from the Haregood statement. The room wasn't too hot but Herringwood's face was pearly with sweat and Wharton's shirt must have been like Toscanini's after a session with Hindemith or Bloch. That, by the way, was when a couple of hours had almost gone.

Wharton leaned back. He took off the spectacles and wriggled his neck in the damp collar.

"Let's put it in a nutshell," he told Herringwood. "You were in a jam. You still are. Don't put on that injured look again. It's common knowledge. If you don't believe me, ask your Shareholders' Association. You had to get hold of Ramplocks and the Haregood woman was your tool. Then you told her to lay off. Perhaps you thought we wouldn't go any further, but let's go on from there. What was your next scheme? Why did you lay her off? Ramplock wasn't dead—not then. What was there to get windy about?"

Herringwood said he wasn't windy. Wharton called him a liar. The kitchen knife was out again and we were once more creeping up the Matterhorn. Ten minutes and Herringwood weakened. Could it be kept confidential? Wharton said it depended. Herringwood hedged. Could his own name be kept out of it. Wharton wouldn't say. Herringwood shuffled on the hard chair and let a little more information ooze out.

"I didn't have any use for her any longer," he said. "I thought she'd crack up and double-cross me."

"So what did you do?"

"I thought I'd rely on someone else."

"Who was that?"

Herringwood said he hadn't got around to it when Ramplock was killed. Then he'd dropped the whole thing like a hot potato.

"All right," Wharton said. "Tell us who you had in mind. You must have had *someone* in mind."

"As a matter of fact I happened to run across Drale. When people are in the same line you're always running across 'em, and he was letting off steam about Ramplock. He was fed to the teeth. I mentioned a merger with us. That's all there was to it."

"What could *his* votes have done?" Wharton asked him contemptuously.

"There were Mrs. Ramplock's, and some of the others held a few. They were all pretty sick about Ramplock."

"You didn't see Mrs. Ramplock yourself?"

"Never. I never spoke to the lady in my life."

I saw a little daylight. It was long before the death of Ramplock that Drale had seen Mrs. Ramplock about her shares.

"Just a moment, Herringwood," I said. "Heaven forbid that I should hint at anything else but a little convenient forgetfulness, but when you say you didn't think of Drale till after you'd finished with Haregood, aren't you—well, rushing too far ahead?"

"I don't get you."

"You saw Drale weeks ago," I said.

"Did I?" His brow furrowed. He shrugged his shoulders. "You can't expect me to get my facts right. Talk, talk, talk for the best part of three hours. Maybe it was some time ago when I ran across Drale. I wouldn't know. I'm getting so I don't know black from white."

That was the sort of slippery devil he was.

"Let's assume you saw him some weeks ago," I said, "and that the talk ran along the lines you've mentioned. What did you try to bribe him with?"

He looked at me as if I'd uttered a blasphemy.

"Bribe him? Why should I bribe him? He didn't like his job; I gave him a hint how to better it. That's all there was to it."

"What was the result?" Wharton asked him.

"Never heard from the fellow. Never a word."

That was about all. I wrote something and handed it to Wharton.

"Keep him here till I've seen Drale."

Wharton nodded, slipped the note into his pocket, and got to his feet. Herringwood rose too and began stretching his legs.

"Don't be in too much of a hurry," Wharton told him as I was going out of the room. "I haven't finished with you yet."

A police car whisked me round to Warbeck House. It was almost two o'clock. Downstairs Enquiries rang up and Drale was back from lunch. I took the receiver and told him I must see him urgently. I hoped it would be a matter of just a few minutes.

I went up to his room. The same table was piled with the same forms. He was sitting there legs well under, as if about to get down to things again. I told him not to get up.

"I'll be blunt," I said, as I pulled a chair to face him. "I'd like you to be blunt too. Keep this under your hat but we've had Herringwood at the Yard. He mentioned your name. Said he'd approached you—or vice versa—to use your influence to effect a merger with his firm. True or otherwise?"

He leaned slowly back in the chair, finger-tips together.

"I most decidedly never approached him. He mentioned something of the sort to me."

"A pity you didn't tell us," I said. "But give me your version now."

"Well, I happened to run across him somewhere—I think it was one day in the Café Royal when I was having lunch—and I must have shot off my mouth about Ramplock. I think I was feeling extra fed-up." He smiled dryly. "I must have been or I wouldn't have treated myself to that lunch. A three bob touch—including beer—is more in my line. Then—well, what you said."

"And you did what?"

"Well, I was fed-up as I told you. Ramplock was driving me crazy, so I nipped down and saw Mrs. Ramplock and tried to sound her. I saw she'd never agree to any changes so I gave the whole idea up. I reckon I'd sort of worked it out of my system."

"And Herringwood never approached you again? Say a week or two before Ramplock's death?"

"He didn't."

"That's all," I said, and pushed the chair back. "But I wish to God you people would tell us all you know and when we ask. This is a murder case. In case you forget it again, tie a knot in your handkerchief or something. Wharton's going to be pretty mad as it is."

I waved a hand and went out. Everything tallied, and Drale, in any case, couldn't have killed either Ramplock or Winter, so what was I peeved about. I didn't know. I went to that Enquiry Office again and asked to use the telephone.

I shoo'd the girl away for a moment.

"That you, George? . . . Our friend still with you?"

"Handy enough," he said.

"Ask him if Haregood knew he was trying to use Drale, and vice versa."

He cupped the receiver. Herringwood couldn't have been shilly-shallying again, or else he had an apt lie, for the answer came back almost at once.

"Neither had any knowledge of the other."

"Thanks," I said. "Unless you want me badly I'll get some lunch around here and then I'll be back. Drale confirmed everything, by the way."

"All clear here in a matter of minutes," George said. "Then I might be getting some lunch myself. Mr. Herringwood doesn't feel like any, so he was just telling me."

I rang off. Now I realised it, I wasn't feeling too much like a big meal myself. Maybe I could get tea and something at that tea-shop. As for Herringwood, I was hoping to God he'd land in jail. I could even assure myself that if he did I'd gladly sing my *Nunc Dimittis*.

Chapter XVII

EARNING ONE'S KEEP

Wharton was still breathing out threats and slaughter, and maybe because he'd had more of Herringwood than I. He was actually wondering if there weren't some obscure charge on which he could be held. He said he didn't like to see him getting away with it.

"Buy a few Herringwood shares and attend the annual general meeting," I told him. "Employ the Broad Street Detective Agency to dig up some more dirt about the hotel deal."

"Mightn't be a bad idea," he told me, but not too seriously. "If I had the money."

I said he couldn't take it with him, and that was reminding me of John Barrymore and Solversen. And then, just as suddenly, I was feeling as if the zest had gone out of things.

"You know, George," I said, "we've had too big a meal and haven't done enough chewing. We're full of information and references and cross-references. For the life of me I can't help thinking we've got the answer somewhere. Don't you think it'd pay us to sit tight on what we've got and try to hatch something out?"

"Might be something in that," he said. "But what worries me is Prince. If I go on much longer I'll be thinking the blasted fellow never existed at all."

Then he sort of stopped in air. I never saw such a state of suspended animation. He was like someone who's blurted out the dangerous truth in one incredible lapse.

"You see?" I said. "Start thinking instead of listening, and you get ideas."

He let out a breath. His shoulders sagged a bit.

"Someone's nicknamed Prince, or called Prince. Somewhere he's right under our nose."

"Let's have the rest of the day off," I told him. "Let's get clean away from the Yard. Go home, or something. Forget all about the case. Then have a good meal tonight and start thinking over a pipe and a bottle of beer."

He thought perhaps he would. I said I'd do the same. In the morning we'd compare notes.

But no sooner was I out of the Yard when I thought of something. There was just one other person who ought to be questioned. Cleeve had mentioned Downe. Drale, in that fit of despair, had been tempted to throw in his hand, and Ramplocks as well. He had seen Jane Ramplock. But her votes wouldn't have been enough. He'd have needed Winter's, and Downe's. I wondered if Drale had ever sounded him.

But I somehow hated the thought of going to Warbeck House again, and all at once I decided to call Daisy. But I waited till I'd got to my club and called her from there.

"Afternoon, Daisy," I said. "This is Travers—the same fellow who took you to lunch."

"Uh-huh?"

"Aren't you going to ask me how I am?"

She giggled.

"You sound all right," she said.

"That's all you know," I told her. "But to get to business. Do you happen to know if Mr. Downe is in?"

Her voice lowered a bit.

"He's in the chairman's room with Mr. Drale." She giggled again. "I just got a ticking off about it."

"No!"

"Yes," she said. "I had the windows open. Mr. Ramplock always liked them open. He was what you call a fresh-air fiend."

"And Mr. Drale likes them shut?"

"Mr. Downe does," she said.

"Well, I won't bother them now," I said. "But don't take that ticking-off to heart. Remember you're coming out to lunch with me one day soon."

"Oh, I forgot to tell you," she said. "I shan't be able to come for over a week. My boyfriend's on leave. He's in the Army."

I didn't know what to say. Even fatuities elude one when you need them most.

"Perhaps I'll see you afterwards," she said. "Cheerio for now."

So that was that. No more information from Daisy over a lunch table. I kept telling myself that it wasn't anything like the end of an episode because it hadn't been an episode at all. And I was old enough to be her father. And yet it had been fun if only because she'd never referred to the fact, and she'd kept that boyfriend under the counter.

But you see the snares and wiles that lie in one's unwary path. Something a little beyond sentiment had insisted on creeping in—the sort of thing, as I've mentioned, that will never make me a cold-eyed sleuth. Even at that moment as the waiter brought me my tea I was having a flashback or two with Daisy instead of realising what it was she had told me. I saw nothing in the fact that Ramplock had been a fresh-air fiend and that Downe, and Drale, were nothing of the sort. But I had to pay. I was lucky to pay with only a night's hard labour.

I rang my wife from the club, then went out to a French movie. I had a good dinner at my favourite restaurant, stood myself a first-class cigar and lighted it at home when I'd opened a bottle of beer, which shows the sort of vulgarian I am. It was then about nine o'clock and my mind's always clearer at night.

I got out paper, found a book to rest it on, hoisted up my knees for a desk, and settled down to some good hard logical thinking. My method is to write everything down. I put a question down and try to answer it, and out of that emerges a train of ideas. You know the kind of thing. Why did Mrs. X's glass show traces of brandy? *Answer*—because she was feeling scared. *Question*— But she was a rabid teetotaller. She told Miss M. she'd rather die than drink strong drink! *Answer*—then someone put brandy in the glass for a blind. And so it goes on. No question left unanswered, and the answer producing new ideas. Or so one hopes.

But that night I had the preliminary idea of placing my chief characters on a kind of map, and having them under my eye. So I found a map of the London Transport system and copied relevant parts. As soon as I'd done it, I thought I had something interesting. Somehow I was seeing people for the first time.

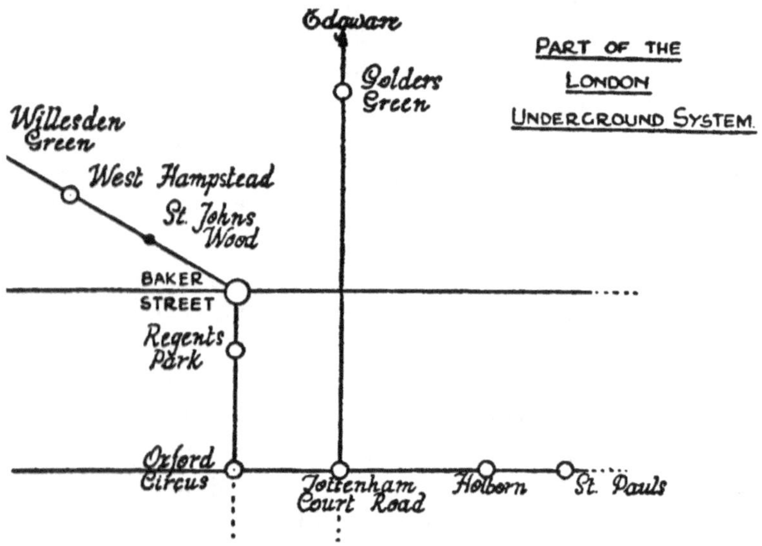

I could see some of them leaving their flats or houses in the morning and making for the Underground, attaché cases in hand or portfolios tucked under an arm. Maybe they'd get a seat. Maybe they'd have to strap-hang, but what they'd certainly do would be to read the morning paper, and, as they neared St. Paul's, peer out to make certain they didn't overshoot the mark. I could see, too, why Drale had his house at West Hampstead. All he had to do was change at Oxford Circus and go straight to St. Paul's. The same applied to Winter. His flat was even handier and nearer, and so placed that he could take the train at Baker

Street or Regent's Park or St. John's Wood. Downe was far-ther out—but still on that same Stanmore Line—and yet quite handy. I wondered if the handiness had influenced him when he applied for his present job. Susan Haregood had been handy too—a straight run to Tottenham Court Road and then a change. Handiest, perhaps, of all was Ramplock. As for Jane Ramplock and Solversen, if they used the Underground, it would be the Watford Line which also came through Baker Street. That would have been handy for Jane Ramplock in the old days when she was staying the night at the Warbeck Grove flat.

That done, I went into alibis. Two people had no alibi for Ramplock's murder, and one of them—Winter—was dead. But when one looked at that map, Susan Haregood's alibi was better than it had seemed. To get to Warbeck Grove that morning she would have had to go round by Tottenham Court Road, with another change at Oxford Circus, and she'd have had to be out of her flat at the latest by quarter-past eight. She might have taken a taxi, of course, and yet somehow I couldn't quite see her kill-ing Ramplock. After that statement of hers I was sure that to go into her alibi was a waste of time. And the rest of the alibis were fool-proof, even if Downe's did depend solely on his wife's word.

I looked at the map again and I wondered who might have seen whom on his or her way to St. Paul's. It seemed that only on rare occasions would any of them have met, even disregarding the crowdedness of trains. Susan Haregood should have arrived just before the three heads of departments, and the overlap-ping was only from Tottenham Court Road to St. Paul's. As for those three heads, they had apparently no fixed hours. Winter had been most off-hand, by what he had said to me. Downe was probably the most conscientious. As for Ramplock, his time of arrival was around ten o'clock, when Susan Haregood had gone through his correspondence.

At eleven o'clock I had arrived at motives and there was nothing for it but to try to disentangle the complexities of those intrigues at Warbeck House. Maybe you'll sympathise with me. If they've been better than a headache to you, then you're in-finitely clearer-headed than I. For the next hour I wallowed in motives, with Herringwood cluttering up the case. I wrote down questions and found answers. I found objections to the answers and then answers to them till spokes so radiated from the central hub that I needed a clean sheet of paper. Midnight came and my brain was swirling. There was a sudden mental darkness with nothing at all but myself in space. I blinked and came out of it, and knew myself for a very tired man. There are times when it's far from cowardly to be a quitter and this was one of them. I poured myself a stiff whisky, gulped down a couple of aspirins and went to bed.

It wasn't ten minutes before I was asleep. I don't remember being particularly restless and it seemed remarkably soon when I woke. I hooked on my glasses and looked at the illuminated dial of my watch. It was just after five o'clock. I put the glasses back, snuggled down and tried to go to sleep again. But I couldn't. The tide of night hadn't ebbed far enough from dawn. A minute or two and I was in that same mental blackout in which I groped for thought. Thoughts came—thoughts unconnected and shifting like the four-dimensional eccentricities of a dream. Solversen needn't have been telephoning from the Lodge; St. John's Wood or Regent's Park or Baker Street; my boyfriend's in the Army; the smell of Herringwood on that Sunday morning; a black moustache like a monstrous caterpillar in Wharton's hand.

They went, and the others that had come with them. I reached for my glasses and switched on the bed-light. I knew I shouldn't sleep so I got out of bed. I plugged in the electric kettle, and when I came back from a tepid bath, it was boiling.

I had a couple of cups of tea, forced the case from my mind while I smoked a cigarette, then took a long time over shaving and dressing. By then it was after six o'clock.

I went into the lounge. The previous night's fug was still there, and I was frowning as I opened both windows. Dawn would soon be in the sky and it was a longish time till breakfast, and I hated the thought of getting down again to the case. I looked through my books and found a volume of short stories which I must have read some years before, for the one at which

I glanced was only vaguely familiar. So I took it to the chair. The room was now chilly so I leaned over to switch on the fire. *But I didn't.*

That was when I remembered something. I couldn't help remembering that Solversen needn't have been telephoning from the Lodge. I saw Winter's flat and I saw that moustache in Wharton's hand. My fingers were at my glasses and then I was getting to my feet. I went to the desk where I'd thrown that map, and I pulled down the flap and drew up the chair and sat there. It was after seven o'clock when I went to the telephone. A sleepy voice said hallo.

"Travers, George," I said. "Mind if I don't come in this morning? One or two things I'd like to try out."

"You're on to something?" He was suddenly wide awake. "Think so, but I'm not absolutely sure."

I was going to hang up but his voice halted me.

"Damnation! But you can't leave me in the air like this! Who've you got your eye on?"

"Well . . . it might be Drale."

"Drale!" He snorted. "Are you mad?"

"No more than usual," I said. "But ask yourself this. 'Who was the only person who saw Prince in the flesh?'"

Then I rang off. And I laid the receiver aside so that he couldn't ring me back.

I hadn't been right, of course. Ramplock had seen Prince, and so had a chambermaid, and so had the desk clerks when he booked himself in and out of the hotel on the night before the murder. But I was somehow aloof from all that. It just didn't matter.

I've written a book or two in my time—not stuff that mattered, but books just the same. And you can't write unless you're part of a book. You live it and eat it and sleep it, and the world outside it is the one that's unimportant. Then the book's finished and its world all at once goes; goes with the snap of a finger, just like that. It ceases to matter and if you think of it at all, it's reminiscently and from that Olympian height we call accomplishment. That's how I was feeling about the case.

I rang downstairs and asked them to send up breakfast as soon as it was on. I left my door open and went to the garage and fetched my car. I had my breakfast and then I rang the Yard. I asked for Matthews to be sent along to my flat, and then I did the crossword puzzle in *The Times*. It was just after nine o'clock when Matthews turned up, and we went straight down to the car. He'd looked curious but I didn't tell him what I thought I knew. I said we had a round of calls to make, and I'd like him to be with me.

We went to that Holborn warehouse and nobbled Harmer again.

"The same old red-tape," I said. "This time we'd like to know what the trouble was that you and Mr. Drale were trying to settle that morning when he was here."

It was to do with the lorry drivers, he said. They wanted double time on Saturday afternoons instead of time and a half.

"Where'd you and Mr. Drale talk it over?"

"Up in my room," he said.

"No need to go there," I told him. "I was in it with you when I was here last time. And so you and he talked."

"That's right," he said. "Then he said he'd see Radvitz and Morgan."

"Who're they?"

Radvitz was a Red and there'd been trouble with him before. Morgan was branch secretary.

"So you went and fetched them."

"That's right. Brought 'em up and argued the toss."

"When did you fetch them?"

"Don't know," he said. "Might have been a quarter of an hour after Mr. Drale got here. Somewhere about that."

"Have any trouble finding them?"

"Don't remember so. Had 'em up there in under five minutes."

"Thanks," I said. "We may have our eyes on Radvitz but keep that under your hat. Not a word to a soul."

"All right with me," he said. He called Radvitz a dirty name and there was quite a warmth in his grip of the hand. I said if I had to see him again it'd be when the pubs were open.

"A longish trip now," I told Matthews. "We're going to West Hampstead."

It was ten o'clock when we got to Estover Road. Number 7 was a smallish detached villa that had recently been repainted. It was a rather bigger place than Downe's but its gardens were not so well kept.

I drew up the car outside it and we went to the front door. A middle-aged woman in apron and mob cap answered the bell.

"Mr. Drale at home?" I asked her.

"Oh no," she said. "He's at the office. He won't be home till half-past five or six."

"We're from Scotland Yard," I said. "We're enquiring about some burglaries round here."

We showed the Warrant Cards and she looked impressed.

"No burglaries here that I've ever heard of," she said.

"You're his housekeeper?"

"Yes," she said. "In a way. I look after the house during the day and have a meal ready for him when he gets home. I've been with him years. I used to do this for his wife—poor dear—before she was killed in that raid."

"I wonder if you can think back to last Monday week," I said. "Was Mr. Drale at home that night?"

"He always is on Monday night. Some gentlemen friends of his always come in and play cards. I have to get sandwiches and stuff ready. I always know in the morning when they've been."

"Plenty of empties?"

"Well, yes," she said, and gave a tentative smile.

"And they were here that Monday night?"

"Oh, yes. I'd have known if they weren't."

"Know the names of any of them?"

She only knew one—a Mr. Cornish who had a chemist's shop in Hampstead High Street.

"It doesn't really matter," I told her. "Thanks all the same. We're sorry we've had to bother you."

"That's quite all right," she said, and gave us a smile as we turned.

We went in search of Cornish and ran him to earth in his shop. He had a good look at our Warrant Cards before he took us to an office at the back.

"This is very hush-hush." I told him. "I can't even tell you names, but we're interested in a certain man who claims to have an alibi. He actually mentioned your name."

"*My* name!"

"That's right. He claims to have been in West Hampstead and to have seen you there at a certain time on the night of Monday last week. Were you there?"

"As a matter of fact I was. Someone I know, was it?"

"He claims to be a customer," I said. "Where exactly were you in West Hampstead on that night?"

He said he was with friends at Drale's house. They had a regular poker school which met every Monday. He'd got there at eight o'clock as usual and the party had broken up just short of midnight as renal. He had walked to Estover Road and back.

"Then our man's alibi looks O.K. after all," I told him, and looked at Matthews.

"Looks like it sir." Matthews said. I held out my hand.

"Sorry to have bothered you, Mr. Cornish. We shan't have to see you again. All the same we'd rather you didn't mention the call. Will you come out with us for a drink?"

He couldn't make it, he said. Too short-handed. I asked what pub he recommended and he mentioned the Haymakers.

"Where now, sir?" asked Matthews when we got into the car again.

"You're going to the Haymakers. I'm going to have some coffee. You'll use the saloon bar, ask if Drale's been in, and get all you can on him. I'll pick you up there at twelve o'clock."

But there wasn't time for coffee. We found the Haymakers, which looked a high-class sort of pub, and when I'd dropped Matthews I went back to the post-office. It took me quite a time to get Herringwood on the line, though I'd asked for a personal call. I told him what I wanted to know. He said we'd asked that question at the Yard. He hadn't known then what we meant and he didn't know now.

"I'm not going to waste time on you," I told him. "At some time before one o'clock this morning we'll be along to see you. If you haven't found the answers then you'll go with us to the Yard. And this time you'll stay a bit longer."

He began the same old shilly-shallying, so I rang off. I drove back to Estover Road and had a good look at the lie of the land. I made a little plan of the area between Drale's house and Ladysmith Avenue which joined Estover Road a couple of houses further on. I was ten minutes late when I went back for Matthews.

He hadn't picked up a lot about Drale. He often spent his evenings in the Haymakers and was a good snooker player. He was classed as being of the sporting type. A little clique played snooker there for biggish stakes. Drale was said to have made a packet over the Derby, but it was significant that Matthews hadn't been able to learn the name of his book-maker.

"Nights in a place like that can be pretty expensive," Matthews said. "Rounds of double whiskies and so on would cost him over a quid a time."

"When he's paid his taxes he's got twelve hundred left out of his two thousand," I said. "There's also what he gets from his holding in Ramplocks. I'd say he could stand it."

"Not so good then, sir."

I said I didn't know. I'd been trying to get a general picture of Drale away from his office. If he was in Queer Street financially, then he oughtn't to be. I'd hoped he was. "You think he's our man?"

I owed Matthews at least a little of the truth. I said I'd picked him as the likely one. But we'd know more when we'd called at Stirling House.

We just made it by one o'clock. We went up the stairs to the first landing and there was the streamlined blonde. She'd been waiting at the end of the corridor with eyes on lifts and stairs. I might have won some slogan competition from the firm by the way she smiled and bestowed that envelope on me. "Mr. Travers? . . . From Mr. Ralph Herringwood."

I had a look at what was inside. It was a short typewritten answer to my two questions.

"Sorry," I said, "but I'll have to see him."

"I'm afraid you'll have to come back later," she told me with a charming regret. "Mr. Herringwood has had to go out."

"Maybe," I said, "but I'd like to make sure."

"But you can't do that!"

I was half-way there. Matthews slipped between her and me. I didn't knock at the door. I walked straight in. Herringwood was seated at that glass-topped chromium desk. He was telephoning. At the sight of me he broke off. The receiver went back and he was getting to his feet. He looked at me as if he'd have liked to spit.

"This isn't signed and it isn't dated."

I laid it on the desk beneath his nose.

"My God! Aren't you ever satisfied?"

"Sometimes," I said, as he picked up a pen and signed. "I may be, for instance, when I see you in the dock."

"I suppose you know you made that statement in front of a witness?"

"Yes," I said, "and I hope he heard it. And by the way, if it was Drale you were talking to, you were just a bit too late. Not that I'd tell him so. We might have the line tapped."

I walked straight out. Matthews closed the door behind us. There wasn't a sign of the blonde.

"Where now, sir?"

I said we'd have to mark time. I'd hoped to ring Downe. As it was we'd better have a meal. Heaven knew when we'd get another. So I drove to a little place in Soho, and we had lunch there. All sauce and no substance, if you know what I mean, but it was a meal and we had a drink with it. It was after two o'clock when we finished the chicory, and I rang Downe from there. I had just one question to put to him, and I said I wanted a plain answer. He gave it to me. He began a question of his own. I cut in with thanks and then hung up.

"Now what, sir?" Matthews asked me with a grin.

"Back to the Yard," I told him. "About time we did something to earn our keep."

But there was just one other thing before we saw Wharton. I was afraid that Flint wouldn't be on tap, but he was. I asked him about that call he'd received that foggy night from Winter. What was the voice like?

"A bit as if he'd got a plum in his mouth, sir."

"Like this?" I said, and cleared my throat, and gave him an extract from *Hamlet*.

"Just about it, sir. Only when he got excited that time I could hardly make out what he said."

"That's when he nearly swallowed the handkerchief," I said.

He didn't get it and I didn't specially want him to. I nodded back to Matthews and we went up the stairs to Wharton.

Chapter XVIII
AFTER THE EVENT

GEORGE WASN'T surprised. Or that was what he said. He also said we'd never make it stick. It was just one of those fantastic things no jury'd ever credit.

"Isn't truth stranger than fiction?" I said. "What about Haigh and his acid baths? Would anyone have dared put that in a book? But the jury believed it right enough."

He was still pursing out his lips and shaking his head. You'd have thought I'd offered him a tumbler of Epsom Salts instead of the case on a gold salver.

"What about paying him a call tonight as soon as he gets home? That's not much of a risk."

He began talking about the Higher-ups: edging the onus off his own shoulders. Matthews gave me a surreptitious wink.

"And have a warrant in your pocket," I said. "I'm pretty sure he'll crack."

"Why should he crack? He's brazened things out before? And what can we actually prove?"

"He'll crack," I said. "I'll bet you a fiver he cracks. He'll be in a dither. That housekeeper will tell him I called. She'll mention Cornish. He'll ring Cornish. Herringwood's been talking to him already. He'll get a message through to him somehow again, even if I bluffed him about the telephone."

He let out a breath. It was like wind from a punctured tyre.

"Well, I'll have a word with the Big Bugs. Just jot down the main facts and what you've been up to this morning, and I'll hear what they say."

It was half-past three by the time I'd finished that. It'd take at least an hour, he thought, so we'd better report back.

So Matthews and I had tea outside. We were doing well for meals so far that day.

"You honestly think he'll crack, sir?" Even Matthews was sounding a bit anxious.

"I won't offer you the bet," I said, "but I'll tell you something that I didn't tell Superintendent Wharton. You're going to be in it too. Let out a word and they'll have your coat off your back."

He didn't look too nervous.

"You're a Londoner," I said. "Can you talk Cockney without overdoing it? Honest-to-God Cockney? Not the stage or novel stuff?"

He could. I tore a page from my note-book and got down to the scenario. We had a rehearsal out on the Embankment in the cold of the gathering dusk. If anyone had listened in, he'd have thought we were mad.

We went back to the Yard and it was five o'clock when Wharton came back. I knew as soon as I heard his steps that the Higher-ups had allowed themselves to be convinced.

"I ought to warn you," he told me, "that it's God-help-you if anything goes wrong."

"That's all right," I said. "My wife's provided for."

He ignored that. He wanted to know when Drale got home.

"Make the zero hour half-past six," I said. "That'll be ample. Have a man report on him from Warbeck House and ring us when he gets to St. Paul's."

He had a look at my plan and began giving orders. Matthews would be in charge till we arrived. His car would be under the plane trees at the corner of Ladysmith Avenue and he would cover the front of Number 7. Higson would cover the back way out to the Avenue, and another car would be there. Wharton and I would arrive at half-past six by the Avenue way, and there contact Matthews. If Drale was in we'd move on to the house.

It was a dark night. In Suffolk they'd call it black as black hogs. We didn't see Matthews when he first stepped out from the denser shadows under those plane trees.

"He's in all right?"

"Yes, sir. The housekeeper went about a quarter of an hour ago."

"Nothing else has happened?"

"Lights on upstairs about ten minutes ago, sir. Then he drew the blinds. Never a sign of light anywhere now, sir. Or wasn't a couple of minutes ago."

"Right," Wharton said. "We'll hear what he has to say. You come behind."

We hadn't flashed a torch and I couldn't tell if Matthews had had luck with that act of ours. Wharton and I moved off, and under the street lamp and on to the overlapping of light and dark. He opened the gate with his gloved hand. The path was visible enough and we were visible too as we made for the front door. I've said I'm not the steely-eyed, cold-blooded kind of sleuth. I wasn't then. My heart was hammering away for one thing, and I wondered if at any minute there'd be a shot. The black snout of a gun beneath an open window and a bullet in my ribs. I wasn't sorry when Wharton was at the door and I alongside him.

He ignored the bell and lifted the knocker. The house had that curiously empty sound. We stood there for half a minute, tense in the silence. Not too far off was the dull sound of traffic and nearer the blaring of a radio, but they seemed to make the silence more intense. Wharton lifted the knocker again. His ear went to the door, and I thought it was funny how he had to take off his bowler hat.

"Give him another minute," he growled at me, "then we'll make an entry."

That was when there was the sound of a shot. It seemed to come from a distance, away at the back, beyond the house. Matthews came running.

"Round here, sir!"

His torch was flashing as he disappeared. We followed him round the side of the house. If Wharton had let me lead we could have moved more quickly but to me he was like an elephant scared of a bog. But we got past the garage and then we heard noises—a sort of scuffling and growling in the darkness ahead. There was the flashing of torches. I shot by Wharton and was making for the back gate. I took a toss over a flower bed, scrambled up with my glasses still on, and got to the open gate.

"Got him all right," Matthews told me. Wharton was suddenly with us. He flashed his torch at the man on the ground. Drale lay with an arm across his face, but I could see the handcuffs. A suitcase lay just behind him where someone had stood it against the fence.

"Trying to shoot his way out, was he?"

"Don't think so, sir," Higson said. "Looked to me as if he was trying to do himself in."

Wharton grunted.

"Got the gun?"

It was a Webley, Mark; dated 1916. There wasn't any silencer.

"Get him away," Wharton said. He was looking down at Drale and there must have been a sneer as he turned to me.

"Doing himself in, eh? Pity he didn't. This'll hang him if nothing else does."

We watched for a minute as two men led Drale away, then the darkness of that long passage-way hid him.

"Better get along to the car," Wharton told me, and we went back by the side of the house. He didn't say a word till we were moving along Estover Road.

"Good job I didn't have that bet with you. Not that I ever thought of it—not when the other man's on a cert."

I could have told him how little he knew—but I didn't.

* * * * *

I didn't hang about at the local station. My job's to find the man, and the rest is up to Wharton. I can even hate the thought of eight o clock on a certain morning and the short drop which answers one man's questions about eternity. But there was still one thing I had to do.

So I took the Underground and went back to my flat, and got to work on my official report. I thought it would be better if I had it out of the way before my wife arrived, and then I'd have some time for tidying up the flat, so I had some sandwiches sent up and opened a bottle of beer. It was best part of midnight before I'd finished it. What I write here is only a brief synopsis. It either omits most of the things you knew or clarifies and correlates the few that you didn't.

THE RAMPLOCK CASE

Motive

Herringwood lay behind it all. He had to get control of Ramplocks or face an irate Shareholders' Association and certain exposure about that hotel deal. But the key to the whole thing was Ramplock himself. And Ramplock was the man we had hopelessly misunderstood—and because Drale had planned it and played it that way.

Drale was undoubtedly driven nearly crazy by Ramplock. Under Sam Ramplock his position had been well-defined and there had been no interference. That he'd appreciated Drale was shown by that bequest of a five per cent holding. But Owen Ramplock made his senior staff much like office-boys. They fed him with information, and he laid down policy and methods.

Herringwood approached Drale just when he was willing to do most things to shift the incubus of Ramplock. He offered a ten year contract as managing director of a Herringwood-Ramplock organisation if a merger could be affected. (*Statement B. by H.*) and an increased holding. Drale sounded Jane Ramplock and had no luck. He also sounded Downe (*Statement to follow*) and probably Winter. He spread rumours, always in strict confidence, that it was Ramplock who was trying to dispose of the firm; and with an attempt to stampede his colleagues into some action and to obscure his own activities.

But Ramplock had become suspicious (*Statement S.H.*). He saw his wife and doubtless Drale's name was mentioned. He had an angry interview with Winter (*Verbal statement D.P.*) and finally he had a show-down with Drale, and sacked him. (*Drale's verbal statement can be so read.*) He must have agreed to buy his interest if Drale so wished and to keep the matter quiet out of regard for past services till the month's notice had expired.

The position before the murder was that Drale would be left with nothing but his holding. He had lost one job and the prestige that went with it, and the hope of a job that would be infinitely better. And it was the despised Ramplock who had exposed him and had the last word.

Ramplock had never wanted any change whatever. He liked himself as the presiding deity. Though he was infatuated with Susan Haregood and had been prepared to sacrifice quite a lot of things, Ramplocks wasn't one of them. And to make his position more secure after he'd dismissed Drale, he proposed a reconciliation with his wife. I think he'd have sacrificed S.H. if it had been necessary. That was why he was so mysterious with her till he knew the outcome.

Drale's motives seemed to me to be ample. A mad hatred of Ramplock after dismissal was ample in itself. With Ramplock dead he wouldn't lose everything. On the other hand he would almost certainly have become chairman of the new company. J.R. had enough confidence in him for that.

Method

Drale created the character of Prince. He had visiting-cards printed, probably in some little, out-of-the-way business. He got himself an alibi for the Monday night by the poker game. After the housekeeper left he registered at the hotel. His disguise was a moustache, glasses and plumpers, all of which could be assumed and discarded quickly. He took care to be seen by the chambermaid, then went home for the weekly game. After it he returned to the hotel, and he left there about eight o'clock in the morning.

The disguise was only for anyone who might see him as he entered and left Warbeck Grove. Once at R.'s door he'd have turned his back on the corridor and become Drale again. R. admitted him. Drale may have rung him on some pretext beforehand, but he shot him at once and turned on the electric fire to delay *rigor mortis*. (*Statement re R. and fresh-air to follow from D.P.*) He put the visiting-card in the pocket and left at once, reassuming the disguise. He took the Underground to Holborn and got to the warehouse at about nine o'clock. He sent Harmer out of the room and rang the Broad Street Detective Agency (*Statement by L.T.*) who had previously done work for the firm. Norris, who took the message, didn't know Ramplock's voice and accepted the message as altogether genuine.

As for that morning in the chairman's room when Drale was supposed to have seen Prince, that must have been adapted from some similar happening when Ramplock really had a private caller.

THE WINTER CASE

Motive

Most of this is surmise but there are also facts. Winter must have seen Drale that morning, or a man curiously like him or with, say, his way of walking. He saw him enter and leave, and he followed him out of curiosity. He watched him from behind his paper in the same train. The disguise must have been removed and he saw him get out at Holborn.

When Drale uncovered Prince for us, Winter was suspicious and began ferreting around. He became sure—even cocksure—that Drale was involved in the murder. That's why he said (*Verbal statement to G.W.*) that he might know who Prince was. Probably on the eve of the directors' meeting he saw Drale and he didn't like his denials or explanations.

He insisted, I think, that Drale must resign at once. But after that Drale couldn't afford to let Winter go on living.

Method

A variant of the Ramplock killing. Drale went to the flat and shot him, turned on the fire more fully, faked the receiver and left. He went by Underground to near the Yard, and rang from a call-box. He probably talked with a handkerchief between his teeth and as nearly like Winter as he could and he took care to be in such a hurry that he hadn't time to speak to anyone who might have been suspicious about the voice. Then he made a plop—boy's toy pistol with a cork?—dropped the receiver, and was at the Yard at near the agreed time, and with an alibi that was unquestionable.

So much for the report. But there were two things that I didn't, and daren't, add.

We'd thought that in each case we'd known the exact time of death, and we were so sure *that we told Anders so.* Possibly Anders's findings wouldn't have been the same if we hadn't told him what we did. Since we were so sure, he probably took it as read. We'd done the same thing once before, and we still hadn't learned.

The other thing I didn't do was to anticipate criticism over Drale's ability to conceive and complete two such murders. But Drale had brains, and I hoped that would be taken for granted. You don't begin life as an errand boy and rise to be virtual head of an organisation like Ramplocks without having brains, and plenty of them. And Drale had held the job down. And had kept the respect of Sam Ramplock. As for the second murder, that, in a way, wasn't Drale's fault. It was something forced on him by Winter.

In the morning I took that report to the Yard. Wharton wasn't free, so I left a message about where he could find me. Just before noon he rang me at the club. Everything was in the bag, he said, and Drale had done some talking. He was so pleased with life, was George, that he asked me to have lunch with him.

That wasn't so generous as it sounded: it was the taxpayer who'd foot the bill. But I was feeling like celebrating so I got him to have lunch at the club with me instead. I never saw him more volatile. What *we* hadn't done or *he* hadn't done was modestly ascribed to luck. He purred when I came back with the correct disclaimer that once more a remarkably good tune had been played on a not-so-young fiddle. Over a second glass of the club port he told me he'd never known a case where I'd been in better form.

When he was leaving I asked if anything had come through about Solversen. He said it was due at any time, not that it mattered now.

"One of your little bloomers—old Solversen," he told me with a gentle reproof. "I never did think he was mixed up in it myself."

I had to chuckle as I watched him go. George wouldn't be George if he didn't make cracks like that. And then I suddenly thought I'd ring Solversen myself. I might have time before he took his afternoon walk.

I told him about Drale and how it would be in the evening papers. I thought he'd be surprised.

"Never did like the feller myself," he said. "Come to think of it, there weren't anyone else."

I felt a sudden deflation. In a way he was right.

"Things aren't always as easy as that," I told him. "Life would be grand if we could be wise before the event. But tell me something, strictly between ourselves. You weren't pulling our legs when you said you'd been a detective yourself?"

"No, son, I don't reckon I was."

"In Quebec, wasn't it?"

"Montreal," he said. "A good ways back."

He might be a liar but he had a good memory. I said I'd be seeing him, and meant it. Liar or not, I liked old Solversen.

I went home then and did some tidying up at the flat. My wife's train was due at Euston at a. quarter to six, and it was just after five o'clock when the telephone went.

"Travers speaking."

"It's me," the voice said, and accepted recognition. "Isn't it dreadful about Mr. Drale! We've just seen it in the papers."

"Uh-huh," I said, and there was silence.

"You didn't mind me ringing you at your private address?"

"Of course not."

There was a little giggle.

"Well, I thought I'd mention Mr. Drale and about my boy-friend. His leave's been cancelled."

"You mean you'd like me to take you out to lunch?"

"Uh-huh."

I might have said something about my wife not letting me. But I owed her a lunch for that information about Ramplock and fresh-air.

"Fine," I said. "I'll give you a ring some time. And give my love to the boy friend."

There was another giggle as I rang off. And then I had to fetch my car. And I was having a quiet chuckle to myself as I went to the garage. Not about Daisy but about Wharton.

He was still sure that Drale had tried to bolt because of the things I'd done that previous morning. He'd even taken credit for some of them himself. But what he hadn't known was this.

Matthews had seen Drale enter his house and then he'd nipped back to the call-box and rung him. I make no attempt to reproduce the accent. It's the substance that matters.

"That you, guv? You won't know me but you did me a favour once and now I'm doing you one—see? About the cops. Two of them was at the warehouse this morning talking to Charlie Harmer: a biggish chap and a long thin chap with glasses. I don't like the cops—see?—so I did a bit of the old Nosey Parker, and Harmer was telling them as how he heard you using his telephone that day when Ramplock got done in. Said you sent him to fetch Radvitz and Morgan and he come back for something and there you was making out to somebody you was Ramplock talking about that Prince that the police was after. That's all guv. Thought I'd give you the tip. So long guv. Good luck."

That was what did it—that and the sight of Wharton and myself coming along that front path. The bag had been packed but we were the final confirmation.

But I didn't chuckle too much. If the Big Bugs ever got word of that little episode, there'd be the devil to pay. Travers would go out on his ear—not that he'd lose any sleep over it. As he'd told Wharton in another context, his wife was provided for. And—something really worth a chuckle—there'd always be a someone to take Daisy to lunch.

THE END

www.ingramcontent.com/pod-product-compliance
Lightning Source LLC
Chambersburg PA
CBHW031011190726